SIX

D0956307

SIX WAYS
FROM SUNDAY

William W. Johnstone
with J. A. Johnstone

PINNACLE BOOKS
Kensington Publishing Corp.
www.kensingtonbooks.com

PINNACLE BOOKS are published by

Kensington Publishing Corp.
119 West 40th Street
New York, NY 10018

PUBLISHER'S NOTE
Following the death of William W. Johnstone, the Johnstone family is working with a carefully selected writer to organize and complete Mr. Johnstone's outlines and many unfinished manuscripts to create additional novels in all of his series like The Last Gunfighter, Mountain Man, and Eagles, among others. This novel was inspired by Mr. Johnstone's superb storytelling.

All Kensington titles, imprints, and distributed lines are available at special quantity discounts for bulk purchases for sales promotions, premiums, fund-raising, educational, or institutional use. Special book excerpts or customized printings can also be created to fit specific needs. For details, write or phone the office of the Kensington special sales manager: Kensington Publishing Corp., 119 West 40th Street, New York, NY 10018, attn: Special Sales Department; phone 1-800-221-2647.

ISBN-13: 978-0-7860-1998-4
ISBN-10: 0-7860-1998-0

First printing: May 2009

10 9 8 7 6 5 4 3

Printed in the United States of America

Chapter One

Them shots across the mountain valley kind of interested me. There was a crackle of shots, and then an answering boom from some heavier artillery. But that boom wasn't on the breeze much, compared to all that crackle and snap.

Curiosity got the best of me. That's my weakness. I turned Critter, my ornery nag, toward the ruckus, thinking I'd at least find out who's shooting at what. Me, I'm a sucker for that stuff and I didn't have much to do. Maybe I'd get to drill a few rounds myself.

But I sort of doubted it. I was thinkin' it was another claim-jumping. This here valley had seen some pretty fancy claim-jumping last few months. That was all anyone talked about at Swamp Creek, the little mining town maybe fifty miles south of Butte that was the heart of this gold-mining district.

"Critter," I says, "that's a bunch of lead flying around, and it sounds like a dozen's ganged up on one, from the way the noise is coming at me."

Critter, he farted. He never did give me much credit for being smart.

I sort of wrestled with myself as I headed that direction. What was some cowboy doing getting into a mining war? But I hadn't been practicing cowmanship for a while now, and thought maybe there might be a job ahead, forty dollars and found, so I proceeded. It was a right peaceful valley, full of sunlight and pine scent on the wind. These here were the Pioneer Mountains, and there were more little gold mines being sunk in the rock hereabouts than I could count. Swamp Creek, the town, sort of mushroomed into a canvas-and-rough-plank place overnight, and now all sorts of entertaining types were digging in there, mostly to mine the miners.

The valley was drained by Swamp Creek, which was named for a big old swamp about a mile above town. It was like that creek got constipated for a mile or two there, and spread out every which way. It was said there was no bottom to it, just black muck and more muck in there, and a person would sink in and keep on sinking until the muck closed over his head. It sure was the only swamp around. I steered Critter toward a rocky gray slope that had a lot of pine forest at its base, and more forest high up, where the jagged mountains stretched toward the blue. That poppin' got louder, so I knew I was gettin' close, but so far I couldn't see nothing.

I was taking myself and my sturdy horse into someplace where lead was flying around, and I argued with myself some. My ma, she always told me to stay outta trouble, and my pa, he always told me to stay clear of women, but they're both gone now, so I get into whatever I get into. I wish I'd paid them more heed, because even though I didn't know it then, I was going to get into trouble and women both.

I rounded a bend that opened on a wide gulch feeding into that valley, and now at last I got me a little peek at what the ruckus was all about.

"Critter," I says to the nag, "I do believe they've got a little claim-jumping party a-going full tilt."

Up in the middle of that cliff was a mine head. All I could see was the mouth of a shaft driven into the side of that big old mountain, a black hole staring down upon me. And blocking that hole was an overturned one-ton ore car, rusty yeller, and a few chunks of metal I couldn't rightly name 'cause when it comes to hauling rock outa the ground, I'm dumb as a stump.

But I hauled up to study the matter, stayin' well out of range of any hot lead. It was plain enough, even to a dumb-ass cowboy. Up yonder were half a dozen hardcases banging away at someone holed up at the mine. That old boy in the mine, he had him a Sharps, with a big throaty boom, while the rest were using lighter artillery, and no one was gittin' anywhere.

Like that feller at the mine was outnumbered but dug in.

It didn't look like any fair fight either, 'cause I seen some hardcases working around to either side, like they're planning to rush the old boy in the mine, coming at him from the flanks where he won't see much until it's too late.

I got the itchy feeling they were gettin' set to shoot that old miner plumb dead, probably for reasons I didn't want to think about, such as ownership. It must be some mine, I thought, to stir up a kettle full of pain like that.

"Well, Critter, you and me are going to buy into this here fracas," I said. Critter, he rolled an ear back and shook his muzzle in disgust. He was telling me I'm plumb nuts, and I never would argue the case, 'cause he and I both agree to it.

Ahead was a mighty stand of lodgepole pine, sticking straight and true into the air, and I headed that way mostly to keep clear of that Sharps up there, and also to get me a better view of the proceedings.

I steered the horse up a grassy slope and into the forest, which was so thick that afternoon turned to twilight, and I let Critter pick his way over fallen timber, which crosshatched the ground. There was no way to escape making a noise as loud as a steam engine, so I just let the nag poke along while I kept a sharp eye out for surprises.

Well, I got myself surprised, all right, when a dude in a dove-gray swallowtail coat, black trousers, and shiny shoes, and with a black silk stovepipe hat, appears from nowhere, pointing a shiny little pepperbox at me, maybe nine barrels in all. A quaint little weapon, outmoded by revolvers, but as lethal as any.

"Hands high," the gent says, so I consider it's my duty to obey, real careful, because pepperboxes are ornery little guns with a habit of shooting off all barrels at once.

I raised my pinkies toward the evergreen limbs above, and smiled kindly. "Just wandering through," says I. "I'm never one to miss a good show."

The gent looked me over and saw a young cowboy, well armed, skinny as hell, with a few acne patches on my cheeks that were some embarrassing, even if half hid by the scruffy layer of beard I'd not scraped away for a week or two. Me, I saw a smoothly shaven face, black hawkeyes, a trim gray mustache, clean white teeth, fancy dark sideburns, and soft hands that had never done a lick of log-splitting, shoveling, ax-swinging, or plow-wrestling. In short, he was some Fancy Dan. He even had one of them gold watch fobs dangling across his middle.

"Who are you?" the man asked, as if he expected a reply.

"I don't like to spell her out," I said. "I never was too happy with the name, so I keep her to myself."

"Nine barrels. Shall I shoot the first?"

"Cotton," says I, all hasty. "It's not a name I cotton to."

"And?"

"You plumb gonna have to kill me dead before I give out the rest.'

He smiled suddenly. "Cotton Pickens," he said. "You've been hanging around Swamp Creek looking for trouble to get into."

I flushed pure red. How anyone got ahold of my rear handle I don't know. I never tell it to anyone.

"This is fortuitous," he said. "I've been looking for you."

Now that was a word I couldn't pronounce, much less figure out. "Put that in words someone like me'd know some of," I said.

"Fortunate," he said. "I heard you are good with a gun, and I thought to hire you."

"Well, I'm not rightly sure I'm for sale," I said. This feller was too clean-shaven for me. My gut feeling is not to trust anyone in a swallowtail coat and a mustache. "But you can give me the what-for."

He shrugged. "This," he said. "We have paper giving us that mine. But that gentleman resists."

"Paper?"

"Deed and mineral rights. We paid the back taxes and bought it at auction."

"But he still figures possession is nine tenths of the law, right?"

"You know some law, Cotton."

"Well, you got to read something in an outhouse, especially when you're as slow to do your business as I am. Outhouses are plumb boring. So I read Blackstone while I'm a-sittin'."

"Frankly, it surprises me. But yes, I'm looking for able men, and you'd fit the bill. Forty a month."

That was a heap of money for some half-starved saddle tramp like me. But I wasn't all that sure about this outfit.

"Now, I don't dicker with anyone that's pointing a nine-shot pepperbox at me. It makes me nervous. And I don't think you've given me a name."

"Sorry," the man said, and slid his pepperbox into a slick little underarm holster, where it lay so close it didn't show under that swallowtail.

"Carter Scruples," he said. "I'm a partner in this enterprise."

That sure was an odd handle. I wasn't sure what scruples meant, but it was something you hid behind most likely.

I quit my twitching, now that the mean little lead-thrower was back in its nest.

"I'm not saying yes and I'm not saying no," I said. "I want to see how this here business is transacted."

He shrugged, and nodded toward the edge of the grove. "Have a look, if you want to risk a shot coming your way."

"I think maybe I will," I said. "But I'm going to leave Critter here, safe in these trees."

I slid down from Critter. He objected some, laid his

ears back, and I yanked the reins just in time to keep him from taking a bite out of this Mr. Scruples.

"Horse needs subduing," Scruples said. "Either that or it needs its throat cut."

I didn't much care for that observation, and gave Scruples a hard look. But he just smiled pleasantly, like everything was fine here in a pine grove while his hired guns were trying to kill some mine owner.

We eased forward until we reached some brush that bordered the slope, and we could see the action above in relative safety.

"You just gonna kill him, just like that?" I asked.

"Not just like that. We gave him his chance to leave peaceably."

"What'd he say?"

"I wouldn't deem it proper to tell you," Scruples said. "In any case, it'll all be over in a few moments."

It looked like it might be. I studied the scene real careful, and found a few gunmen creeping and dodging up that rocky grade, hiding behind talus. An occasional boom from that big Sharps kept them from rushing, but it was plain a rush was coming, and one man with one long gun wasn't going to hold off a pack of gunslicks. Especially since now the two at the flanks were edging in, taking advantage of cover to stay out of sight.

A few of the gunslicks down below the mine head kept popping away with their carbines, just to keep the mine owner occupied, while them stalkers at the flanks was creeping along the rocky cliff getting ready for the potshot.

Then most everything happened at once. The ones in the middle upped and clambered that steep slope, while the ones at the sides opened fire, and now there were more than six in sight, maybe eight or nine, all a-jumping and dodging toward the mine head. The Sharps didn't boom at all, and I wondered if the old boy in the mine had bought the ticket. Lotta lead flying around up there, whanging off that ore car. Then the whole lot of gunslicks whooped up that slope, and the damndest thing happened. It was sort of shocking actually.

Old miner, he let fly with a couple of sticks of DuPont Hercules with a cap and some spitting fuse wired together, and next thing I know, there was a hell of a eruption as that thing went off, and I seen a couple of bodies fly upward like rag dolls and flop to the earth, no doubt extinct. They sure looked surprised up there. Not a one of them was standing. The concussion had flattened the whole lot. It knocked Scruples and me off our pins, too. Then I heard a maniac laughing up there, behind the overturned ore car, laughing like a bucksaw slicing wood. I have to give those gunslicks credit. They upped and ran toward the mine head and the whole thing happened over again. A couple of sticks of dynamite with a spitting fuse sailed out. I got smart and stuck my fingers in my ears, and tried to hit the ground before the thing went off, but didn't make it. The blast knocked me flat. This time, four more of those dudes were writhing on the slope, or tumbling down the talus. Durndest thing I ever did see.

I guess that did it some. The rest of them slicks, they hightailed downslope just as fast as they could scramble, leavin' them dead sprawled around on gray rock. Those two flanking ones just quit and come tumbling down that grade. There was four lyin' mighty still up there, and four more come stumbling into the woods, all deaf as stones and some bleeding red all over.

That's when I saw her. She was just about the most

beautiful woman I ever did lay eyes on, a blonde wearing black satin from chin to toe, one of them fancy dresses with more buttons than I can count. She had one of them picture hats topping that soft blond hair, and I just stood there and stared. Where'd she come from anyway?

Scruples, he went over to her and she tucked her arm into his.

"Win some, lose some," he said to her.

She smiled wryly. I ain't seen a smile like that on a lady like that ever before, and I just stood there staring and rocking on my feet. I was dumbstruck. There just ain't any women like that in the whole Territory of Montana. That sort of woman, she's tied up with J. P. Morgan or Vanderbilt, or one of those that live at Newport and have got a lot of gold to toss around. But there she was, being led away by Scruples.

They all forgot I was there. The whole lot drifted off, those bloodied-up gunslicks, the man and woman, and in a bit I saw Scruples and the blonde get into a shiny black carriage drawn by a pair of trotters, and the rest climb into a spring wagon that was parked around a bend, and the lot of them rode away. I watched them bounce and lurch across open fields until they reached the wagon road that ran up and down the valley, and then they slowly wound their way toward Swamp Creek. And next I knew, someone up in that mine was cackling like a goose.

Chapter Two

That was it. Scruples and his blond beauty rode away in a shiny black carriage. High up that slope, there were bodies sprawled in the rocks.

That didn't seem fittin' for some country boy like me. Maybe they weren't dead. Maybe they could be helped. But I had me a problem. The minute I stepped out of the pines and onto that rocky slope, that big old Sharps would bark.

"Critter," I says to my nag. "I've got me a job to do, and it scares the britches half off me."

Critter clacked his teeth and yawned. So much for admiration. I thought maybe Critter would salute.

I dug into my kit lookin' for a white flag. If I was going to step out of them trees, I'd need to be waving some white. But I didn't have no white. Just some old cotton underdrawers that started out white, but now was a sort of yeller gray. Well, yeller gray would have to do, so I tied the legs of them drawers to a handy stick, crept up the edge of the grove, and waved the thing around a bit.

I didn't see no action up there, or hear some damned bullet sail by me, so real cautious, I crept out on the rock, takin' my time, and waving my yeller-gray drawers around, and makin' a lot of noise so's not to surprise that mining bastard up there.

But all I got was a mess of silence.

Well, I thought, it's now or never. Just as a precaution, I undid my gunbelt and hung it over my shoulder as a further peace offerin', though I didn't say nothing about the two-shot derringer in my boot. I did a slow climb over talus toward the lowest of them gunmen, and found him sprawled in the rock, plumb dead. He'd been punctured here and there. So I clambered up that rough gray rock to the next, and found he'd expired, too, and was missing an arm. It wasn't no pretty sight to look at.

The next one was over on the flank, and was one of them two that was creepin' in on the miner. I was gettin' out of sight of the mine head when a voice filtered down to me.

"Stay in sight," the owner of that voice said. I took it for plumb good advice.

"Just checkin'," I said.

"He's dead, and so's t'other on your left."

"You mind if I come up and palaver a little?"

"You ain't one of them. I saw you ride in."

"That's right, I ain't. But I thought to take care of the wounded and maybe plant the dead, long as the rest of them hightailed out of here."

"No tricks. I got a few more of these little DuPont bombs."

I had yet to see this fellow. Somehow, he was hidden in the shadows of the ore car, and probably as forted up as a man can get.

I made my way up the talus slope, and finally reached a small flat in front of the shaft, where all the mining stuff lay around and about. The miner, he appeared from somewhere in all that tangle of iron, and that old Sharps was staring at my navel.

"Howdy," I says.

He didn't reply, but grinned toothlessly. He was an old boy, wearing more dirt on him than cloth, and peering at me from bright blueberry eyes.

I got mad. "That's the second time today I've stared into a barrel, and I don't like it. First time, I was looking at an entire pepperbox, and that sight ain't for the fainthearted."

"Sharps is empty anyway," he said, setting it down. "When it comes to fights, I prefer some DuPont." He said it *DOOpont,* and even a dummy like me got the idea he was talkin' dynamite.

He had a row of those bombs there just inside the shaft, and he fetched one to show me his work. "Two sticks of DuPont Hercules, this copper cap in there, with six inches of Bickford fuse crimped in the end, plus a mess of tenpenny nails to do a little damage, all wired nice. Now, this here fuse burns thirty seconds to the foot, so these are ten-second fuses. That's so no one picks one up and throws it back at me. Pretty smart, eh?"

Tell you the truth, I was plain itchy standing there next to that thing. I know short guns, and I'm not bad with a long gun, but this thing he was waving around was big enough to kill Paul Bunyon.

"Maybe you oughta set her back in there a piece," I said.

Those blueberry eyes glimmered and glowed, and he whipped a lucifer across some rock, lit the fuse until she sparked orange, and then tossed her off to the right. He dove into the overturned ore car, and so did I, just in time. That sucker lifted the ground from under me, and shot tenpenny nails everywhere. I was right grateful Critter was nowhere near.

"Agnes Cork here. What's your handle?" he said.

I could hardly hear a word, and waited for my eardrums to quit dancing.

"What did you say it was?"

"Agnes Cork, my boy."

"Now wait just a minute here. You ain't no Agnes."

He nodded. "Joseph St. Agnes Cork," he said. "They was trying to line up a few saints when I was born. Now what's your handle?"

"Cotton."

"That's half a handle."

"Agnes, I can't bear to give you the rear half of my handle. Just can't, so you've got to take me as I am."

"Well, invent a name. I just need some pants to go with the shirt."

"Invent a name?" Truth to tell, I'd never thought of inventing a name. But it wasn't a bad idea.

"Sonny, I'll invent one for you. You mind that?"

"Sure I mind. I'll invent my own name, Agnes."

It sure was strange, calling that mining bastard Agnes. I decided to change the subject.

"No one's coming around to plant those four, so it's up to me."

Agnes nodded quietly. "You have a good heart, Cotton."

"Maybe you can help me. It's all rock around here."

Agnes nodded. "Glory hole about fifty yards that way. Miner named Walrus Wank hit a pocket there, but it petered out after a few feet. Still, nice little eight- or ten-foot hole in the wall."

When we reached the first body, Agnes pulled his

pockets out and collected a few coins. The man's revolvers were nowhere in sight, and probably got blown into the next county. "They owe me," he said. "I'm charging them for the powder I blew. Must of spent forty dollars defending my mine, and they'll pay. Any more, I'll give it to you to take to Swamp Creek."

"Fair enough," I said.

We carried the dead gunslick over to the glory hole and laid him flat in there, after chasing a rattler out. The man sure was perforated. I think about five tenpenny nails had done for him. It was grim work, and I didn't like it none, and besides that, it plumb wore me out. But it didn't bother Agnes none, and after a while we got all four of the gunmen laid out in that little burrow hole, and Agnes had collected thirty-seven dollars and one revolver with a bent barrel.

"That evens it up," he said.

"We gonna pile up some rock here?" I asked.

"Naw," he said. He hiked back to his mine, told me to get well back, and brought one of his DuPont specials, but this one with no tenpenny nails dressing it up and a longer fuse. He lit the thing with a lucifer, tossed it into the mouth, and walked swiftly toward his own mine, arriving exactly when it blew, and after the dust cleared, and my ears quit howling, and I could stand up again, I looked over at that glory hole and there was nothing there except a mess of rock. It was plumb amazing.

Agnes, he just he-he-heed his way back to his own place. He sure had a laugh that made me wonder whether I'd get outa there alive.

I sure didn't know nothing about mining, and I thought I'd better find out.

"How come they were trying to kill you?" I asked.

Agnes, he pulled some tobacco lying loose in his pocket and stuffed it under his tongue. "Just for the fun of it," he said.

"They own this mine? That's what Scruples said."

Joseph St. Agnes Cork, he just cackled. "That wouldn't a got anything if they killed me," he said. "Gold pinched out some whiles ago, and now she's nothing but a hole in the cliff."

"No gold?"

"Pocket mine. Gold along here is in pockets. Clean out a pocket and there's nothing left."

I was getting testy. "So you fought 'em for nothing?"

"Oh, I didn't say that, boy. You got a thing or two to learn about mining. I loved that fight. Now I can sell this here hole for mebbe ten thousand simoleons. Now I got what I needed, and they handed it to me. A man fights off ten, twelve claim-jumpers, why, that hole of his must be worth a lot of moolah."

"You mean you're going to defraud the buyer?"

He grinned, and those blueberry eyes sparked bright. "Oh, I'll salt her a little, and we'll see. A man digs a hole for better part of a year, he ought to get paid for it, right? I'm just angling for some pay, and that Scruples bunch handed it to me on a platter. Until they showed up, I was plumb discouraged."

I didn't like this none. Cork was a crook.

He started cackling again, and I had a mind to get out of there. Critter and I thought to help someone outnumbered ten to one or so, and now four gents lay in their graves and a bunch more were full of nail holes.

"Cotton, you stick around here and I'll teach you some about getting gold out. You want some johnny-cakes? I'm of a mind to eat."

I had nothing better to do, so I nodded. "I'm going to fetch my horse Critter, water him, and bring him up here. He likes griddle cakes and he'd be plain unhappy with me if he got a whiff of johnnycakes and he couldn't sink his buck teeth into a couple."

"Does he haul ore cars? I'll put him to work."

"No, Critter ain't never had harness touch him."

Agnes Cork was makin' me huffy again. I wouldn't let no miner lay hands on Critter. Trouble is, Cork was a miner, and they ain't half the man any cowboy is. I worked down the talus slope, plunged into the dark forest, found the nag chewing on bark, and brought him back up there to the mine, where he laid his ears back and snapped a time or two at Agnes, and then tried to kick him, too.

"Horse is just like me," Agnes said, and laughed that mean laugh again.

The miner set to work mixing some cornmeal and water while I scrounged up some firewood. There sure wasn't none anywhere near.

But in time, along about sundown, we got Critter and ourselves fed.

"You got to git now," Agnes said. "I don't allow no one around here disturbing my sleep and slitting my throat. Anyone stirs around here, he gets a knife up to the hilt."

"We'll vamoose," I says, eyeing his little shanty, which was the most disgusting-looking dump I ever laid eyes on. If I set foot in there I'd catch leprosy for sure. "But afore I go, you mind telling me about these claim-jumpers? They offered me forty and found, and I'm just thinking about it. Sure beats starving."

"Oh, Scruples. And his lady friend. They got that Palace Car in town."

Well, that explained something. Sitting up a slope from

Swamp Creek was a regular Pullman Palace Car someone dragged overland, probably using fifty oxen and some braced-up wagons. It was right fancy, purple lacquer with gilded letters on the side, and when I got a peek or two at her, I could see wine-colored velvet drapes in there, and heaven knows what, my being too dumb about all that to know a flush toilet from a two-holer.

"What about all that paper? He told me he's got a legal right."

Agnes cackled. "You got a few things to learn, boy. Scruples, he's in cahoots with the mining district recorder, Johnny Brashear, and pays the old souse to find fault in a claim." He eyed me, sizing me up for a ten-year-old. "Mining districts get born pretty casual, long before the government moves in and surveys a place and makes it legal. Miners themselves set up districts, adopt some rules about the size of a claim, stuff like that, and this gets put in a ledger, and usually the government gets around to recognizing this stuff years later. But bribe a clerk or two, and you pretty much turn it all cattywumpus."

"Your claim's valid?"

"Bet your ass, sonny boy."

I didn't cotton to being called sonny boy, but it was better than being called Cotton, so I just glared at him a bit.

"So them in that Palace Car, they're not up and up?"

Agnes Cork, he began wheezing so hard I thought he'd choke.

"How come no one's fighting 'em?"

"It's that woman," Agnes said.

I couldn't make sense of that, but it sure did make me curious about her. She was just about the first woman I'd seen in a long time that made my britches go tight. I didn't know they made women like that. She was some better than Sarah Bernhardt. I seen a picture of her once, and thought there sure is some world out there I ain't never seen.

"Boy, you go back to pushing cows around until you're growed up enough to walk into a mining camp. Now, it's getting dark, and I kill anything wandering around my mine in the dark, and I don't ask questions neither."

I think that was a message aimed my way, so I loaded up Critter and climbed aboard, wanting enough light so he could pick his way down that slope without busting a leg. Leastwise, I got out of there without getting shot, and Critter didn't bust nothing.

And I wandered toward Swamp Creek wondering whether to hire on. If all sides was as crooked as it sounded, it wouldn't matter none which one paid me wages.

Chapter Three

I was scrapin' the bottom of my purse in that mining town, and I was wonderin' where my next chow would be coming from. This wasn't no cow town where I could hook up with most any cow outfit, move into a bunkhouse, and fill my belly. No, this here Swamp Creek high in the mountains was different.

It rose up mighty fast, first canvas buildings, then log, and now some sawn wood was showing up here and there and the place was looking like it might stick around a while. There was false-front stores doing a trade. They was a saloon ever' few yards, a few whorehouses with them red lanterns rocking in the breeze, a few flophouses where a miner could lie on a bedbug pallet for two bits a night, and a few little whitewashed cottages where folks lived pretty decent.

Now there's plenty of work available in a mining town, and sometimes for two or three dollars a day, too, king's wages, but the stuff you got to do is plain disgusting. If it's hard-rock mines, like in the Swamp Creek district, you've got to go down in some black hole for ten hours, choke on fumes, hope the whole thing doesn't cave in, and spend the whole time hammering and shoveling. The noise is so bad that you're half deaf time you get out of that hole and breathe some real air and see some night sky.

Most of them miners, they're big and tough. Even the little ones are big and tough. They come from all over the world, places I can't even pronounce, and half of them got names I never heard of. Soon as the shift ends, they head for their favorite saloon and toss down boilermakers, or some such. Like most cowboys, I learned the hard way to treat 'em good. Now most cowboys, me included, we think we're pretty tough. Sometimes we work hard, like brandin' time. But truth is, mostly we're just getting carried around on our nags and hardly use our muscles. But miners, they shovel sixteen tons of rock a shift into ore cars, year after year.

So the first time I got into a little punching match with a miner, he just about hammered me down a posthole. It was an education. Once, while sitting in a two-holer, I read about the Seven Wonders of the World and the Colossus of Rhodes. I ain't got much schooling, and most of it was sittin' in one crapper or another. Most cowboys got educated that way. There was always something to read in there, right next to the corncobs.

This here miner I took a lick at one foolish night in a saloon, he was that Colossus of Rhodes in the flesh, and for certain the Seventh Wonder of the World, eight feet tall and five feet wide. I was laid up for a week and black and blue for a month. It might not have been so bad if I'd been alone, but there were a dozen cowboys watching me and hooting me on, and they got to see the whole show. We all thought we was tougher than a bunch of rock grubbers, but boy, did we learn fast.

Since then, I've been mighty smiley around them miners, because I don't want to mop up buckets of my own blood. But now I was plumb out of money in a mining burg, and the options weren't good. I could muck rock for two dollars a day, or I could leave town and hope to eat rabbits and squirrels on my way somewhere else. It was depressin' to think about. I've been down in one of them little holes once, and that was enough. I looked at that rock above me, and wondered when a thousand tons of it would land on my head. You sort of get to appreciate daylight down there. Even a cloudy day seems mighty nice when you get out of one of them holes.

Maybe I could find something else for a while. I stared up and down that muddy street, wonderin' how to feed my face, and not coming up with much. Well, it was then that a job found me. Some tough gunslick with greased-down black hair, he stops me outside the Eagle Saloon and asks me if my name is Cotton.

I owned to it reluctantly. I can't seem to keep anything quiet, includin' that name.

"Mr. Scruples, he wants to talk with you," this lantern-jawed gent said.

"Oh, I don't think so," says I.

"Unfinished business, Mr. Scruples says. You can meet him at the Palace Car. But don't delay. If he doesn't hear from you, he'll make other plans."

Unfinished business would be that job offer, and I wasn't of a mind, not after seeing all those bodies scattered around and Agnes Cork tellin' me what Scruples was up to. But I overcame my reluctance, mostly because I wanted another glimpse of that ice blonde. That would be worth the whole trip. Just one little look. Just a few words. Just thinkin' about her made me itch in the britches.

I wasn't too keen about this whole thing, and thought maybe to have a drink first, a little liquid courage, so I headed into the Mint Saloon, and laid my last dime on the plank bar and got a mug of tap beer. The stuff tasted like creosote, and I thought maybe the Saints had brewed it. They didn't drink it, but they wasn't opposed to making money any way they could, so they cranked up their distilleries and pumped out Valley Tan, and beer, too. Their teamsters delivered it regular to mining camps, and without drinking half their load.

I sat real quiet on a stool and listened to the gab around me, and it turned out that the Mint was the place to pick up word about all them little mines. This wasn't a miners' bar at all, but one where prospectors and small-time operators and loners gathered. These gents, they mostly had beards and weathered faces the color of an old saddle and battered slouch hats. Now you take a miner, he's white as a fish belly, and that's because he hardly sees daylight.

Somehow or other, word had leaked out about Agnes Cork's fight, and those bearded fellows, they were listening hard, and I listened hard, too.

"That Scruples, he sent a regular army after old Agnes, and they got whupped," one said.

"I don't know how long he can hold out. Next time, they'll try something different."

"Cork told me he filed proper on that pocket, but Scruples don't let that slow him down. Scruples tried to buy him out for a few clams, but Cork, he didn't budge. He said he'd sell for ten thousand."

"Must be a pretty good pocket. Agnes Cork, he don't

lack for anything. He's paid up at the Mining Supply. I was in there when Cork bought a case of DuPont and some fuse and caps, and a new pick, and he just laid down gold coins."

"Coins? Not ore? He must be makin' some bucks."

"You think ten thousand's a bit high for that pocket?"

"Guess we'll find out. Scruples, he's going to try again, I'll wager. You just gotta wonder what's up there in that hole."

Me, I just studied each man, trying to get some handle on him. Mostly, they were loners, I thought. I didn't hear anything bad about Scruples, except he was lookin' for a bargain. We all look for bargains.

"How does Cork get his ore out of there? You'd think Scruples would just jump the mine when no one's around there."

"He must have some secret way of getting it out. Truth is, I've never seen a load leave that mine."

"Whatever it is, he ain't going to tell us how he does it," one of them said. "That's a hell of a hole he's got there. Them tailings keep on growing, so he's hauling a lot of rock out of there. He must be in there a quarter of a mile."

It was funny, because I had the answer, straight from Agnes Cork himself. There wasn't no ore. But I kept my mouth shut and sipped that rotten beer, which tasted like horse piss. I had no idea why Cork's mine went in so far, if the ore had pinched out and it was just a pocket.

Well, I finished up my mug and took a leak in the alley, climbed onto Critter, and headed up a steep hill toward this here Palace Car, which glowed purple and gold in the late afternoon light. It sure was out of place, with no railroad anywhere near. But there it was, on the crest of a hill, lording over Swamp Creek, as if whoever lived there owned the whole place. And maybe they did.

Well, there wasn't no hitching post up there, but as soon as I got close, some gunslick with a pair of Colts hanging from his hips butt-forward climbs out of the shadows. I watch him close, thinkin' maybe he'll pull one of those short-barrel .45-caliber irons on me, but he simply stared up at me. "The man wants to talk with you. I'll take your horse."

"That's Critter, and he don't like bein' taken anywhere."

"I'll take him."

"No, I'll ground-rein him like always."

"I'll take him."

"You tell Scruples I'm not interested," I said, starting to turn Critter away.

But this dude, who's got greased-down hair like the one in town, he grabs my bridle. "I'll take him," he said.

Critter kicked the hell out of him, and the dude dropped to the ground howling, and when he came up he was waving that revolver in Critter's chest.

"Lugar, stop."

That was Scruples, who was standing on the observation deck at the rear of the Palace Car.

Lugar, he gave me and my nag one of those you're-dead looks, and sulked off toward a barn and pen downslope some. I knew he was itching to spray some lead around, and not just at Critter neither.

"Mr. Cotton, come in."

I didn't really want him to be calling me that, but I wasn't going to admit to being Mr. Pickens either, so I just marched up them iron steps to the platform at the end of the car, and on in.

Holy cats, I ain't ever seen such a place, and I ain't got

the words for it. There was a mess of red velvet drapes
sort of pinned up with gold tassels, and shimmery stuffed
furniture I think my ma called brocade, and damned if
there wasn't a big old grandfather clock in a walnut case,
and Venetian blinds on the windows, and a mess of them
books, all leather and gilt, and vases full of daisies and
whatnot, and a mysterious hallway along one side that
went to other rooms in the railroad car.

And that blonde, she was nowhere in sight, and I figured it was all for nothing. I'd have given a month's top-
gun salary just to see her with her hair down and flowing
around her shoulders. But hell, that's Pickens' Luck, and
if I planned to live a while, I'd better just get used to it.
My supply of women was pretty much limited to the red-
lamp variety.

"We like comfort," Scruples said. "And if this district
runs out of ore, we'll take our comfort with us."

He motioned me toward a narrow corridor along one
side, and we emerged into a compact dining area with a
kitchen at the other end of the car. I warn't feeling very
pleasured by it. This place was full of stuff, like oil
paintings on the wall and tablecloths. I'd heard of them
tablecloths, but this was the first I'd ever laid eyes on
one. This here one was a mess of white cloth laid over a
table, just waitin' to sop up stains. And napkins, too.
I'd seen a few of those, but not these white ones sitting
in rings of something that looked like silver. Maybe it
was pewter. I hardly knew one from another, except it
wasn't gold. But there was gold around there. Them picture frames looked to be gold, and them spoons and
forks, the handles was gold anyway. And them plates
was purple and gold, like the colors outside.

Without asking, he poured me some coffee from a

fancy jug, or whatever it was, and handed it to me. He poured one for himself, and motioned me to sit, which I did, sinking into a soft leather cushion. I sure had no notion why people lived like that. It seemed a mess of work to me, and no time off to have a beer.

"We have an investment company that's buying up mining properties in the district," Scruples said. "Mostly properties that are delinquent in paying taxes, or have faulty deeds. The problem is, it's hard to remove the previous owners from our property after we acquire it. You saw exactly what can happen. The loss of four of our men sets back our plans, and we'll have to push to return to schedule." He paused. "We intend to own the entire Swamp Creek Mining District."

That coffee, I'd never tasted the like. It was like them beans got burnt. It was strong enough to stain the rear end of an antelope brown. But I sort of liked the flavor, and thought maybe if I roasted some Arbuckle's beans hard before grinding them up, maybe I could do her.

Scruples, he looked me over amiably, his gaze focusing on me to see how I was responding to all this here stuff, so I just gazed back, wishing that blonde would show up out of one of them closed-off rooms. I didn't half mind this man Scruples, even if he was as real as a three-dollar bill.

He smiled. "We lost about half of our work force," he said. "And that's where you come in. I've made inquiries and found you're handy at a lot of things."

I sort of knew what he was driving at, but long as he was using big words like inquiries, I'd have to sort it out later.

"You could quickly become a top man with the Scruples Company," he said. "Maybe the straw boss. We've

ten or fifteen evictions ahead of us, and then we'll own
every mining property we think has promise."

"What's evictions?" I asked.

"Oh, persuading people like Mr. Cork it would be
wise to pack up and leave."

"That's all? Just talkin' people into leaving?"

Scruples smiled in a way as if he thought I was
dumber than a stump, and maybe I am.

"By whatever means," he said.

I knew right then he was working around the truth of
it with a mouthful of fancies.

"You mean push 'em out at gunpoint," I said, "and
using them guns if I have to."

Scruples smiled. "It's worth a hundred dollars a
month to you."

Holy cats, that's more money than I ever seen before,
and it made me itch. But I'd have to use my six-guns to
kill people just for hanging on to the mines they started
up. I thought about that, and I thought about the two
slicks I'd met today, the one near the Mint and the one
he called Lugar, and I didn't much like the idea.

"I think not, Mr. Scruples," I said.

"I don't ask a second time," he said.

I collected my sweaty old hat and stood up, and holy
cats, that blonde walked in, and her hair was down
around her shoulders, and I plumb stopped whatever I
was doing right then and there.

Chapter Four

Well, I'd wandered up the hill and dickered with this here Scruples, and there she was, standing there and smiling, and I went weak at the knees.

"Mr. Cotton," she said, extending a creamy hand.

I hardly dared take hold, but I managed it, and pumped away until it occurred to me I oughter stop.

"I'm Amanda Trouville, and pleased to meet you."

I just gawked there, not being in control of my senses, and words just wouldn't fill my mouth or even come into my poor old head.

I guess you'd call her a golden blonde. Least, that's how it come to me. She had that soft blond hair, my ma used to call it dishwater blond because it had a bit of light brown in it, but you couldn't use that there word, dishwater, on Amanda Trouville. It just didn't fit. That flesh, my ma used to call it peaches and creamy, and maybe that fit well enough. Peaches, that was pretty good. Her eyes, they were purple, I'd make an oath to it, first purple peepers I ever seen. But that hardly describes her. She was above medium, and curvy, but not too curvy, and well formed, far as I could tell. She wore a simple gray dress, and darned if it didn't have pleats in it, something I hardly ever seen, and it was unbuttoned a bit at the neck, where that peachy flesh sort of disappeared.

I was half crazy, and was thinkin' maybe I'd better just vamoose now that I got a good look. She was a rich man's woman, and not for the likes of old Cotton.

"I've heard so much about you," she said, makin' me more nervous than I've ever got in all my life. What'd she hear? Probably no good, for sure.

"Do sit down, Cotton. I'll have some coffee with you."

Scruples, he just settled a cup and saucer before her.

"Cat got your tongue, Cotton?" she asked, and them purple eyes sort of took me in, scraping over me like I had no secrets left.

"Well, ma'am, I was just wonderin' how come you're Trouville and he's Scruples, or maybe I'm just getting myself into more trouble here."

"Oh, we're not married, Cotton. We're partners. We're equal owners of an enterprise. We're in business together."

Well, there's business and there's business, and I didn't dare ask what sort of business.

"Our company's called Transactions, Incorporated. Carter and I believe that all of life's a transaction."

"Ma'am, I don't know one end of that word from the other."

"Oh, of course you do. Transactions are agreements. We believe in negotiating agreements with others, and that's how we live. Our personal arrangements are a transaction. I am his lover and he supports me. He pays me a thousand dollars a month to go to bed with me. But it's not an exclusive contract. I am free to made my own arrangements."

I was getting mighty flustered here, and I sort of

thought maybe I'd gotten into something I couldn't get no handle on. I thought there's married people, and people who go to whorehouses, and people who work in whorehouses, and I didn't know anything else was floating around except old maid schoolmarms.

She didn't look mean neither. I always thought them women were hard as a Dutch oven, but her gaze was sweet, and she had little smileys around her eyes. I sure couldn't make no sense of her, but I didn't have to. Every time she shifted around, all I could think about was what was hidden from my poor eyes.

Carter Scruples, he must of seen me making moon eyes, because he sorta took over.

"Amanda, Mr. Cotton doesn't think he'll join us."

I hated like hell to be called Cotton, that not being my real handle, but I just shut up and smiled.

I'd gotten what I came for, a look at this here blonde, and I figured it was time to get out.

"I'm on my way, sir."

"Oh, don't go!" Amanda said. "We need you."

I didn't have no answer to that. Truth is, I didn't much care for this Transactions company and what they were up to. I think she read it in me, because she started in on me.

"Our company's going to control the Swamp Creek Mining District quite soon, Mr. Cotton. There's the two big mines, and all the outlying ones. The big ones are proven, and have lots of reserves, but the smaller ones are only now being explored. We pick up the rights to them at auction, mostly because their claims are faulty, and it's going to pay off. The claims on the two big mines, they're both faulty, too, and we'll have them in a few months. But we need professional staff, good men who'll help us. That's where you fit in."

"I'm not sure I'm following you, ma'am."

"It's miss, not ma'am. The last thing I want from life is marriage."

"What is it you want, ma'am?"

"Lovers," she said.

Me, I get dizzy mighty quick, and I was getting plumb loose on my pins just then. I looked at old Carter, and he was just smilin' away like he'd heard it all before.

Scruples just smiled. "You probably don't approve of us. It doesn't matter. We make a fair offer on the smaller mines, some of them hardly proven up, and if the owners resist, we apply some muscle. We certainly don't want anyone to get hurt. Usually, a little show of force is all that's needed. And then we record a new claim that'll stand up. We've gotten five smaller mines that way, and we're having them evaluated. Some will be worthless, and that's why this business is a risk. But once we have the small operations up and running, and get a revenue stream going, we'll tackle the Big Mother Mine. That's the crown jewel of Swamp Creek, and it's yielding a clear profit of half a million a year, with no sign of pinching out. And the Fat Tuesday Mine's not far behind."

He was making it sound like some regular business deal, far as I could tell, but I got to remembering what old Agnes Cork told me, all about Brashear, the crooked clerk for the district in cahoots with this bunch, and it wasn't so regular at all. And all them gunslicks out there at the Cork place, they were fixing to kill old Agnes and take over.

I got to my feet, and pushed that fancy cup and saucer away. "I guess I'll go collect Critter and head down the hill," I said.

"Wait!" she replied.

I didn't much care to, but I thought I'd hear her out.

She came right up to me and peered into my eyes. "I guess we're not paying you enough," she said. "So here's some incentive. Each time you clear out the squatters from the mines we've got, you can spend one night with me."

That hit me in the pit of my stomach. I could hardly manage it.

"Each success, one night. I think you'd like that." She smiled. "I'd like it, too."

I sure was getting into places where I ain't been, and I couldn't hardly make sense of it.

"Your hundred a month, plus your pleasures," Scruples said cheerfully.

"How come me?" I blurted.

"Because of your big gun," she replied, and laughed sweetly.

My mouth, it was so parched I couldn't hardly reply. She smiled and beckoned me to one of them rooms in the Palace Car I'd not seen when we were going from rear to front. I followed her to a door, and she opened up, and there was a small but fancy bedroom with a big old bed in it, and just room enough to get around in there. It sure was a purty place, with lots of quilted stuff and things like that, but that's not what caught my eye.

Above the bed was a big long oil painting of Amanda, spread out on some sort of couch I hardly ever saw before, and she wasn't wearing a stitch. She was just lying there, all golden colored, with a little smile on her face, and her lips parted a little, and the rest of her sort of waiting for the evening to begin. I just plain stared, not having seen anything like that, not even in some saloon, where they got naked ladies in paintings, but them ladies usually got some gauzy thing sort of protecting them a little. But not Amanda. All of her was just plain caught in oil paint, and I took off my hat and stared.

"Well, all right, I guess I'll do her," I said, pushing aside all them objections that'd been crowding in my mind.

Just one night, I thought. I'd get some old miner to move along, and have myself just one night with her, and just the thought of it made me want to get the job done in two seconds.

"Then we have a transaction," she said.

I wasn't so sure what all that was about, and must have showed it.

"There are a few details still to be worked out," she said. "But it's clear enough, isn't it, Mr. Cotton? For each trespasser you remove from our mining properties, you get one night, and only one, with me."

She smiled. There was more in her purple eyes than business.

"I'll get right on with it," I said.

She motioned me to the cozy parlor at the rear of the Palace Car, where Carter Scruples was waiting. He had donned one of those neck scarves, danged if I could re- member the name, but ascot came to mind from some- thing I'd read. First time I'd ever seen one.

"I'm glad, Cotton," he said. "You have certain valu- able skills we happen to need."

He meant I knew how to handle a gun, which I sure did.

"You just give me a list," I said.

"Well, we need to look at a few details before this is finalized," he said.

I knew it. There was always a few strings. You cut a deal with someone, and next thing, they're adding a few strings. It's the damndest thing how a deal gets worked upon after the handshake, and not before.

He eyed me cheerfully. "Once you're in our employ, you'll follow our direction without cavil."

I sure didn't know what a cavil was. "I don't have any cavils," I said.

"Objections. You'll proceed agreeably as directed. Agreed?"

"No wiggle room?"

"You can always discuss it with us, if you think something won't work. We're not some sort of Prussian militarists here."

"What if these here people I'm evicting get excited, like Agnes Cork?"

"You will remove them by whatever means."

"And confiscate their property," Amanda added. "We consider it payment for rent."

"What else?"

Scruples frowned slightly, as if a little bit perplexed by the human race. "It sometimes happens that someone wants to abandon his agreement with Transactions. We can't permit it. Once you're in, we expect absolute loyalty until such a time as our goals are reached. The earliest you can seek release is one year from today."

"That's a long time some fella can't even quit."

"Then don't join us."

But Amanda, she was winking at me and fooling with a button.

"Anything else?" I asked.

"If you should betray the trust we place in you, you will be considered to have gone over to the other side, and we will deal with you."

That riled me some. "I'm not some switcher, and there's no call for you to accuse me. I join up with some brand, I'm loyal to the brand. I got one other question. You got the same deal with the other ones, the fellers out there in the barn?"

"Our arrangements are confidential, and that applies to you, Mr. Cotton," he said.

"You mean I can't even open my mouth?"

"Exactly," said Scruples.

"Just so you know," Amanda added.

"We've built our company on agreements we've entered into by our own free will. If you agree to this, it's by your own free will," Scruples said.

He was sure talkin' like some lawyer, but there was Amanda, her eyes bright, and that wasn't no pout on her lips.

"All right," I said. "It's a deal."

We shook on it. It made me feel funny, shaking on that.

"Well, then. This is the time to plan," Scruples said. "We've got eleven primary targets, and thirty-one secondary ones. We'd like to move fast on the primary ones. There's a lot of good ore escaping us because we can't get these miners out."

"I'm your man," I said, swelling up. I liked being handed a big job.

"The Hermit Mine. There are six partners plus two women up there. They're well dug in on an ore seam and cleaning it out just as fast as they can. They've got themselves fortified, and working two shifts, and are probably pulling a thousand dollars a day out of it. Their claim's flawed, and we bought it at auction."

"How much help will I get?" I asked.

"We have only three effectives. One of our men's wounded."

"They got any surprises for us, like Cork?"

"We don't know. They're armed, mostly with shotguns."

"You tried to evict them before?"

Scruples sighed. "We haven't been fortunate in our selection of men," he said.

"I'll get 'em out," I said.

Amanda, she grinned, and up and kissed me right in front of Scruples himself, and I got all rattled.

"Dawn?" said Scruples.

"I'll go out there and scout," I said. "You draw me a map."

He didn't need to. He handed me a printed map of the Swamp Creek District, and drew an X on the Hermit Mine.

"All right. I get 'em outa there and then what happens? You got a crew and a foreman that's gonna mine?"

"Oh, no, we'll shut it down. Seal it up."

"Shut her down? How come?"

"We know little about mining, my friend. We're speculators. We'll shut them all down. When we control the whole Swamp Creek District, we'll sell it."

For a fortune, I thought. For more money than old Cotton ever thunk about.

"All right. The Hermit Mine's first. And then you'll tackle Agnes Cork."

Chapter Five

When I drifted out into the twilight, it was stepping into the real world. Inside that there Pullman Palace Car, things sure didn't seem natural. Critter, he trotted up and bit me on the shoulder, just to let me know I'd ignored him too long and he wanted some hay.

"I bite back," I told him, but he just bared his teeth and sawed his head around.

I peered around some, now that I was a hireling of the Transactions company. I sure didn't know how I stepped into that, but I guess I did, and I'd have to clean my boot soles. This here railroad car was perched on a little hill on the edge of the big swamp, and there were two or three structures around it. I took one to be a bunkhouse. Another was a two-holer, and the third was a barn and stock pen. They were all hammered up from rough-sawn wood, with battens over the cracks, and looked like they'd blow away in a weak wind. But that was a mining camp for you.

Carter Scruples and Amanda Trouville were not here to stay. Anyone could see that. But there weren't no mining towns I ever heard of that intended to stick around, except maybe Butte, north of there a piece, which had so much copper under it that they'd never get it all out. There was even brick buildings going in up there, so some folks were planning on sticking around.

I led Critter to the pen and loosed the cinch and pulled my saddle off. I found a hay fork and loaded up a manger. Then I pulled his bridle off and cut him loose. He farted and headed for the water trough, kicked away some jackass in there, and settled down to some serious drinking and munching.

"That one should be shot," said Lugar from off in the darkness somewhere.

I ignored him for the moment, untied my war bag from behind the cantle of my saddle, and then hung the saddle on a wall peg.

"That's the bunkhouse?" I asked.

Lugar grunted, so I headed that way, and stepped into a gamy hellhole. These here employees of the Transactions Corporation hadn't soaked their flesh in a tub for a long time, and their duds was worse-smellin' than my own. Home Sweet Home, I thought.

"That bunk taken?"

"They're all taken," Lugar said.

I took it anyway, setting my war bag on it. Lugar and three more men stared at me. One had a left arm wrapped in a bloody rag.

"I joined up," I said.

No one said nothing. It was the damndest welcome I ever got.

One porker had just cleaned his Smith & Wesson, and was dry-firing it, letting the barrel edge my way as he clicked off a few. If that there seven-inch barrel wandered an inch more in my direction, there was gonna be a bunkhouse brawl about thirty seconds after I arrived, and Porky was going to get the worst of it.

But he eased his piece away, smiled at me, and holstered it.

"I guess I'll answer to Cotton," I said, hating it. I couldn't think of no good name for myself.

I waited some, but no one volunteered a name.

"Some feller called me Cottonmouth once," I said. "Them two in the parlor car, they hired me to get some jobs done."

"You the new straw boss?" asked a skinny gent, scarce beyond his boyhood pimples.

"I don't know. I'm just hired to get her done, and done quick."

"What's your pay?" asked the one with the bloody arm.

"Top wages," I replied. No sense in bein' modest.

I hadn't got a name out of the lot, except for Lugar. So I started on him. "You got a handle?"

"You've already heard it."

"You allergic to talkin' with a new man?"

"They come and go," he said.

I didn't recognize any of these. I'm handy with a six-gun, which is why I got myself hired, and I sorta keep track. But none of these looked familiar. If they were any good with their pieces, I'd probably know them. The only one that looked like he might be pretty good was Old Bloody Arm.

"You got a name?" I asked him.

"Garfield," he said.

That was a mighty peculiar choice, seein' as how Garfield expired three months after taking office.

"And you?" I asked Skinny.

"Arthur," he said.

"And you?" I asked Porky.

"Cleveland," he said.

"Well, all right. Call me Washington," I said. "I'm the Father of the Country."

They smiled some, but their teeth was so gray, I had a time makin' it out in the middle of that gloom. There was a little fire going in the potbelly, and it threw a little light from the cracks around the door.

The whole lot was amateurs. These weren't gunslicks with reputations. They were just toughs, or thought they were. Most likely, they were too dumb to make it in the crime business. They got to wear revolvers and shoot at miners for forty a month and found. Given the looks of this bunch, it was a wonder they could name a few presidents. But it was a wonder that I could, too. Just goes to show the value of outhouse readin'. I always read the newspaper before puttin' her to other use.

I looked over their rigs. There wasn't a fancy cut-down and oiled-up holster in the lot, just workaday leather for carrying iron, worn high on the hip. But Cleveland had him a black wool suitcoat hanging on a peg behind his bunk, and I suspicioned he had a hideout in a breast pocket and would be a handy backshooter. So this wasn't no gunslick bunch, just some thugs makin' some bucks by shooting miners. Scruples was hiring cheap—unless they got the same deal from Amanda I got . . . but the thought was so repulsive I couldn't hardly stand it. She had to draw the line somewhere.

"You from around here?" I asked, real general, because people are mighty touchy about personal questions like that. But I thought to make a little talk, just to get an idear about this bunch of misfits.

No one said nothing, so I did. "Me, I've been driftin'

around Wyoming and Montana, lookin' for work. Guess I found it," I said. "They want me to take on the Hermit Mine, and gave me this here map. You fellers in on this?"

Truth to tell, I didn't know if I was in charge or not. Scruples, he never made me boss. He just said, go do it. No one said nothing. This was a real mouthy bunch.

"They's six men and two women helpin' out over there and they got shotguns."

Lugar yawned. "We know all that, Cottonmouth. We were digging out buckshot for a week."

"You tried it?"

"I told you, we were doing surgery on ourselves."

"What time of day did you move in?"

"Afternoon."

"I'm going in at night."

Lugar bared some yellow-stained teeth. "Good luck," he said.

That was right friendly of him.

"And I'm going to look it over right about now," I said.

No one volunteered to go with me, but I hadn't expected them to. I'd do better just sliding around in the dark.

I took a long look at the maps, hoping I could make sense of the land when I got out into the night, and then stuffed the maps in my shirt.

"See you," I said, and slipped out the door.

Oh, that fresh air was just fine with me. I thought it'd take an hour or so just to get the stink outa my duds.

The Hermit was a mile out of town and up a grade, and I chose to walk it. I didn't want no trouble for Critter. That crew didn't give me any confidence, and I was thinkin' I'd mostly want to do these jobs alone. The dangerous one was the skinny one, Arthur, not Fatso. Lugar was mouthy, but looked pretty careful to me when push came to shove. I got to wonderin' how Scruples picked up that lot. He sure was scraping the bottom of the barrel. Him and Amanda didn't know much about mining towns. They couldn't have hired worse men. That told me something about Scruples. He was probably new to this game.

I like to think I know my way around at night, but the truth of it was that I got powerful lost trying to find the Hermit. There wasn't no moon to help me, and the few lamps in town were long snuffed out, and it's hard to pace a mile with nothing but stars to guide you, and I got so turned around I scarcely knew where I was. But then the old moon began to shine behind some ridge off to the east, and pretty soon it yellowed over the top of a ridge, and I got some idear of where I was. I'd gone too far, so I backtracked a bit, and turned up a gulch I thought was likely, and began hiking up a two-rut road that looked used enough.

I wanted to see a bunch of things, like where they bunked and whether someone was guardin' at night. I was thinkin' it'd be best to jump a mine like that around midnight and move in so fast that no one's awake and grabbing for iron. Pretty soon, I saw the works ahead, a regular head frame poking into the sky, and some log buildings, and a heap of tailings, and some ore cars, so I was getting the layout in mind.

That's when them dogs got me. Next I knew there was five, six of them snarling dogs comin' after me, some barking and the rest snapping at me bad. It was like I was gonna be dinner for a pack of wolves. One leapt at my throat, snapping teeth at me. I knocked him off, but he whirled around again and he was jumpin' even as the others were biting my legs and snapping at my arms. I sure was in a fix. Two, three others just stood back and barked, wakin' up anyone around there. I was too busy knockin' dogs off to know what to do, but somehow I got my revolver out and began knocking dogs with the barrel, slashing this way and that, sending 'em howling. But now I was bitten bad, and hot blood rolled down my legs, and a dog or two had got a sleeve and wouldn't get loose, so I was losin' and maybe about to get eaten.

I saw that one leaper comin' at my throat, so I shot him. He yelped and fell in a heap, and I whirled around and shot another comin' at my neck, and he whined and shuddered and went limp, and then ever'thing happened so fast I couldn't make no sense of it. But next I knew, two big arms came around me from behind and caught me in a steel grip like I was fish in an eagle beak. I bucked and jackknifed, and all I did was make them arms go tighter. They pinned my arms to my side, and my gun went flyin' somewhere.

Then another one of them miners comes around in front of me.

"Kill my dogs, do ya?" he said. He slugged my chin and then slammed my gut and then hammered my pinned-down arms until I was half crazy, and then knocked my head again, and there wasn't nothing I could do, not with some two-hundred-pound miner behind me pinnin' me and turnin' me into a target.

"Dat's what you get for killing dog," one said, and punched my nose. I felt blood runnin' down my lips.

"Dis here's a lesson," he said. "Next time I kill you."

Whoever pinned my arms tossed me down and the pair started kicking me. I felt some pain in my rib, and knew one boot had stove me in. Them dogs circled around, but didn't dive on me.

"Dis here gun's mine, and so's the belt," one said, yanking my gunbelt off me. "Dat's for da dog you kilt."

I lay there on my back, all busted up, with a couple of loose teeth, blood dripping from a few holes in me, and so sick I thought I'd faint.

"Tell Scruples dis mine ain't his," the miner said. "Next time, we go get him and do dis to him personal."

They stared down at me. I stared up at the moon. I'd hardly gotten a look at the pair, but they were both bigger than me, and twice as strong.

I saw one of them pick up the dead dog and pull it close in his arms, and croon to it.

"You was the best one," he said. "You done good. You gonna get buried right."

Then, suddenlike, there was only silence. Them miners and their live dogs left. I didn't know how I'd get back to town, and up to the bunkhouse, but I had to before something else finished what the dogs and miners had started.

I wasn't fit to stand up for another half hour, and when I finally got up, I wished I hadn't because I hurt more places than I knew I had. I was too sore to get mad. I'd get even with those bastards some day, but not now. In the space of a few minutes I'd learned how to hate ever' miner that ever lived.

I took one step at a time, feeling the ground come up through my stockin's, and that's how I walked back to Swamp Creek, one foot at a time. I decided I didn't like this job a whole lot.

Chapter Six

I think I got back to that bunkhouse around dawn, but I don't rightly remember. I mostly just piled into a bunk and was lost to the world. But I did hear some yakkin' about me from the rest. I was too far gone to know or care.

Next I knew, old Scruples hisself was standing over my bunk staring down at me like I was some piece of bone some mutt dug up. I stared back up at him, hurting too much to say anything. Besides, there wasn't nothing to say. He could read the whole story just lookin' at blood and bruises and tears in my shirt and pants.

"You failed," he said.

That wasn't an encouragin' word. My teeth was too loose to talk back, so I just stared back.

"We thought you'd have what it takes," he said. "But obviously, you don't. We'll have to resort to other means."

I wondered what that was all about, but I didn't care. I just wanted to close my eyes and hope all that pain, comin' at me from every unknown part of my body, would go away. The worst was in the ribs. I know one or two was stove in because of that kick from that miner. That hobnailed boot busted my chest.

"I'm taking you off top-dog wages," he said.

I thought we had a deal, but I couldn't put that in words, so I just stared back up at him. If he had the right to change a deal whenever he felt like it, so did I. But it would be a while before I could do something.

"What happened to your gunbelt?" he asked.

I mumbled something through busted teeth and swollen lips.

He smiled suddenly. "They have it." He chuckled. "They took it from you. Not only did you get pounded by some skinny miner, but he took your guns."

I gargled down some bile and lay there, staring at the bastard. Then I remembered what they said, and made my mouth work some. "They said you're next if you come after them," I muttered. "Told me to tell you."

Oddly, this had its effect. Scruples didn't laugh. He probably was thinkin' what would happen to that smooth face of his if they came after him, and maybe all the rest of him, too.

"That tells me all I need to know," he said. "Since you're of no use to us for a few weeks, you'll be on suspended wages."

Only then did I glance around the bunkhouse, but none of them others were in with us, so they weren't hearing this.

"We'll charge you for your room and board and horse feed when you're back on salary," he said. "You have our permission to stay here."

That was some transaction, all right.

"Broken rib," I muttered.

"There's no doctor in Swamp Creek. So live with it."

Then he was gone, out the door, into the sunlight, and there was nothing but the stink of the bunkhouse there for me. I wanted to get my rib bound up, some tight wrap around me just to keep things from movin' around in there. I supposed I was lucky it didn't poke into my lung.

That pain, it just kept comin' at me, and I just had to take it. I settled back on the bunk, wondering which stink was the worst, mine or the bunkhouse's. It was a toss-up. I lay there wondering how I'd get some guns and a gunbelt. I'd probably have to borrow money for that, too, from Scruples, and he'd have me in slavery for a year.

But then the door creaked open, and there was Amanda, wrinklin' her nose.

It was cool out, but she left the door open some to air the place.

"Carter says you need some help," she said.

"Broken rib. Can't hardly breathe sometimes."

"You want it bound?"

I nodded.

There wasn't no sheets in there, so she went off to the Palace Car to get one, and I thought maybe Transactions, Incorporated, wasn't so bad.

She had a sheet and scissors when she returned, and soon was cutting away my shirt and undershirt, because I sure couldn't manage it.

"There?" she said, pointing to a bad area, bulging red and turning purple.

She tore the sheet into wide strips and set to work, wrapping it around me, and finally making little tails she could tie things with. It did feel some better once she got me wrapped like a mummy. It put me in mind of our deal, and I managed a smile, but she wasn't lookin' at me with those purple eyes, and maybe she had forgotten.

"Dogs got me," I mumbled.

"We need you. Get well," she said, and vamoosed.

I watched her walk out of there, thinkin' it would be a while before I had my night with her. She sure was all business. In fact, I thought she'd charge the sheet to my account, too. Everything in her life was a transaction. I finally did get to know the meaning of that word.

I had the feeling she wrapped my chest to protect their investment. It didn't have nothing to do with Cotton.

They were some pair, her and Scruples. I didn't know beans about them, and sort of wished I did. They were Eastern, and they had some money, and they sure had an attitude. I wondered if his ma and pa ever put a dime in the church collection box when it came around. And what her ma and pa did that they'd raise a daughter like her.

That was a puzzle. They were makin' all this look legal, too. They got papers saying they had bought flawed claims at auction, though I durned well didn't remember no auctions of mining claims around there. But they had all this legal paper, so they could claim it was all up and up, and if they got into trouble the courts would back them up. But it was all a fraud, leastwise that's what old Agnes Cork said, and them two miners at the Hermit seconded that. So why bother with a lot of legal paper? I sure didn't know.

I settled back in that bunk, and wished for some fresh air to drive away that stink in there, and I watched the clouds go by, but the window was so grimy I could hardly see out of it. I thought I might get up a little in a few days, and maybe start walkin' again, and begin with the gunsmith or the hardware to see about a new gun. A new one takes some gettin' used to. You don't just buy one and stuff it in your holster. You got to get to know it like a lover, know every inch of it and how she shoots and slides in and out of the sheath. You got to know all that, and whether the trigger's stiff and slow, and whether you need to do a little filing on the mechanism to get her to speed up. But hell, I didn't even have a revolver now, and not enough to get a new one neither.

I sure didn't see much of them others, Lugar and all them so-called presidents. I wondered where they went and why they couldn't give me a real name. They'd come and go, hardly ever speakin' to me, but sure busy with something. Cleveland, the porky one, he just grinned at me as if I was fly-bait. Arthur, the skinny one, never even glanced my way. And Old Bloody Arm, Garfield, plain ignored me.

Those days went pretty slow. I lay there, wanting to get healed up. The rest were gone, and no one said where to. The only one that looked after me was Lugar, and that was because he was ordered to by Scruples. Lugar made sure I got fed and watered, and got helped out to the two-holer. But I wasn't eating much; it hurt to down anything and feel that busted bone moving around in me.

After a few days, I couldn't bear it, and forced myself to get out into some fresh air and hobble around. The clean air done me good, and the next day I hobbled down the slope and into Swamp Creek, just to see the sights. The town was full of miners. They mostly wore dust caps and dungarees and hobnailed boots, and I was plumb respectful. They had persuaded me that they ain't to be messed with.

Swamp Creek was a rowdy little town, even in broad daylight, when the saloons were all roarin' and the gamblers were all at their green tables, and they was a drunk leaning into a wall every few yards. There wasn't no law in Swamp Creek, except for a town constable the miners put in there to keep the lid on. But the constable was an old drunk hisself, and he didn't have a jail neither. But he had a lockup even so. They'd planted a piece of mining rail in the ground, and given the old boy some leg irons, and that was the jail. That didn't sound like much, but it was no fun bein' leg-ironed to that post in broiling sun, or through a winter's night, so even if it wasn't much, it kept the lid on Swamp Creek. But real law, sheriff law, that was some distance away, in Butte. And that's how everyone wanted it. That was the thing about any mining town. It wanted the law just as far away as it could get.

I kept a sharp eye out for them Hermit miners, fearful of a repeat performance, but they was all busy up there blowing ore out of their mine. I knew I wouldn't recognize them, and I'm not sure they'd recognize me, except I was so stove up. But things look different by daylight, and there were lots of stoved-up men in Swamp Creek. Those Hermit Mine boys, they was probably all about seven feet tall and shoulders wide as an ax handle. Me, I'm cowboy sized, which is about medium.

Now, all this time I'm wondering what my bosses are up to. Scruples, he vanished somewhere, and I hardly saw Amanda, except when she was taking some air. But something was goin' on, even if I didn't have a clue. There wasn't no more raids on what they called trespassers in the mines they claimed to own, and things was pretty peaceful. But I didn't believe for a minute that things was going to stay quiet. Whatever Scruples was up to, I'd find out soon enough.

Then one afternoon, a new man showed up in the bunkhouse while I was takin' my siesta, and we looked each other over. I thought maybe I knew who he was, though we'd never met. I knew because of his habits. First thing he did was open the one window and the door. He chose a bunk in the corner, got a scrub bucket and some Fels Naptha, and scrubbed the hell out of the whole area. Then he washed the old blanket lyin' there and hung it out to dry. This one, he was thin and neat and clean. He had fingernails so clean they actually looked white. He was shaven close, too, and I imagined he scraped his jaw every morning. He wore a shirt so clean I couldn't see one food stain on it, and even his britches was clean and washed. But that interested me less than his rig, which was a well-oiled gunbelt that he tied low on his left leg. Left-hander then, which fit with what I knew.

"I'm called Cotton," I said.

He smiled. "Your reputation precedes you," he said, and I wallowed that around in my head for a while, not knowing what to make of it.

"I always use my entire name, which is a rarity in my trade. I am Rudolph Costello Glan."

That's who I thought. Scruples had hired himself an assassin. Glan was the cleanest man in Montana, and the dirtiest backshooter alive. He didn't get into no fights; he simply stalked and killed, usually with a high-powered rifle. It sent a small chill flowing through my busted bones.

"I think I heard of you once," I said.

"I'm afraid I haven't heard of you," he replied.

I didn't think I wanted to be heard of by someone like Glan.

"I'm just a wandering cowboy," is what I said. "Some miners learned me to respect them, which is why I'm laying around here."

"I don't teach anyone to respect me," Glan said. "Except at the last."

I watched him get settled. In his war bag were changes of clothing, and several bars of soap, and some witch hazel so he'd smell good.

"You mind if I leave the window open?" he asked.

"Suits me," I said. "But the rest, they'll close it. They can't stand fresh air with no stink in it."

"We seem to share the same tastes," Glan said.

I wasn't so sure I shared anything with Glan. "Scruples, he got some work for you?" I asked.

"I have a contract with Transactions, Incorporated, which requires my confidentiality," he said. "I'm afraid I can't discuss it."

"Pay and anything else?" I asked, riled up some.

He simply smiled.

He didn't say nothing, but I sure as hell knew he had his own little contract with Amanda, and he was looking forward to collectin' real soon.

I shouldn't of got heated up. It wasn't none of my business. But I did. Even if she made her own deals, I didn't much like it. Banged up as I was, I still thought of Amanda as belongin' to no one but Scruples and me.

"You going to be well enough to help out soon?" he asked politely.

I got the feeling he was hoping I wouldn't be. "Pretty quick now, but I don't even have a rig, and there's no gunsmith in town."

"Pity, isn't it?" Glan asked.

There was a miners' cemetery outside of town, and I thought there'd be some new graves in it pretty quick.

Chapter Seven

A few days later, Carter Scruples sent for me, and I hiked upslope to the Pullman Palace Car. He let me in from the rear platform, and there was Amanda, too, perched in a fancy chair with fabric that looked like spun gold. They were both in good cheer. She was wearing purple, to match the enamel of the palace car.

"How are you?" he asked.

"Gettin' around now."

"We're going back to work," he said.

I didn't know whether that was good or bad, the way I was feeling about this whole outfit.

"We're going to drive off trespassers from our property. Two more gents are coming in tonight, and with Glan, we'll have what we need."

I wondered who the gunslicks might be, and whether they were Glan's caliber, or just another bunch of thugs. At any rate, things was pickin' up some, and they was fixing to put me back into the middle of it. I guess they got over being mad at me.

"We've waited too long. Every day we're not in control of our property, we lose money. We're going after the Hermit Mine again, and this time there won't be any errors."

He didn't quite say they were my errors, so I smiled some.

"You're going to ride in this afternoon and deliver this envelope, and wait for an answer," he said.

"Ride in?"

"Certainly. No one's going to shoot you in broad daylight. You'll be unarmed, and one glance at you will tell them what they need to know."

One glance at my face would show them a lot of black and blue, not to mention some purple and sickly yeller and some puffed up red.

"I guess that's gonna tell 'em who they kicked and pounded," I said.

"Exactly. It's just what we want."

"I don't know if I want to go in there without no guns."

"Safest thing that could happen to you. Wear a gun and you might get shot."

"I'd rather walk naked into a whorehouse," I said.

Amanda, she smiled some. I was gettin' all full of thoughts about Amanda again, just seein' her sitting there, looking so pretty she could melt an iceberg.

"Wait for them to read the message and then tell us their response," he said.

"What's in it?"

"Anyone not out of there by dawn tomorrow's likely to be shot. Of course, we don't quite say it that way. The wording is, trespassers must leave before sundown and anyone who stays does so at his peril. But they'll understand perfectly well that firearms will be employed."

"Shot?"

"On sight."

"Isn't that pushing things some?"

"Part of your contract with us is to obey our direction unquestioningly." He stared at me, waiting for me to get riled up, but I didn't give him no satisfaction.

"I'll do her," I said. "But I'd like a gunbelt in my saddlebag."

"No, nothing. No saddlebags. When you get back, I'll give you a gun. Take your pick. Those men who foolishly got themselves killed the other day at Cork's mine left a few spare weapons around in the bunkhouse. I'll sell one to you and take if off your wage. But not until you're back."

I guess I was lucky not to foolishly get myself killed that day.

"Come show me all your bruises tomorrow night," said Amanda.

Oh, that did it all right. I was half thinkin' just to quit and get out while the getting was good, but now she got her claws into me again. I went a little wobbly at the knees.

Scruples, he handed me a white envelope, and I took it. He cocked an eyebrow, like it was something he didn't want said out loud, and I nodded.

"Back in a couple of hours," I said.

When I stepped out, there was Critter all saddled.

"Someone should kill this horse," Lugar said.

Critter, he nipped his hat and waved it. Lugar knocked a fist into Critter's jaw, and snapped the hat to his head. I wasn't in no condition to knock a fist into Lugar's jaw, but he saw it in my eyes, and grinned.

I get on with some trouble, because it started my ribs howlin' at me again, but pretty soon I was steering my old nag down that hill and up the road, which ran up the valley, to get to the Hermit Mine. I wasn't feeling very good about it, but if I wanted to draw my pay I'd just have to keep on going.

I thought Scruples was right. Come in there by daylight with no weapon and they'd palaver. But that didn't make me feel any better. I still wore more colors on my face than anyone else in Swamp Creek, and it made a lot of fellers in town point and smile. There is them that enjoyed my misery.

Actually, it felt good to be on Critter, ridin' up a sunny valley in clean air. I guess that stink in the bunkhouse was gettin' to me. Not even Glan could get rid of it, and he tried. He was the best-washed man-killer I ever met. It was like he was scrubbin' sin out of him day and night, but at least he smelled good.

I passed lots of two-rut roads heading off toward mines, and a big road that went up to the Fat Tuesday Mine, which employed a bunch of men and was raking in a bonanza. Some gambler from New Orleans named Argo got ahold of it in a poker game, and quit his gamblin' to run it. He had two shifts runnin' and word was he was thinkin' of adding another shift, so it would be pulling up rich ore all day every day. I wondered how them miners felt about it. They got three dollars a day, a lot of money, but they spent most ever' day down in that pit.

"Critter," I says, "I ain't ever going to be a miner."

He farted, which is his usual way of agreeing with me. There come a place I thought would take me to the Hermit Mine, but it was hard for me to remember. There was snow up high on the mountains, and a lot of pines up there, and gray rock, but it didn't look the same by daylight as it did that night. It sure was pretty.

But I turned anyway, thinkin' this was the road, all

right. I half expected to get jumped or shot at, and I sort of hunkered low in my saddle, trying to avoid the worst. But we just trotted along, up a long grade, and then a steeper slope, and then out on a hanging flat. I could see the Hermit Mine ahead, and no one stopped me, and that didn't make no sense. But I sure felt eyes on me, or maybe a spyglass or two, watching me come along. It was just another sleepy afternoon around there.

I was movin' closer than I got that night, but no one was waving a rifle at me, so I just kept on. There were a few buildings there, rough board affairs, but one with windows looked like a place to bunk. They sure weren't spending money on comfort. There was a shaft bored into the slope, and some rails goin' in. There were a couple of storage sheds, and what looked like a powder bunker off a way, notched into the stony slope. And still no one gave me a holler.

I finally reined up Critter at a hitch rail and got down. I was lookin' around when a woman stepped out the door of a little shanty. She wore a blue bonnet, and looked kinda wiry.

"Yes?"

"I'm looking for the manager."

"He's in the pit."

"Someone in charge up here?"

"Yes, I am."

I looked her over. She looked like an in-charge woman all right. I wondered if she was in charge of her husband, too. I didn't never see a woman in charge of anything 'cept a whorehouse before.

"Well, I'm supposed to deliver you this here envelope and wait for an answer."

She eyed me closely, her steely gaze taking in my

purple and blue and green face, and she smiled slightly. "You're the one," she said.

"They didn't improve my ribs none."

She was sort of enjoying that, but she took the letter and opened it and slowly digested the message.

"Tell those bastards in the railroad car to go to hell," she said.

"I'll do that, ma'am."

"And if you show up here again, we'll bust the rest of your ribs."

"They tell me you're trespassin', ma'am. This here is theirs, according to the papers they got."

"Sonny boy, you're working for crooks," she said.

That riled me some. Not the working for crooks part, but getting called sonny boy by this female armadillo.

"And if any of you show up here again, watch your back," she said.

At that point, a boy wandered out of the shack. He looked to be nine or ten, and was lugging a revolver, which he brandished.

"Luke, don't shoot that thing," she said.

"I'm protecting you, Ma," he said, and swung that barrel toward me. I was sure getting the sweats.

"I'm just here to talk, kid," I said.

"You're stealing the gold mine."

He swung that barrel around at me, and I bailed off of Critter, who began to buck.

"Luke!"

The kid pulled the trigger, and the revolver barked. The recoil threw the kid's arms up and unbalanced him. I didn't know where that bullet went, but I cowered behind Critter. This sure was a new one for me.

"Luke, hand me that!"

The boy docilely handed the old revolver to his ma,
who slid it into her paw and kept it aimed my direction,
just on general principles.

"Now git back to your lessons," she said.

The stinkin' little fart was grinning, but he meandered back into the rough-sawn wood shack.

"Too bad he missed you," she said.

I came out from behind Critter. The cuss knew what
I'd done, and bit me.

"That horse should be shot," she said. She eyed me,
like she was going to start a lecture, and then that's what
she did.

"You're working for crooks and maybe you're one,
too. They're in cahoots with the mining clerk, Johnny
Brashear, and they scheme up ways to beat people out
of their own mines. Mostly, it's a sealed auction, not
even announced to the public, and next thing a person
knows, he's lost his mine and he's a trespasser. That
crook Brashear gets a cut, and your bosses take the rest.
I don't know whey they bother with legal paper. All they
need's a few owlhoots like you and they'd take over."

"I rightly don't know either, ma'am."

"What're they paying youse to drive away owners, eh?"

"Fancy wages, but I haven't seen none yet."

"You never will. They'll welsh on you."

The thought had occurred to me, but I wasn't gonna
admit it, not to her anyway. That kid and his revolver
still riled me some.

"I got to feed the shift coming up to daylight, so you
get out of here. Tell them two, Scruples and the whore,
no dice. And tell them, if they start trouble here, it'll end
at their railroad car."

I nodded.

"You were lucky all you got was some broken ribs and loose teeth," she added.

An ore car erupted from the black mine mouth, followed by three grimy men. No sooner did they spot me and Critter but they was liftin' shotguns parked around there somewheres and coming at me like I was a bull's-eye.

"Scruples sent him," she said.

They were a grimy lot, but they gathered around me studyin' my face and seeing how it looked purple and blue and green.

One, a big brute, simply smiled. They all raised their twelve-gauge shotguns until three bores, they was pointing at me, and I about kissed the world good-bye.

"You got the message," said the big one.

I sure did. Critter, he was muttering and snapping his teeth, but I tugged on the rein to quiet him down.

"The company, it's got more men coming in, and they ain't friendly," I said.

"Neither are we," one of them replied.

They waved me off, so I turned Critter down the road, feeling my back itch.

I sure would have a few words of Carter Scruples and Amanda, too.

Chapter Eight

They was waitin' for me when I got back to the Pullman Palace Car, and I got let in before I even had Critter took care of.

"Well?" Scruples asked.

"Oh, they got the message, all right, and she says they'll take the fight here if you mess with them."

"She?"

"Woman who runs the office and feeds 'em."

"But you delivered the warning, right?"

"Yep."

"You have anything else to tell us?"

"Nope," I said. I decided not to talk about that little brat that pretty near blowed my head off.

"Then we're covered. They've been warned they're trespassing. They've been given time to pull out."

He sounded like he wanted to make it all legal.

Amanda, she was sittin' there looking so pretty I could hardly stand it, but she wasn't sayin' much. I was wondering if maybe she'd invite me in for the night, but she was just busy with her knitting needles makin' a pink sweater. I hardly ever seen a woman knit before, and I couldn't see how she was making them stitches. I looked at her sort of hopeful, but she just smiled all blond peaches and cream like.

But then she set aside her needles and stared at me. "Did they say whether they'd be leaving?"

"Well, not exactly. She said they'd come after you if you messed with them."

"That's all?"

I didn't know whether to get into the rest. "She said you're, aw, you know."

"I don't know, Mr. Cotton."

"Crooks." I felt my ears redden.

"I imagine we are," she said. I plain stared.

"Confidence man, confidence woman," Scruples said. "The old shell game. This is the biggest one we've tried."

They had me there. "What's a confidence?" I asked. Another one of them big words I never learnt up to grade eight.

"Swindlers," Scruples said.

"I don't know that one neither."

He smiled. "You're the perfect employee," he said.

I got all puffed up with that. No one in my whole life ever called me perfect before. I decided it was time to get myself armed.

"In that case, how's about that gun?" I asked.

"Oh, the gun. I've several in my office. Some of those gents who braced Cork had spares, you know. Come along, and we'll put you in business."

I followed him down that long corridor to one of them rooms, and it proved to be an office, all right. A little oak desk and a black typing machine in there, and gray account books and red law books and stuff. But hanging from a coatrack were three gunbelts. Scruples motioned toward them, so I went for a look. The one Colt Frontier was so beat up I didn't much like it. Another was an ancient Dragoon, a ton to wear and lift and shoot. The third was a shiny Colt Baby Dragoon, a cap-and-ball thirty-one-caliber model with an octagonal barrel. It felt fairly tight, and the hammer came down square on the nipple. I didn't want the thing; I wanted brass cartridges, not powder and caps and balls and wads, a gun that wouldn't fire every time it rained, and a gun needing a lot more care than I wanted to give it.

"These don't do me much good," I said.

Scruples shrugged. It was plain he was putting his chips on Glan, not me, and it didn't matter what I thought.

But then Amanda showed up in the doorway.

"Try that belt with the smaller Colt," she said. "I think you'd look very good in it, big boy."

"Oh, hell," I said, and I tried it on. It shore wasn't anything I wanted to wear, but there she was makin' moon eyes at me, and I just sighed and nodded. The well-oiled belt fit, and the holster hung about right.

"Twelve dollars against your pay," Scruples said. "But you get some extras."

He handed me a red can of DuPont powder, a box of caps, a box of .31-caliber balls, and a pasteboard box of patches.

"How 'bout if I just borrow her for a few days until I can get me a real gun?"

"No, Mr. Cotton, this is it."

"You look just wonderful, sweetheart," Amanda said.

Oh, hell, what's the use of fighting anything? I just swallered a little and smiled. At least I had a shooting iron strapped on me.

That's how it ended. They eased me out the rear door onto the platform, and I hopped down them steel steps to the ground. They'd put that old Palace Car on a bit of track cobbled together from mine rails and mine timbers, which is how they got her leveled up. But it sure was a strange way to live, like they was ready to roll away in a moment.

I put Critter in the pen and hayed him. There was a couple of new nags in there, one of them a looker, with good blood showin'. The other was even uglier than Critter, and looked just as mean, too. Horses say something about their owners, so I looked 'em over real careful. The good-lookin' chestnut one was brushed, and the mane was roached and he didn't have a scratch. I thought maybe it was a Morgan, but I don't know nags that good. The other, it was a big walkin' wreck, and showed scars on the flanks where the owner's rowels had dug into flesh. Its mouth was sore-looking, from someone yanking the bit around. It looked mean, and I steered clear, not wantin' to catch a horse hoof right where I was savin' up delights for Amanda.

I tossed my saddle on a peg and headed for the bunkhouse, wonderin' what the company had brung in.

It didn't take me long to find out. They was two new ones in there, in addition to Glan and the three presidents, as I called them. This new pair was big and little, and I saw at once how it was with them. The big one, he'd taken my bunk under the window, and was sittin' there just waiting for me.

I liked my bunk under the window, because it gave me some fresh air, which was in mighty short supply around there. But now this big galoot was sitting there grinning at me. I knew the type. He was a street fighter, a brawler, who never learnt a dirty trick he didn't like. This was an eye-gouger, nut-pounder, ear-biter, toad-stabber, hair-yanker, knee-buster, and toe-stomper. And he showed it, too. His nose had been flattened more times than it could remember, and now it was a big wad of pulp. He had more cuts and scars on him than an army sergeant. He didn't have one front tooth, up or down. They'd all been knocked out.

"I guess that's my bunk," I said, knowing what was coming.

"I guess it was, laddie," he replied, his voice an odd whistle without those teeth.

"I guess first come, first pick," I said.

"You can pull me off of it, me boy," he said, sort of smirky. "I'm game."

He sat there cracking his thick knuckles. His fingers were about the size of my wrist.

Truth to tell, I wasn't in no mood to make a contest of it. My ribs were still bound up, and my face still looked like an old T-bone steak.

"Game's been postponed," I said. That would let him know a thing or two. This wasn't over.

"Youse is a thmart laddie."

"Busted ribs," I replied. "I'm Cotton."

"Arnold," he replied.

"That's all?"

"Arnold is all thish man wants for a name."

"That's better than two of 'em," I said, wanting to be reasonable. I'd want this brute on my side in a fight.

I looked the other one over, and damned if he wasn't pretty near a dwarf. He wasn't no dwarf, but he didn't get much ahead of four feet. He was plumb delicate, but eyeing me with brown eyes that was neutral. He was decidin' whether I'd do or not. He'd taken a bunk over near Glan, and the pair of them looked to be the real gunslicks in the outfit. That little feller had him a gunbelt of black leather with two little guns hung from it. They was little short-barreled items, maybe thirty-two caliber. You had to be pretty close to do any damage with a rig like that, but maybe that's how this little feller liked it.

"We all have pseudonyms around here," he said.

There was another of them words I'd never heard of. "Soodo what?" I asked.

"Noms de guerre," he replied.

I sure didn't know what he was yakkin' about. "Cotton here," I said.

"Front or rear," he asked.

I wasn't about to admit to nothin'. "Take your pick," I said.

The little guy smiled. Nice even white teeth. He owned that fine horse out there.

"Call me The Apocalypse," he said.

"Mind if I just call you Pock?"

"Of course I mind."

This was getting plumb difficult. "That a nice Morgan horse you got out there?"

"How did you know it is my horse?"

"It sure don't belong to him," I said, jerking a thumb at Arnold.

"You're smart," The Apocalypse said.

I was damned if I would call him that, but I'd settle it later. It looked like old Scruples had a full house here now. I eyed the rest while I got myself settled in the bunk across the aisle. Not that I wanted that stinkin' bunk, but I needed to heal up before makin' an issue out of it. And it'd pay to watch Arnold in action before I settled his hash. They usually had some weakness or other.

It was some crew in there, thugs like them presidents; an all-around tough son of a bitch like Lugar, a brawler like Arnold, a sniper like Glan, and an in-close man like whatever the hell he called himself. And me, just a country boy good with guns, at least if I had any. They was all lookin' at that old Baby Dragoon cap-and-ball revolver, and maybe smilin' some. I was small potatoes, far as they was concerned. I didn't mind. No one was payin' me no never mind.

It looked to me like Scruples had himself a bunch of trespass enforcers that could deal with most any outfit, 'cept maybe the two big ones, the Big Mother Mine and Fat Tuesday. It sure stank in that bunkhouse, and I hoped to get 'er over with quick.

Long about after we licked up some sowbelly and beans for our supper, Lugar gave us our marchin' orders. Scruples, he was still goin' after the Hermit Mine; they must be blowing some good gold ore outta there because it was tops on Scruples' list. Lugar, he never told us he was the straw boss, but he's the one come to tell us what we'd be doing in the morning.

"We're going to drive them trespassers out for good," he said. "Live or in coffins, don't matter any."

The deal was that we'd go there at dawn, shoot any dogs, and move in close enough so Glan could put his marksmanship to work, and then simply shoot anyone in sight until they called it quits.

Scruples was gonna have the Hermit Mine all to himself and Amanda before sundown.

"Any questions?" Lugar asked.

"You gonna give them a chance to pull out?" I asked.

"They had their chance."

"What if they raise their hands and quit?"

"They had their chance."

That didn't sit well with me, but it didn't bother the rest none.

We'd leave at dawn and the sun would come up blood red.

Chapter Nine

We left for the Hermit Mine around dawn, while dew was still glistening on the grass. We passed quietly through Swamp Creek, still mostly asleep except for a drunk sitting on the boardwalk in front of the Opal Saloon. The clop of our horse hooves echoed hollowly from the rough-sawn board-and-batten buildings lining the sole street. Scarcely anyone noticed the passage of some of the strangest-lookin' hombres in the territory.

There was Lugar, skinny and tall and sprung like a rat trap, leadin' the parade. They'd made him the straw boss. He had Garfield, Arthur, and Cleveland behind him, three good-for-nothing thugs with real names I'd never know, all of 'em off of some waterfront somewhere back East. They wasn't good for much, but now they all had shotguns, which were handy for crowd control. They didn't know the front of a horse from the tail, and flopped around in them saddles like the Eastern dudes they were.

I was in the middle there, still pretty useless, with that little pocket Colt hangin' from a borrowed gunbelt. I'd healed up but hadn't gotten any speed back, so I was mostly along for the ride. Then there was Rudolph

Costello Glan, elegant and clean-shaven and cool, the best man with a long gun anywhere. He was carrying a long-barreled Sharps in a sheath, and could hit a bull's-eye at a thousand feet. His target would be dead before he heard the shot.

Then there was Arnold, the street thug, floppin' around on that abused nag, looking for something, anything, to pulverize. He was wearin' a derby and a brown tweed suit. He'd be a good man in a brawl, but this time he was given a special mission: them dogs at the Hermit Mine. And trailing along was that little feller who called himself The Apocalypse, dressed up in black ready-mades from a clothing store. Danged if I knew what that was about, but those were mean little baby guns hangin' from his waist. He reminded me of one of them small-pecker men always trying to make up for it.

We rode on through town and out past the two big mines, Fat Tuesday and Big Mother, and we could hear them shovin' ore cars around up there, and then we heard the rattle of a car dumping tailings over the cliff edge. That's where most of the gold in the district was coming from.

We sure were some bunch, clopping along that dirt road that sunny morning. Me, I almost didn't feel a part of it. We was supposedly goin' to evict some trespassers, but half of these fellers was just itching to kill someone, especially someone big and defenseless who wasn't gonna fight back none. Maybe it wouldn't happen. Maybe they'd all be gone, or maybe we'd just see to it they loaded up and left.

But I didn't really believe that. This here morning would see some blood spilled. Them miners was too dumb to git out while they could. Me, I wanted only one thing out of it, my night with Amanda, and then I'd see whether to stick with Transactions or not. The thought of her made me itchy all over again. Tonight should do it. We'd get rid of the trespassers, and I'd be a part of it, and that was my pay, signed and sealed. That nude painting of her come to mind, and I could hardly concentrate. Old Critter, he knew it and snarled at me.

It sure was strange, only one complete name in the bunch. Glan, he didn't mind using all three of his, and didn't mind lettin' the whole world know how he was called. The rest of us, we hardly owned to any name. Lugar, I'd never heard no more of that name. He was just Lugar. And them three thugs, I wondered if they even had names. They just invented one whenever it came in handy. Maybe they growed up in some whorehouse where the brats never got a last name. And Arnold. Another one-namer, like me. I wasn't gonna tell no one my last name was Pickens and I'd been named Cotton Pickens, which made my teeth ache. And then there was The Apocalypse, another made-up name. If I'd read up the Good Book, I might figure it out, but in my mind he was the little fart with a name like death.

We got into the open country out of town, and it was coming up a mighty fine day. The sun spilled over the mountains and golden light tumbled into the valley, drying up the dew on the grass. It was just a dandy morning, a good day to be alive. We passed the roads going up to three little mines, Lilly Langtry, the Lola Montez, and the Florence. I knew what them fellers had in mind when they named their diggin's after women they dreamed of. Them three was on the list Scruples and Amanda was wantin', so I supposed we'd be heading up them two-rut roads someday soon. But the Hermit was a bigger prize, with six miners running it, and that's what we'd take over this fine summer morning.

We got to the turnoff, and Lugar turned us toward the Hermit, so we quieted down some, and was more alert. Critter, he liked it. He kicked any horse come near him, and Arnold, he says that Critter should be shot.

"I agree," I said. "Along with anyone that shoots him."

Arnold just grunted.

We got maybe a half mile up that road when the dogs found us and come barkin' down, the same three as gave me away that night. They was a bunch of mean mutts, snapping teeth at us and tellin' the world we was comin'.

Lugar, he nodded at Arnold, who avalanched off his nag since he couldn't get down graceful, and waited for them dogs to come in on him. They sure enough did. First was a big brown one with a square jaw, snappin' at Arnold. He just ignored them dog teeth and grabbed that mutt and snapped its neck. It quivered once and quit livin'. Arnold waited for the second, a liver-spotted white hound that come streaking in on him. This one he booted quicklike with them hobnails and sent that mutt flyin'. When it landed, Arnold whacked its head with his fist and it just quit right there. The third, a big black with wolf teeth chopping and smacking, came after Arnold hard, and Arnold let him sail past, grabbed it by the tail, lifted that thing up, and whirled him around and flung him good. That there black, it landed in a heap and didn't get up. So much for them dogs. Arnold, he just clambered up on that sore old horse and kicked its ribs in. Them three thugs, Garfield, Arthur, and Cleveland, they was snickering pretty good. I was sort of wishing Arnold had done it to them, and not those good dogs.

It was uncommon quiet again, but we pushed on

toward the mine, up some steep grade until we topped a
flat and could look across to where the Hermit was sittin' against the mountain. It sure was quiet there. Maybe
them miners had pulled out, got the message and was
two counties away by now.

We went a little farther, but then Lugar, he called a halt.

"All yours, Glan," he said.

Glan nodded, stepped down from that good horse,
pulled his extra-long-barrel Sharps out of its sheath, ad-
justed the sights, and settled himself behind an old log that
would make a bench rest. He wasn't in the fancy-stand-
up-shooting business. If he could shoot more accurate
with his barrel resting on something solid, he'd do 'er.

Me, I didn't like none of this here stuff.

"You gonna go in and tell 'em to get out?" I asked
Lugar.

"You done that already," he said.

"Yeah, but we need to tell 'em to load up and git."

Lugar sighed. "Who are you? Scruples?" he asked.

I seen how it would be. But there wasn't a thing I
could do about her now. It was all in motion and I was
just a watcher of whatever was gonna happen.

We were sittin' there some while. There was a nice
breeze that morning. I watched a monarch butterfly flit
around that meadow and then disappear somewhere. It
was collecting its dinner, I imagine. Some crows were
scouting us, and anyone alert to the world could read them
crows and know something was riling them up. Critter, he
was nipping grass and getting it all mired up in his bit.

Then at last there was movement up there. I saw that
little dark-haired brat of a boy come trippin' out of the
shack, and almost dance because he got loose of his

schoolin'. Then I saw Glan steady that Sharps, and I tried to stop him.

"That's the boy," I said. "Let him go."

But Glan just eyed me like I was a dead fish, sighted down that rifle, and squeezed.

That boy, he collapsed like a sack of potatoes, squirmed once, and lay still. That there shot echoed up into the rock and sent the crows to squawking.

"No!" I yelled.

The boy's ma tumbled out of that shack, screaming, runnin' toward the boy, yankin' her skirts up, and then Glan, he shoots her, too. I could see that one better. That bullet turned her face pure red, and she fell acrost that boy and lay there quiet. It was awful quiet.

Nothing more happened.

Lugar came over to me. "Anyone else in those shacks when you was there?"

I shook my head. I just wanted to get on board Critter and cut loose, but there'd be a bullet in my back if I did.

Arnold, he got down on all fours and puked. There he was, the roughest in that crowd, heaving up his guts into the grass. Dogs he could deal with; a woman and a child, that was what emptied his gut. I swallowed back my bile, because I was almost there, too.

After a while Lugar nodded, and the bunch moved up to the mine buildings. That woman and boy, they just lay there, covered with big black flies and a lot of red. There was nothin' else to see. The men, they must have been deep in that hole in the side of the cliff.

"Seal it," Lugar said. He nodded to them thugs of his, and they carried the dead woman and her boy into the hole a ways and left them there. Then the one called Garfield, he finds the powder magazine off a piece, and gets some sticks of DuPont, and some fuse and a copper cap, and he makes some charges. He must have worked some in Butte, because he knew what to do with powder. It's a big job, and he makes about three charges that he sets up in the mouth of that mine, with long fuses, and then he motions us to get away and lights them fuses. We hurry down the slope to where we were, and that's when them charges go off and the mouth of the mine vanishes in rubble. There's no one left around there.

"Clean out the shacks," Lugar said. So we go up there and throw clothing and food down the two-holer and freed a mule from its pen and let it wander. Pretty quick, it looked like miners just quit and took off. Transactions, Incorporated, had itself another mine. It was all peaceful there, with no one in sight, and any miners back in that shaft trapped behind a wall of rubble. I saw that old monarch butterfly flit by, lookin' for dinner.

I wasn't feeling good. I'd get to spend the night with Amanda now, but I didn't feel like it. I wished Amanda would just get out of that valley so I'd never see her again. We rode back to the bunkhouse real quiet, and Lugar, he went into the Pullman Palace Car to report to Scruples, and we didn't see him for a long time. No one felt like eating. I didn't think I'd eat for a week. It was a real quiet afternoon. I couldn't take the bunkhouse no more, so I hiked off a way and lay down in some clean grass and stared at the sky.

Tomorrow they'd go after Agnes Cork. Glan would kill him, too, easy as shooting a deer.

I didn't want to go into that bunkhouse, so I just settled there in the grass away from the railroad car and watched the dusk thicken. Sometime I'd have to go into that bunkhouse. I had to go feed Critter, too. But I just couldn't do it.

I got to hearin' something like a drumbeat, a steady thump, thump, thump that seemed to come from below somewhere, and then that drumbeat came closer and got louder, and I couldn't make no sense of it. It sounded like some funeral, that steady, mournful beat of a bass drum. I watched as men poured out of the bunkhouse to see what was happenin'. Glan, he picked up his rifle and sidled away, and the rest, they went for their weapons. And that thumpin', it just got louder. Something real bad was happenin' and I sure didn't know what. I checked my Baby Dragoon, which I still wore, and waited.

Then I saw something strange. Six men were carrying something big and flat, and on it was something. And behind was a crowd, and someone in that crowd had him a bass drum strung to his shoulders and he was hammerin' soft and steady.

Lugar, he shouted a few orders, and pretty soon all them in the bunkhouse was spread across the path in a loose line—the thugs with their scatterguns; Arnold, clenching his meaty fists; the little killer called The Apocalypse, makin' himself small in a corner near the Palace Car; and Lugar himself, out front with a pair of revolvers slung from his hips.

And still the drummin' came along, and now I saw what it was comin' in there. It was them six miners from the Hermit Mine, and on their shoulders was a big door torn off its hinges, and on that big plank door was them two bodies, the woman and the boy, lyin' there for all to see. And half of Swamp Creek was walkin' behind.

I thought maybe my life was about over, and I lay lower in the grass above, where no one would see me.

But them miners weren't armed, and no one in that crowd of people from Swamp Creek was armed. They was all comin' to lay the blame where it belonged.

The miners, they just kept comin' along, closer to the line of fighting men Lugar had thrown across their path. And that drum just kept on beating, like a heartbeat, and no one stopped or even slowed, even with them shotgun bores pointed straight at the miners.

That was the same bunch as stomped my face in and broke my ribs, so I wasn't feelin' very quiet while all this was happening. I remembered them hobnailed boots and ham fists hitting on me. But now they weren't looking for a brawl.

They'd laid the woman and boy out on the board, carefully folding the hands across the chests. But the blood was there, and the clothing was the same as when they was shot so sudden. I glanced at the Pullman car in time to see Amanda and Scruples peer out, and then suddenly drop the velvet curtain across the windows. They'd seen what they wanted and weren't going to look no more.

And still, the marchers came on. I hoped Lugar had some sense. There wasn't a one in that crowd that was armed, far as I could see. But who could say what a bunch like that would do? The miners carrying the door came on, straight toward the Palace Car, ignorin' those shotguns and revolvers. It was plain that they'd got themselves out of the mine, and brought the woman and boy with them, and it was plain they knew where to come. But what might happen next, I sure didn't know.

Chapter Ten

Lugar, he showed some sense. Them miners carrying the dead woman and boy, they just kept on a comin', with the crowd and that drummer behind. At the last moment, Lugar motioned them thugs to hold off and collect around the metal steps of the rail car. So that bunch of Swamp Creek people just swarmed in, with that drum hammering like a heartbeat. I don't know as I ever saw anything like it.

Them six that carried the door must've been down in the Hermit Mine when they got sealed in, and now they was out and paradin' two dead people. They got there to the railroad car and lowered the door to the ground. They hadn't done nothing to wash up them two, and the clothing was soaked with dried-up blood. People was collectin' there, lookin' down on the woman and boy, and I sure didn't know what would come next.

Then Carter Scruples, he walks out on that platform, and if it was quiet before, it got a lot quieter now. He stared at the two dead, and at the miners, and they stared back at him, knives in their gazes.

"This is a great tragedy. I don't know why you brought

them here. Something bad happened, and I share your sorrow," he said.

Them miners, they didn't quit staring. I sure didn't know what to expect.

Then Amanda Trouville shows up on the platform, too. She's got a shawl and put it over her hair and wrapped it over her shoulders. She peered down at the woman and boy on the door, and clutched Scruples, and sighed softly.

"Someone's wife and son," she said. "This is a sad day. I'd like to pay for their burials if you'd let me."

No one said nothing.

She sure looked pretty, all soft and tender, with that lace over her head.

All them thugs was collected at the foot of the platform, makin' a wall between the crowd and her and Scruples.

"May God watch over them both," she said.

I don't think she or Scruples wanted anything bad like that to happen, and now they were feelin' bad about it. But who could say? Not long ago, they was tellin' me they was confidence men. But they sure looked sad, standin' there in that quiet.

Scruples, he dug into his pants and pulled out some coin. "Here's two double eagles to see them buried," he said. "Maybe the whole town should take up a collection, and I'd like to get it started. This is a loss for all of Swamp Creek."

No one of the miners stepped up to take the proffered gold coins. So Amanda, she got them coins and stepped down off the rail car and laid the coins on that door, right between that mother and her boy. Then she slowly retreated back to the platform, and into her railroad car.

Nothing much happened for a while. That crowd, it

didn't know what to do. But finally, them miners got in position and lifted the door carrying the dead, and walked quietly down the slope and into Swamp Creek, while the crowd drifted along behind. It was over, whatever it was.

I peered around from up there on the hill. Glan, he was at the barn, his rifle out, his good horse saddled. He'd been ready to get the hell outta there. Now he was stuffing that Sharps back into its sheath.

From where I was, I could see that crowd drifting into Swamp Creek. They all were heading for the Mint Saloon, and pretty soon them miners carried the dead right in there. I knew it wasn't over. That whole crowd could turn itself into a lynch mob in no time at all. A drink or two would do it. And then they'd march back up the hill, with some coils of hemp in hand.

I hadn't done any shooting of a boy and a woman, but I shore felt like I had. I lay there in the grass, knowin' something had changed in me. I'd gotten tied up with the wrong outfit. I ain't very smart, but I knew enough to stay outa trouble. But now I was in trouble. Just bein' with this bunch was the biggest mistake I ever made. I wasn't no killer of women and boys. And this business of jumpin' claims and takin' over mines that this outfit had no right to, it bothered me real bad.

Them thugs, they'd gone back into the bunkhouse, except for The Apocalypse, who hung around lookin' for someone to kill. I headed for the barn and threw a saddle over Critter, who kicked at me because I'd been ignoring him. I went into the bunkhouse, where most of them boys was stretched out on the bunks, not sayin' much. I threw my truck into my war bag and started out the door.

"Where you goin' with that?" Lugar asked.

"I'm puttin' it on my saddle," I said.

"You quitting me?"

"I am."

"No, you aren't."

"I'm going to the railroad car," I said.

Lugar followed me around. He watched me tie my truck behind the cantle, and head over to the Pullman Palace Car, like he was gonna keep me there if he felt like it. He wasn't gonna do it because I would shoot the son of a bitch if he tried.

I walked right up them metal steps and knocked on the door.

Scruples eyed me through the drapes and opened a crack.

"Quitting," I said.

"You can't. You've made a contract, and you owe us for a month's board, horse feed, and that revolver."

"I haven't seen a thin dime," I said.

Amanda, she appeared at the door. "Cotton, you come back in an hour, and I'll enjoy your company."

That still made me weak in the knees. She stood there, still in that lace shawl, and I was some smitten all over. But it just didn't work no more. I couldn't be spending time with her and thinkin' about that dead woman and boy. I just couldn't be takin' my pleasure with her, not ever.

"Bye, Amanda," I said.

Scruples smiled. "Leave the revolver," he said.

"That's mine; I earned it."

"Our mistake," Scruples said, and shut the door in my face.

I was their mistake, all right. Lugar, he heard it all and didn't stop me. I drifted out to the barn in the gathering dusk and climbed onto Critter, who shivered under me. Critter, he always knows when something's up.

"Horse should be shot," Lugar said.

I eased out of there, fearful that the straw boss would backshoot me, but he didn't. Scruples thought he'd made a mistake hirin' me, and he had, and Lugar knew it. So I let Critter ease himself down that road, until my itchy feelin' left me, and I came down into Swamp Creek, which was quiet but not peaceful. It seemed like the quiet before a thunderstorm to me. I knew I'd not be welcome in town, and might get myself strung up, so I eased through there as quiet as I could, all the while wonderin' where to go. Damned if I knew. I didn't have a dime to my name.

And then I knew. I'd ride out to Joseph St. Agnes Cork. He'd spare me some flapjacks. And maybe I could tell him a thing or two about what would be coming his way.

And then, right there in Swamp Creek, with people starin' at me as I steered Critter through the twilight, I knew what was about to happen. I was switchin' sides. I'd try to keep Glan from pumping a bullet into Aggie Cork, for starters, and after that I'd see what I could do to get that Pullman Palace Car outfit clear out of Swamp Creek before anyone else got hurt or busted.

It shore felt good. But feelin' good didn't make it any better. I'd likely end up six feet under. But a feller had to do what he had to do, and switchin' sides was what I had to do. I'd left Scruples and Amanda with nothin' more in mind than getting away, but now I was comin' around to the rest of it.

That is, if anyone wanted me. I didn't think that them miners would have much use for me, seein' as how I was working for Transactions, Incorporated, until then.

"Dammit, Cotton," I said to myself. "You sure stepped into the dog doo now."

Critter, he responded with a long loud fart. That was his biggest compliment. I hadn't heard him cut loose one of them for a long time. We jogged past them big mines, the Fat Tuesday and the Big Mother, which was workin' two shifts steady, and made a lot of noise night and day, and pretty soon we was out in the country, with the stars beginning to pop up and the smell of pines drifted down off the mountains. There was still a lantern lit here and there, a bunch more mines, but we kept on goin'. Cork's mine was pretty near the last one in that long string of 'em up and down Swamp Creek Valley. It was a right pretty evening, and I was lookin' ahead to a good visit with Aggie, providing I didn't get shot at first. You never knew about them old bachelor miners. One moment they're fine; next moment they're pumping lead at you.

I cussed myself for switching sides. Dumbest thing I'd ever done. I knew I wasn't born too smart. And now I was going to prove it once again. That bunch there, Glan and The Apocalypse, and that brawling brute Arnold, they could turn me into worm-bait in about one minute. And me with nothing but an old Baby Dragoon bouncing on my hip. By the time I pulled the trigger, and the cap blew into the nipple and ignited the charge in the cylinder, and that load took fire and pumped a ball out the end, they'd have about six rounds in me. About all a Baby Dragoon was good for was holding up banks.

I got to the turnoff. I think it was anyway. Nothing looks the same in the dark. But it was as good a turnoff as any, and there was woods ahead, like I remembered, so I steered Critter in there and he about had fits he was so happy. Of course I didn't know how I was gonna tell old

Aggie Cork I was there, but I settled on shouting some, and after he shot at me a couple of times he might listen.

It was the place all right, and some moonlight was helping me. I parked Critter in the woods again, and then I yelled up that slope to the mine.

"Agnes, it's your old friend Cotton," I said.

There wasn't no reply.

"It's Cotton," I yelled.

That damned shotgun of his went off, but I was too far away.

"It's Cotton and I want to talk."

This time, I saw something fly through the air with sparks spitting from it, and I dove to the ground just in time. One of his DuPont Specials, it blew off firing ten-penny nails all to hell and back.

After my ears quit ringing, I yelled at him again.

"Dammit, Agnes, I want to talk. Let me in."

"Boll Weevil is what you are. Working for Scruples."

"I quit them."

A long silence followed. I was feeling pretty mournful.

But then he worked up to what he was gonna do. "You walk up here by your lonesome. With your hands high up in the sky. If there's trouble, you're gonna be full of nails."

I went and did her, all right. I sure didn't know what I'd do if one of them bombs spitting fire from the fuse sailed my way, but it didn't. I got up there to the shacks and the mouth of the mine, and didn't see him.

But he says from somewheres, "Turn around slow so I can see your backside."

I did it, twice for good measure.

Then he appeared from somewhere. "How's old Cotton?" he asked.

"Hungry. I want some flapjacks."

"Now you're talking my language," he said.

"Yeah, and I got a few more things to tell you, too."

I wasn't sure I wanted his flapjacks. They were made from some blue sourdough goo that he let percolate for years at a time so it'd get real ripe, but I didn't have no choice. I had a reg'lar hole in my belly by then.

"You fry and I'll talk," I said.

He was agreeable to it, so that's what he did and what I did. By the time he had a stack for me to eat, he knew all about what was happening down the valley, and about Rudolph Costello Glan, and what was in store for Joseph St. Agnes Cork.

Those were the most gawdawful flapjacks I ever put a fork to.

"And what're you gonna do?" he asked.

"Keep you alive," I said, not so certain I could manage it.

"I can keep myself alive, so go to hell, Cotton," he said.

"You're stuck with me," I said.

"No I ain't. You're fired."

"I'm sticking. And them were the worst flapjacks I ever ate."

"Oh, all right," he said. "At least you're honest."

Chapter Eleven

Aggie Cork was scouring out the tin plates with sand while I was skunkifying the neighborhood after all them flapjacks.

"I 'magine we oughter go," he said. "Nothing here no more."

That was my thinking, too. It was twilight, but there was still light enough so that a bullet from Glan could knock out our lights.

"You got any place to go?" I asked.

"Hell, yes, dandy little shut-down mine three miles toward town. Scruples and them, they scared off the owner, Bob Brass, and no one's seen him since. It's a good little pocket mine with plenty of ore left. He called it the Lola Montez Tunnel, honor of the lady he loved. They shut it down, but maybe we could sneak in and start her up."

I cut loose with another fart, and yet another. Cork eyed me. "That's how I kept people out of here," he said. "But it don't matter now."

"How come it don't matter?" I asked.

"I ain't got anything to live for," he said. "Pinched-out

mine here I was hoping to unload on some sucker, and nothing much up the road."

"How'd you take up prospecting, Aggie?"

"I lost my sweetheart in the fight at Chickamauga, and it ain't been the same since."

I was trying to figure that out, and thinkin' maybe I didn't want to partner with this here lonesome miner after all, when he got me squared away.

"My sweetheart, my honeybunch, Emmy Lou, she was in the outhouse there, doing her business while that battle was raging half a mile away, and a Reb minié ball came straight through the quarter moon of that one-holer and in one ear and out the other. Wasn't for three more hours till they found her, and it took three weeks to get word to me, and my life hasn't been worth spit since then. There just wasn't nothing to do after that, 'cept get a mule and a pick and go off on my own somewheres."

He carefully put out the fire now that dark was closing in, and pretty quick we was in darkness. Then he was collecting his few possessions.

"Why don't you leave that there blue stuff behind for the next fellers?" I asked.

"Leave my sourdough starter behind? I've been using that since I was first on my own, age thirteen, and it's just gettin' good!" he said.

"Well, it didn't poison me," I said. "But it tried."

I helped him load up his two mules, one of which he'd named Emmy Lou in honor of his lost love. But he put his DuPont and his caps and fuses on the other mule, the one named Richard. That was the worst name for a mule I ever heard. One bit of wisdom I got from my ma was, never trust any Richard.

After we got Emmy Lou and Richard loaded up, I

drifted down to the woods and got Critter, who bit my shoulder in gratitude, and we joined up on the two-rut road along there, walkin' in starlight and laying farts behind us, which was sort of a policy in case someone was following. But no one was.

"Old Bob Brass's mine's a dandy," he said. "I figure Scruples probably just killed him and dumped him some-where, because Bob Brass was a catamount who wouldn't quit. Maybe we can work the mine real quiet, and Scru-ples won't notice, and we can keep ourselves in beer," he said. "If we ever find old Bob, we'd owe him a share."

There wasn't no road up to that mine, just a trail I couldn't see, but Aggie knew where to go, and he steered us off the valley road and through some foothills and up a canyon to the lonesomest hanging valley I ever did see. And there was the mine, driven horizontal into a red cliff, like the rest around there, and a well-built mortared rock house. The mine mouth had been piled with rubble to keep fellers like us from taking Scruples' gold from him. But I figured old Scruples, he owed me a little wage, and I'd help myself here if I could.

Aggie knew right where to put stuff. He eased the powder into a vault off a way, and put the caps and fuse in another place, and then we carried his truck into the rock house there. The moon threw solemn light into it, and I reckoned I saw a ghost gliding through there. I just hoped it was a friendly ghost, maybe old Brass himself, helpin' us get settled. But I drew my Baby Dragoon and walked through there, ready to deal with anything, but all I saw was cold white moonlight and a thick layer of dust.

"I think maybe your friend Brass's behind that rubble in the mine," I said.

"How so?"

The things that had happened only that dawn flooded back to mind. "That's where they put the woman and the boy," I said.

"We'll know pretty quick," he said.

Maybe even the next day, when we would begin the hard work of pullin' all that red rock out of the mine mouth. If there was murder to be seen, we'd see it.

I put Critter out on good grass, and he began knockin' it down, and then I pulled out my bedroll and found me a good corner in that stone house.

"Is there neighbors around here?" I asked.

"Mines? Three or four nearby. Mostly one- or two-man deals."

"I'd better go around and let them know we're here," I said.

"I knew you'd find some way to get out of mucking rock," he replied.

He shore knew me better than I'd thought.

We had a good rest that night, feelin' safe up there for the time being, and next morning Aggie Cork made some more of them flapjacks with that blue stuff, and I knew I'd put Critter to shame all day. But I got it down, and it fueled me, so I saddled up and rode along the foothills toward the mines down the line, steerin' clear of the valley road below. This was plumb pretty country, long grassy slopes, gray ridges rising up toward snowy peaks, lots of dark timber up a way. Plenty of water, too, sparkling little streams tumbling out of the high country. And the day was mild, too, so Critter and I, we were having a good time and I didn't have to muck rock with old Aggie.

From some places, I could see clear down to the valley road, and what I saw that morning put a chill through me. There was a bunch of horsemen headin' up the valley, and even though I couldn't make out the details, I still knew it was Scruples' bunch, and there was only one place they could be headin' and that was Aggie's old place. So they were going to push him off, just like they said they would.

I thought to warn Aggie, but we were far from the old mine and he could take care of himself, and he had a stone house to get into if trouble started, and he had them DuPont and tenpenny bombs if he needed to defend himself. So I kept on riding toward the neighboring mines I seen ahead a way, and pretty soon I helloed one place and got no answer. It was pretty much like all them little mines there, but this morning it stood real quiet. So I steered Critter toward the next, which I could see ahead, and it was a bit bigger, maybe five or six men running that one, but it was quiet except for a yapping dog that Critter finally kicked. After that, it stayed about six feet away from Critter's hooves.

The same was true of the next mine. That was small, a one-man glory hole, but no one was around there either. They didn't show no signs of being took over by Scruples. He always sealed up the mines he'd stolen, but these were all operating mines. It just was that no one was mucking ore there. I got off Critter and looked around there, and shouted into that shaft in the red cliff, but all I got was echoes. I got back to Critter and cut loose with a big one as I was getting on board, and Critter, he turned his head around and gave me a pained look.

"Critter, even since I got on to them blue flapjacks, you ain't King of the Hill no more," I told him. He cut loose himself, but he was no match for me, and he knew it.

I pushed on toward town, riding past the two big mines and the stamp mill they shared. The mill pounded the ore to dust, so the gold could be leached out. The big mines owned it, and the smaller operators took ore in for custom milling, and pretty soon they'd get a check, or the gold itself if they wanted it. It worked pretty well, and no one was complaining.

I got near to Swamp Creek, and then I saw where most ever'body was. They was out on Boot Hill buryin' that woman and her boy. There were maybe two hundred crowded around a single grave there, and I knew where them miners had come, and I knew also where that Scruples bunch going up the valley were going, and I thought there'd be hell to pay this day.

There sure was a big bunch at that buryin'. It looked to me like most every miner in the country had come to it. Most of them was wearing black, but a few of them old prospectors was so poor they didn't have nothing. But they all managed a black armband, saying on their sleeve what they thought in their hearts. There wasn't many women in Swamp Creek, but most ever'one there was standing at that grave. The women wore big floppy hats, but the men stood bareheaded, the wind riffling their hair some.

I didn't see no preacher, at least no one with one of them collars. Swamp Creek didn't have any that I'd ever heard of. But someone was leading the prayers and all that. It looked like the hardware man, Joshua Belknap. I guessed he was good as any.

They'd carpentered one wide box for both the mother and the boy. It was made from mine plank, there being no casket makers in that little town. The bad thing was, I didn't even know the names of that ma or that boy. But that surely was the husband standin' there right beside the box, and the rest of the men from the Hermit Mine was right there, too. I thought I'd better go there, not because I wanted, but because none of 'em knew what they'd find when they got out to the Hermit Mine.

I rode closer some, and then bailed off Critter and left him to munch on grass, and edged up to the crowd. I guess they was pretty focused on the buryin' because they didn't see me, at least not at once.

"And so we commit the mortal remains of Matilda Lovelace and Willis Lovelace to the love of God and the joy of eternity in heaven," the man was sayin'. So that was Lovelace standin' there seeing his wife and boy planted that morning.

I thought when it was over, I'd slip up to one of them six miners and tell him the bad news. That mine of theirs was taken over while they were here burying their own. But my plan didn't ever get that far. Someone there spotted me standin' at the back of the crowd, and began nudging the others, and pretty soon there was a big bunch turning around to have a look at me, and it was only then that it sunk into my head that they thought I was one of Scruples' crowd, and they didn't like it a bit. And worse, I was wearing that Baby Dragoon, and was the only armed man at that funeral. It sure didn't look good, and I cussed myself for being so dumb, but I took off my old hat as a mark of respect, and hoped to get through this here buryin'.

But it just didn't go that way.

Eventually, that feller who was doing services just stopped. And then he walked over to me, the whole black-clad crowd watching.

"Why are you here?" he asked, and didn't wait for no answer. "You are not welcome here."

"Killer," said one of them miners. "Killer of a woman and a boy."

I hardly knew what to say, because this whole thing was blowin' up and those people in black were fixin' to maybe string me up with some hardware store hemp, and plant me there, too.

I took one look, and pretty quick saw that them miners was beginning to come around close to me. They didn't know what they'd do, only they was fixing to do something. And it didn't matter none that I had that Baby Dragoon; it didn't matter one little bit, because it would have been worthless.

I hardly knew what to do. Critter, he was most of a city block away, but I thought to head that way and git on him.

Those six miners, the widower, and a hundred more behind, they knotted up around me, and I knowed I'd never been in a jam like this one. Them bruises on my face, they was most healed up, but it was like wearin' a brand. And if they roughed me some, they'd find my ribs still bound up tight where they was broke by these same men.

But now it was oddly quiet. The buryin' had stopped, and this bunch was around me like a thundercloud.

They were measuring me for some hemp; I could see it plain.

"I quit them. I didn't do no killing. I come here to tell you something."

There wasn't a sound among them.

"This morning I saw them Scruples men ride out to the Hermit Mine. They're takin' it over right now, while this buryin's getting done."

I heard nothing but a barking dog over in the field, yapping at Critter.

"I quit and rode out to Aggie Cork to warn him he was next. He and me, we're partnered up and out of there. We got us another place. Go on and ask him. I'll take you there."

Lovelace walked up real close to me. "You was with the bunch killed my woman and boy?"

I took a breath. "I was with the bunch that watched it done by a sharpshooter named Glan."

"Then you're as guilty as him."

"I told the straw boss, Lugar, don't do it. But they went ahead, so I quit."

That man that was doing the reading from the Good Book and all, he stepped into the quiet.

"Mr. Lovelace, let's finish with our services now. We want a proper burial now. We've come to honor Matilda and Willis. We'll decide what to do with this one later." He stared at me. "You, sir, stand right there. We're not done with you."

I eyed old Critter, drifting farther away, and wondered who'd own my horse next.

Chapter Twelve

What happened next was, I got mad. I stood there with the steam buildin' up in my boiler, ready to pick a fight as soon as they done with the buryin'. My pa, he always told me, don't get mad, get even. But I was too far gone to care.

By God, I had six shots and I'd use them all before they strung me up.

The talker, he wound it down, ashes to ashes, dust to dust, and all that. I felt sorry for that Lovelace, losing a wife and a boy to that killer. But there wasn't nothing I could do about it now.

Finally, they got it over, and then turned to stare at me, like they was thinkin' who else they could bury that day. They're all just staring, men, women, and children, most of the town of Swamp Creek.

So I just waded in.

"I come to warn you that they took over your mine. I come to tell you you'd get shot, more killed, if you go out there and face men like that. I come all the way over here to tell you that, and it don't make no difference to you.

Well, go ahead and get yourself kilt then. I done what I could. I'm getting out of here."

They could see the heat in me, and that probably counted for more than what I was saying. But the silence seemed to melt some. No one said nothing, but I could tell it was over.

"I'm holed up with Aggie Cork. You want us, we're at Bob Brass's place," I said. "They was fixing to kill Aggie, so we quit his place."

Lovelace himself, he come over to me. He didn't shake hands or nothing. Instead, he put that big miner hand on my shoulder and squeezed a little. We wasn't at the handshaking point yet, but he let me know maybe I wasn't all skunk.

There was a bunch of miners there, watching all this. I imagine most of them small operators had come in for this, and now they'd maybe share a beer in the saloon, or ride back out to their mines. That's how this district worked: a lot of little outfits, and two big ones. They were tough men, all right, used to being alone, but no match for someone like Glan, who'd simply shoot them one by one and then Scruples' bunch would take over another mine. I'd heard there was already half a dozen missing men in the Swamp Creek District, and there'd soon be more. Some probably took off, once Transactions, Inc., came around, but there were others who got themselves buried somewhere. It was big country, and there'd be places where bodies would never be found.

I took hold of Critter's reins, but he laid his ears back and butted me. That was his notion of friendly. I rode out of there with all them miners staring at me, but not so bitter now. What those six miners would do about the Hermit was their business. I'd warned them, and they

knew what they faced now. It was up to them, not me. I
headed up the valley under a lonely sky, keeping a sharp
eye out for Scruples' men. They had no quarrel with me;
I'd quit is all, so I wasn't too worried about meeting
them. But maybe I should be.

Scruples didn't have enough men to defend every
claim he jumped, so he was just blowing up the shafts to
keep people away. His powder man wasn't very good at
it, if them six miners at the Hermit could wade through
the rubble and get out of that hole. But probably good
enough to shut down every glory hole they jumped.

I rode slow up that valley, keeping an eye out, because everything in Swamp Creek was lookin' mean
now. It sure was a fine day, with puffball clouds hanging on the peaks. Critter, he liked the weather so much
he lifted into a bone-jarring trot, a real ass-pounding
trot, just to let me know the sun was shining. I was
heading back to the Bob Brass place, but didn't want no
one to see it, because we'd made a sort of hideout of it.

I was a couple hours up the valley when sure enough,
there came the Scruples bunch, coming toward town. I
didn't like it much, but there wasn't nothing I could do.
Half of them fancy horses could run faster than Critter.
But I wasn't in a running mood. I was just gonna sit
there in the middle of that trail and let 'em come, which
they did. At least Lugar did, with the three presidents,
big Arnold, and The Apocalypse.

"You fellers look mighty busy," I said, opening the ball.

"I still think you should shoot that horse of yours,"
Lugar replied. "Want me to do it for you?"

"It'd be hard on you," I replied.

"Nice day," said The Apocalypse.

"Blowed off a few," Garfield said.

"Finishing up," I said. "Them six miners got themselves out of the Hermit, so I guess you didn't do the job."

"Well, it's sure done now," Garfield said. "It's blowed so tight it'd take a week to clean out. And them shacks, they're all firewood now."

"Shut her down good," I said.

"We're painting signs on those places now," Lugar said. "Skull and crossbones. That says it."

"I guess it sure does," I said. "Pretty smart, going up there when that bunch is burying the woman and the boy."

"Scruples, his idea," Lugar said. "We shut down Cork's mine, too. He wasn't near there. Guess he bailed out after all. I'da liked to kill him after what he did to us."

"Where's Glan?" I asked.

"Scouting. We shut down three more glory holes. Pretty near every miner in the district's in town now."

"Blow the mouths shut?" I asked.

"No one's gonna work them until Scruples gets them sold. We painted warnings on all of them." Lugar eyed me. "You should have stuck with us. Scruples is some put out, and when he gives the word, you'd better be somewhere else."

"I guess I will be," I said. "And what's Amanda up to?"

No one responded. Funny thing. Mention her name in that crowd, and no one wanted to say nothing.

"Glan, he's out prowling?" I asked.

"I think before the day's out, he'll put a few more trespassers off of Transaction claims," Lugar said. "He don't seem to care for us, so he just drifts away, like he's his own boss."

That didn't sound good to me. It sounded like a bullet out of nowhere to me, a bullet that could end my days or Aggie Cork's days without us ever having an inkling it was coming.

"You think that's right?" I asked.

"I don't think."

"Scorched earth," said The Apocalypse.

I took me a close look at that little guy with his deadly little guns. The revolver was supposed to be the equalizer, making any little guy the equal of a big guy, but this one made a small target, too. I wouldn't want to tangle with him.

"That's what Carter Scruples is saying?"

"Thirty days. He wants this whole district in his pocket in one month," The Apocalypse said. "He came over to the bunkhouse and gave us a plan, and some incentives."

There was another of them words I never heard of. "I don't know what them are," I said. "Like gold?"

"The faster we clean out the trespassers, the more we get. Too bad you quit, Cotton."

"Well, I thought to grow potatoes," I said.

Lugar smiled. "Someone should shoot that horse," he said.

They put spurs to the flanks of their horses, and I watched the death squad ride by, and then meandered up the valley. I knew Lugar would post someone to see where I was goin', so I rode past the trail up to Bob Brass's place and kept on until I was out of sight, and then doubled back real quiet. I sure didn't like it that Glan was roaming around there, and thought I'd better check up on old Aggie. Maybe moving in to that place wasn't a good idea. Aggie Cork knew how to fight, but he didn't know nothing about snipers turning a blue sky black.

I drifted overland, staying off ridges, and finally come

down on the Brass mine, which was awful quiet. Old Aggie hadn't moved any rock out of the mouth of that shaft. I didn't like it none.

It sure was a nice day. It'd warmed up good. I could see them heat shimmies rising from the stone house. Something told me things weren't right, but I couldn't see what was wrong. I just get that itchy feeling sometimes, and I've learned to respect it. So I took my time. I was up on the far side of a hogback lookin' over the ridge and keepin' myself small. With Glan on the loose, and Scruples tryin' to sweep the upper valley while them miners were at their buryin', I knew anything could happen.

But if Glan was waitin' for me, I sure didn't see it.

I touched heel to Critter, and he got us over the hogback and down the long grade to the mine. I was keeping an eye out, but there wasn't nothing to see. Aggie Cork was nowhere around there. But his mules was out on the pasture, so I knowed he didn't go nowhere. I got off Critter and put him in the deepest shade I could find, and headed on in to that house, that Baby Dragoon in my hand because I didn't want no surprises.

"You come just in time," Aggie said.

He was on his bunk, bleeding to death.

I slid that Dragoon back, and knelt beside him. He was pale and breathing ragged, and there was a hole through his right lung, and he plainly had only a minute or two on this earth.

"I'm sorry," I said.

He nodded. "That sniper you told me about. Him."

"Glan is his name."

"Never heard the shot. Just hit and fell, and after a while I crawled in here."

"Anything I can do, Aggie?"

He shook his head. He was fadin' fast.

"Anyone to tell?"

He shook it again. "I'm alone."

He was breathing hard, and blood was gurgling from his lips and his chest, too.

"Take me down to the Mint Saloon," he said.

"I will, Aggie."

"And go after that bastard."

"It's a promise, Aggie."

He nodded, and then sagged and fell from life. One moment his spirit was there; the next it was gone. It sure was quiet there. I stood, and stared out the window upon that sunny mountain valley, shimmering in the golden light.

I didn't think much of gold and what it done to folks just then. Killin' a woman and a boy and a harmless old man. I knew right then and there that it was going to come down to me against Rudolph Costello Glan, and me against that whole crowd, and the crooked man and woman runnin' that deal.

I found a piece of canvas and some rope, and I carried Aggie to the canvas and wrapped him tight in it, takin' my time to knot things up. He was warm and limp, and his eyes just stared off at nothing. But I finally got him wrapped, and then I fetched his mules and his pack-saddles, and I rigged things up and put Aggie up there on the packsaddle.

"I hope it don't hurt none to ride like that," I said.

There wasn't much else to bring. But then I did see something I wanted. Aggie had fixed himself half a dozen more DuPont firecrackers, and I wanted a couple of them. I slipped two into the panniers on Aggie's other mule, one on either side because I didn't want them rubbin' on each other. Then I took the rest of those tenpenny bombs and hid them away from the rock house and the mine head, actually in a canvas-lined pit behind the outhouse, and threw a little dirt over the top. I'd know where to come if I needed some powder fast. They sure made me itchy.

I loaded my truck behind the cantle of my saddle, and took the mules by the lead ropes and went slow down the trail to the valley road, wondering if a shot by Glan would darken my lights, too. I sure was in a grim mood, no matter that this was just about the prettiest valley on earth.

The Mint was where old Aggie went when he wanted to spend a dime on a mug of beer. It was where the small-time miners gathered, to drink, tell tales, show off some chunks of ore, or do deals. There was also the Miners Exchange, where the hard-rock miners from the big mines collected after each shift. But they were paid men, while the Mint was the place for men who were going it alone.

We walked to town real slow, Aggie and me, and I kept checkin' to see whether Aggie was riding well. And checking everything in sight, my gaze studying this and that as if my life depended on it. Which it did.

It had been a long day, and wasn't over yet. I reached Swamp Creek about the time the sun dropped below the western ridges and the purple shadows were crawlin' across the muddy street. People stopped and stared. There was no hidin' what was wrapped up tight and tied down to the packsaddle. And sure enough, even as Critter and I slowed down at the Mint, a crowd followed. I didn't much care for them getting too close to them panniers on the pack mule, but there wasn't nothing I could do for the moment.

By the time I got down, there was quite a crowd, includin' Johnny Brashear, the mining district secretary, who was eyin' me and that bundle and makin' noises. But I ignored him, and carried Aggie inside, through the double doors. There was a lamp throwing light and shadow over the tables and the bar. I carried Aggie to a table and eased him down real careful, and then waited for all these miners to collect.

"It's Agnes Cork," I said. "He was shot in the chest by someone with a rifle."

"That's a good story," said Brashear.

I knew straight off, I'd be wrestling with the district secretary, too. He was Scruples' man, for sure. And also what passed for law in Swamp Creek.

Chapter Thirteen

These independent miners clustered around the table, but none of them was much feelin' like opening that canvas and havin' a look. It sure was quiet in there. Some of them from the Hermit Mine was there, but I didn't see Lovelace, who'd lost his family.

They weren't trusting me neither. I didn't blame them any. In their minds, I was still one of Scruples' men.

"He was just about gone when I found him," I said. "His last wish was to be brought here. Take me to the Mint, he said, so I did."

"Did he say who done it?" someone asked.

"No. It just hit him from somewhere." I wanted to say that Glan done it, but I didn't have any proof.

"Where was this?" Billy Blew, the saloon man, asked.

"A closed-up mine he was holing up in."

"What mine? Not his own?"

"No, he quit his own. This one belonged to someone named Bob Brass. It was shut down, and made a hideaway."

"That's a Transactions mine," said Brashear. "Trespassing, were you?"

"Holin' up," I said. "We were partnered up. I told him they was after him, and we got out of his place."

"Likely story," said Brashear. He was law in Swamp Creek, a deputy of the sheriff up at Butte. And in Scruples' pocket, too.

It made me mad, but I kept myself in check a little.

"I'm hoping you boys will help me bury him," I said.

"Something we got to do," the barkeep said.

"I want to see in there," Brashear said. "Just to know what's what."

It was a fair enough request. It was up to me to untie that canvas, so I did. There was a dozen men watching as I untied the cords and finally pulled the canvas free from Aggie Cork's face.

"Him all right," Brashear said. "Pull it down some."

I did until the bloody shirt and the hole in Aggie's chest came into view. No one said nothing.

Brashear took a long look and started playing lawman. "How'd you know where to find him?"

I was in for a grilling, but this was murder and Brashear was on good ground, askin' questions. I told him how I'd gone out to Cork's place to warn him, and how he quit the place then and there, and said he knew a place we could hole up.

"You went and tole Cork that the outfit was coming at him again?"

"I told Aggie they've got a sniper called Glan, and Cork didn't have no chance against a man with a special-made Sharps."

"You betraying your former boss, eh?" Brashear said.

"I guess quitting a bad outfit's not something you'd do, right, Brashear?"

He sure didn't like that, and didn't bother to give me what-for.

"I'll help you," said Wally Deaver, one of the Hermit Mine owners. "Aggie was a friend—and looks like you're a friend, too."

I nodded, and tied up the canvas around Aggie once again. Some of them men stepped outside, and pretty soon some had spades and a pick and I knew we'd get Aggie buried proper.

There was ten of us, including Billy Blew, who shut down the Mint for a while, and we carried Aggie Cork real gentle to the same plot where they'd all just buried Mrs. Lovelace and the boy.

We took turns, three of us working at a time, and pretty soon we got the grave hollowed out of that clay.

"I guess you'll say the words," the barkeep said.

I'd rather slide down an avalanche, but no one else was gonna say nothing. I don't have enough words to fill a shot glass, but there I was. I felt like a cornered rat, but they was all waiting and staring, even Brashear, who was noting everyone that had pitched in to help dig that grave, so he could report it all to Carter Scruples. One thing about this: From now on, Scruples would know what side I was on. And what side everyone standin' there was on. It was sort of air-clearing—like opening up them windows in his bunkhouse to let the stink out. But from now on, I'd have me a bull's-eye sort of pinned to my chest by Scruples.

"He didn't have nobody," I began. "So we're it. We're the friends to see him off. I guess I just want to wish him well, better times than he had in this life, where he run out of luck most everything he did. So, I guess that does her."

They was standing there waiting for more, but I couldn't think of a thing to say.

"You were a good man and a true friend, Aggie Cork," I said.

That was the thing they needed.

"Amen, amen to that," they was muttering.

We lowered Aggie in, and shoveled the clay over him, and went our way to the Mint again. But Brashear, he hightailed out, and it was plain where he was goin'. Carter and Amanda would hear the whole story in about three minutes.

Back there at the Mint, Critter was standing at the hitch rail snapping at horseflies, and the mules was there, too, kicking at flies, which made me plumb nervous when I thought what was in them canvas bags hung from one mule.

We went into there, and they treated me to a mug of beer, and now that Brashear was gone, they opened up some.

"They gonna knock us off, one by one, and jump every claim in the district," said a young guy, Mike Pulaski. "I don't know how to fight it, not with snipers waiting to kill me."

"Their goal is to jump every small mine in thirty days," I said.

"You know that for sure?" Pulaski asked.

"Scruples told me so. After he cleans you out, he's going after the Fat Tuesday and Big Mother."

"I can fight some pistoleros, but not snipers," said Deaver. "Some guy waiting to shoot me, he's gonna do it sooner or later."

"His name is Glan. Rudolph Costello Glan. He works alone, and floats around like a ghost, and leaves bodies behind and no evidence he done it," I said. "But the company's got more men, including some new little killer I never heard of, calls himself The Apocalypse. Get in close to him, and you're likely breathing your last and seeing the last sunlight you're gonna see."

"You know that for a fact?"

"No, but I know the type. And they got another new one, a brawler named Arnold. I don't know him neither, but he'd gouge out an eye and knee you where it hurts, and bust every bone in your body."

"We're miners. He ain't gonna do that," another one said.

"Want to give him a try?" I asked.

"Any time, any place."

"There ain't no hospital here for you."

The man laughed. "You mean for him," he said. "Mucker Mack," he said. "Call me Mucker."

I liked Mucker, if I did think he had no brains in his head.

"I don't fight," he said. "I don't know how to swing a fist or land a haymaker. I got my own way, and it's the old bear hug. You want to know how Mucker Mack works? I give 'em a hug."

I'd never heard of fightin' like that, and thought anyone with a jackknife could deal with Mucker, but I didn't say nothing, and besides, I liked him. Maybe he'd squeeze Arnold a little.

These were tough miners, all right, them that was sober, which was maybe half. And that sorta gave me an idea.

"Seems to me, you want to stop this killin' and jumpin' your claims, we should put some heat to them two up in the Pullman car," I said, sort of casual.

They stared. Some sucked the foam off their beer and sipped.

"They ain't expecting it. I've got a couple of Aggie Cork's grenades sitting on that mule out there—"

That's as far as I got. Them miners bailed out of the Mint and put fifty yards betwixt that mule and themselves. I didn't realize Aggie's bombs were that touchy.

But eventually them miners crept back, eyin' that mule something nervous, and expecting hell to bust loose. I guess old Aggie knew what he was doing. One by one, they picked up their ale mugs and began sipping again.

"I wonder which of you fellers won't be here tomorrow, and which one of you'll vanish the next day," I said.

There sure wasn't no sound in the Mint Saloon just then. They was all thinkin' the same thing.

"I guess we could walk away," said Mike Pulaski. "Just leave our hopes behind and stay alive. I've got a good mine going, clearing about a hundred a day. That's more money than I've seen before."

Those independent fellers had some tough choices to make. It wasn't gonna be safe for them to work their little mines no more, not with Glan lurking around.

"We could fight back," said Wally Deaver.

I wanted to butt in there, but I kept my yap shut. These lads were miners, not gunmen. Every one of Scruples' little army was a killer. The miners couldn't do much alone. And the law, such as Brashear was, wouldn't lift a finger, not with Scruples owning the deputy.

It sure was a mess of bad choices. Every one of 'em was sipping suds and wondering how it would be to step out of a dark mine into daylight and take a bullet through the chest.

Then the double doors of the Mint swung open and

two gents walked in, big and little. The big brute was Arnold, lookin' rougher than a corncob on the butt, and the little was The Apocalypse, maybe four and a half feet, nail thin, maybe a hundred pounds wet, all in black, with twin holsters high on his belt, each with a snubby little black revolver parked in it.

It got real quiet in there as them miners started staring at that pair. There wasn't a man in there that didn't have it figured out who employed Arnold and The Apocalypse. But just so's to make it clear, I greeted them.

"Well, if this ain't something," I said. "This here's Arnold, he's the heavier one, and the other calls himself The Apocalypse."

The Apocalypse ignored me and ordered two ales from the barman.

"How do you like to be called?" I asked him.

He ignored me, and slowly eyed the crowd, taking its measure.

"That handle's too long for a country boy like me," I said. "Guess I'll call you Pock."

"No, you will call me The Apocalypse, every syllable, and leave none out."

I took his meaning. He wanted to prod me into a fight and get it over with. Old Arnold, he was around to keep them miners in check. Brashear had rushed up to the Palace Car, told his tale, and Carter Scruples didn't waste a moment sending this pair after me.

"Whatever you want, pal," I said. "This here gent's been hired by the Transactions company."

"Don't call me pal, Pickens," he said.

Somehow he knew my name, which made me mad. I didn't tell no one my name, but this one knew it. I just ignored him.

"And Arnold here, he's from the East, and you wouldn't want to mess with him," I said to the miners. "Not if you want your eyeballs and ears and teeth and knees and fingers and hair."

Arnold preened himself, sort of. I didn't doubt that he could flatten two or three miners at once, and leave them disabled for life.

The Apocalypse eyed me mildly. "Mr. Scruples said that in the contract, anyone who quits him is against him. Isn't that true?"

"I 'magine so," I said.

"I just wished to clarify matters," The Apocalypse said. "You know the contract, do you?"

I nodded.

"Then you know what happens to defectors."

"What's a defector? Talk English, Pock."

I sure didn't like going against this one with an old Baby Dragoon hangin' from my hip, but he got me riled up some.

"A traitor, my friend, a traitor. Does that shoe fit?"

I pitched ale in his puss and charged him. I wasn't gonna get into a gunfight with this one, so I barreled in before he could lay his dainty hands on them shorties, and knocked him flat and stayed right on top. When he did finally get one of them out, I was sitting on him and pointing my Baby Dragoon right into his eyeballs.

Arnold, he didn't do nothing. His orders were to keep the miners off, and let the gunfight happen. Only this time, there wasn't gonna be no gunfight. The Apocalypse didn't make no headway under 170 pounds of me sittin' on him.

I pulled them snubbies out, and checked for hideouts,

finding another down around his ankle, so I collected that one, too.

"All right, this sawdust down here's smelly, so's you get up and tell old Scruples that your guns got took and The Apocalypse didn't get the job done."

"You're a dead man," The Apocalypse said.

"Sooner or later," I agreed.

Chapter Fourteen

I looked around at them fellers in the Mint Saloon, who was sitting mighty quiet, and wonderin' whether they had it figured out yet. There wasn't nothin' between them and death from a sniper's bullet, unless they quit their claims and got out. This wasn't just claim-jumpin', it was plain murder.

I wasn't no better off either. I'd took them popguns from The Apocalypse. I wished to hell he had a real handle, but if that's what he called himself, that's what I'd call him. Arnold and him, they backed out and into the dark, and I wondered whether I'd get myself shot if I stepped out, too.

I looked at the man's stubby revolvers, thirty-two-caliber and short-barreled. I took a closer look at them bullets in the cylinders, and saw how each had a little cone cut into the lead, so that they'd flatten big when they hit flesh and put a fifty-caliber hole in a man. The Apocalypse might have toy guns, but he'd turned them into cannons.

Well, guns get shot both directions, I thought. If he messed with me, he'd get some of his own lead back.

I sucked up the last of my suds and decided that the best defense is a good offense.

"I guess I'm going to have me a visit to the Pullman Palace Car," I said. "There ain't no stopping this claim-jumpin' unless we put the heat on the jumpers. Anyone comin' along?"

They stared and said nothing. Maybe that was best. These were miners, not gunmen, and they'd just get themselves kilt.

"If you go back to your claims, you'll get yourself shot. Maybe you should all hole up somewhere safe."

"And let them take our mines from us?" Pulaski asked.

"Up to you," I said. There was no sense pushin' these hardrock men.

I set down my empty mug and fixed to leave. I hardly knew what to do with all them popguns, so I stuffed 'em in my pockets. I didn't go out the front neither. I went to the back door, where you go to piss in the alley, and then worked around to the front, keeping to the dark. But I saw no one lurking around, so I eased out, got Critter and the mules, and headed out of town. But as soon as I got away from the buildings, I cut over to the creek, and tied Critter and them mules in a patch of cottonwoods. Then I got them two bombs of Aggie Cork's and began working my way toward the hill with the Pullman car on it. Them bombs sure made me itchy. I wasn't even sure how to get the fuse lit proper, but I had some lucifers with me I could scratch on any rock. Only trouble is, matches make light and I'd likely get myself shot at getting one of them things lit and thrown.

They were hefty little devils, two sticks of DuPont, a copper cap with a fuse crimped in the end, and a mess of nails wrapped around the sticks with wire. I studied the hilltop, and especially the pen and barn and bunkhouse. A lantern was lit in the bunkhouse, and there was a couple lit over in the Pullman car, so I thought them people were in residence. But I didn't doubt they'd post a guard or two now, especially after a whole crowd of miners come up that hill, carrying the body of the mother and boy.

There wasn't much of a moon, which I took for a good omen. I edged closer, and then decided it was time to settle into the grass and just let the night progress a little. After watching clouds chase the moon a little, it all paid off. Back on the slope above the railroad car, someone lit up a cigar or a cigarillo. Flare of light, orange glow, light out. So they had a guard up there after all. Maybe more. I'd think Scruples would be itchy enough to post a couple more, and have them do night shifts. I'd also guess it would be one of them hooligans, maybe Arthur or Cleveland. Them names sure entertained me. I thought maybe I should call myself Lincoln, but pretty quick I thought twice about that one. I'd just be old Cotton.

There wasn't no mosquitoes or I'd a gone crazy lyin' there. But it was a quiet night, and pretty soon them in the bunkhouse blowed out the lantern. There was still lights up in the railroad car, and I wondered what Amanda was up to. I thought maybe I'd better not wonder. She sure could set off the itchy twitchy in me. She had some sort of power over me I didn't like. But maybe a couple of sticks of DuPont Hercules would educate her about jumping claims.

One bomb at the bunkhouse, the other under the railroad car. I didn't know what sort of damage that would do. Not much, I thought. It wasn't like sticking the stuff into a hole drilled in rock, which would catch the force of the explosion. But maybe it would scare 'em enough so that they'd wonder whether their claim-jumping was worth the risk.

Problem was, I'd need a sheltered place to light the fuse and throw the bombs. So I crawled upslope some more, until I reached the pens. Them horses were all starin' at me, so I settled down to see if someone noticed. Someone did, all right. A dark figure come out of the barn, and began comin' toward me. I saw the glint of a revolver in his hand. The place was well guarded, all right. I dug around until I got one of them little stubbies in hand. It was sort of handy, a barrel that short. And I just lay there in the grass on my back, that popgun aimed at the guard. He was working along inside the corral, lookin' for someone in there, and so he passed me by. I couldn't see which one of them lowlifes it was, but he finally gave up and headed back into the barn.

I waited some, and then started crawlin' toward the bunkhouse. If I had only time to get one lit and throwed, I'd toss it at the bunkhouse where them hardcases was livin'. Maybe if two sticks of DuPont were to turn that place into kindling, them that survived would look for fighting money somewhere else.

There just wasn't nowhere that would shield me once I struck a lucifer. I'd just have to scratch the match and throw one of Aggie's bombs and hope to light out before anyone thought to shoot at me.

Them lights in the Pullman snuffed out, too, and now it was quiet around there, at least until I made a little noise.

Off in the hills, I could hear the Big Mother and the Fat Tuesday goin' strong. Them two scarcely quit, and ran one shift after another. And the mill was stamping ore twenty-four hours a day, making a steady thump near Swamp Creek. This was some district, with two good mines and a mill like that.

I edged closer, until I figured I was close enough to light the fuse and throw it and hightail it. The clouds gave me my chance. The moon vanished for a moment, and it was plenty dark, so I stood up, got the fuse where I wanted her, flicked my thumb over that lucifer until it flared, and then held it to the fuse. It took a moment, and I sure was flinching with the thought of a bullet coming at me, but then that fuse started hissing real serious, so I pitched the thing and saw it land thirty, forty feet from the bunkhouse. I didn't stay around there, and started down the hill when it blew. The concussion, it knocked me right off my pins, but none of them tenpenny nails drilled me, so I guess I'd gotten far enough away. It sure was a blast. It lit up the whole hillside, cracked so loud my ears hurt, and blew the logs of that bunkhouse in.

That sure did it. It blew shingles off the barn, and made the ground shake under my body. First thing I heard was a lot of screeching from the corral, and I knew them tenpenny nails had cut up a lot of their horses and mules. There was fires starting up, and I needed to get to cover, especially since them employees of the Transactions company was pilin' out of that ruin, wavin' revolvers and shooting at every shadow. I guess them logs was thick enough so that most of those thugs survived, and they sure did come out shootin'. They was wearing their long-handles, mostly stained gray, and wavin' them revolvers. It wasn't a good idear to hang around, not with lead whistling past my ears.

I was disappointed. I thought maybe Aggie's bomb would blow that bunkhouse to kindling instead of just denting a log wall, and I thought I'd put them hooligans out of business. But at least I'd served notice to that outfit. They couldn't go jumpin' claims and killin' honest folk without the war returning to their own pigpen.

The lead was sure flyin', so I crawled fast, just about the time some of them hooligans in longhandles come down the hill carrying Greeners. I made the valley road, crossed it quick, and headed for the river bottoms and the cottonwoods in there, and then stood real quiet. Only then did I realize I still had Aggie's other bomb right there in my hand. Meanwhile, over to the Fat Tuesday, the steam whistle starts blowin', just on general principles, so Aggie's bomb started some commotion and everyone in the whole district was wonderin' what it was all about.

Two or three of them gunfighters, they had buckets and was dousing the fires.

I could see them up on the hill, collectin' now and talking things over with old Scruples, who was wearing a bathrobe and slippers, and pretty soon them hooligans was haulin' stuff out of the weakened bunkhouse and into the barn, where they was gonna camp for the night. And now there was a couple more sentries posted around, itching to shoot anything that moved. Then they got the fires put out, and darkness settled over that outfit up there, and them gunfighters was all lyin' around in the barn.

I was thinkin' maybe to go back there and toss that other bomb that old Aggie Cork put together, and was sort of weighing the options when everything changed.

What changed was the sudden appearance of cold steel stuck firmly into my back.

"Nicely done," said a voice I thought I knew. "Now you stand very, very quiet, and maybe you'll live."

A hand reached around and emptied my holster of that old Baby Dragoon, and then the hand patted my

pockets and extracted them two little popguns I took off
The Apocalypse, and then that hand sort of get aholt of
Aggie's bomb, which I was carrying in my left hand,
and sort of took it all from me.

"Don't move, my friend," the voice said, and a hand
slid down around my ankles and got that hideout popgun too.

"Yes, excellent tactics. You may slowly turn around
now."

I sure enough knew that voice by then. It was the one
person who wouldn't be in that bunkhouse, who hated that
bunkhouse, and who floated around entirely by his lonesome. The one who dressed in clean duds and didn't stink.

"Hello there, Glan," I said, only halfway friendly.

"You and I think alike. It's a pity we're on opposite
sides," he said.

"I haven't chose up sides yet," I said.

"That only means they haven't offered you money.
You have your price, and they'll pay it."

"Who's they?" I said, playin' dumb for the moment.

He laughed softly. "Mine is five hundred a week. Now,
I would have done this a little differently. If you really
wanted to kill them, you would have slid the dynamite
under the floor of the bunkhouse. But you contented
yourself with tossing the sticks against the side. Did you
really intend to spare them?"

He was just letting me know how dumb I was, so I
just agreed with it.

"No, I'd of blown them to bits if I could. They've
killed a mess of good miners."

"Ah! You need a little more training, young man.
There's no room in this business for mistakes. Such as
letting me walk right up on you. While you were busy

watching the hillside, I was busy watching you, checking out your horse, and noting how you were armed. That's why I command a good price. I can quit the business any time, you know. I could go to San Francisco and run a whorehouse if I wished."

"I don't think I ever had that in mind, but I wouldn't mind visiting one," I said.

"Well, what do you think I should do with you?"

"I've been kinda wondering the same thing, Glan."

"Maybe we should leave it to Mr. Scruples."

"Your choice," I said.

"Well, then. You go fetch your horse and I'll follow along. Now, I've already had a look in your saddlebags. You're mighty poor, aren't you, boy? I imagine a good meal would suit you just fine right now."

"I'm not one to refuse a good steak," I said.

Well, I got Critter and the mule and we sort of drifted up the slope to the Pullman Palace Car, and Glan, he had some sort of signal that let him through the guards. Just about when I was getting real nervous about someone taking a potshot at me, Glan blows a little whistle, and we just walk on in there.

And sure enough, we get to the Pullman Palace Car, and it's tilted a little bit because the blast knocked it off its rails. That baby's solid steel, and I was glad I didn't try to blow it to bits. I mighta knocked in some windows, but I hardly would have dented that outfit.

"Nicely done," Scruples said. He was standing in his robe and slippers at the end of the car. I sure didn't know who he was talkin' to, Glan or me.

"Come in, Mr. Pickens."

That got me riled up again. I don't much like him knowing my name.

Chapter Fifteen

They sure knew more about me than I knew about myself. I didn't never tell anyone my last name, 'cause it's nobody's business. But someone sure knew about me and I was ready to hang a noose around whoever tattled on me.

Just then, in comes Amanda, and she's wearing something gauzy, several layers of white stuff I never knowed the name of, except it sort of doesn't hide as much as it pretends to. She wanders in there to that rear parlor, and her hair's undone and fallin' around her shoulders, and the lamplight, it sort of wanders through all that gauze and I'm staring at whatever is shiftin' around in there, namely Amanda herself, just as sweet and curvy as in that painting over her bed in her boudoir, and the steam heat in that rear parlor raises upward about a hundred degrees.

"Why, if it isn't Cotton," she said.

"I don't want no truck with you," I said.

"Amanda, Mr. Pickens is the gentleman who recently caused the little uproar," Scruples said. "Mr. Glan caught him and brought him up here for our attention."

Glan smiled. "He still had one of these," he said, waving the remaining bomb.

"Ah, Mr. Glan, perhaps it's not a good idea to have that device inside here."

Glan looked wolfishly at Scruples and Amanda, as if he were deciding whether to obey, and finally smiled slightly.

"Here," he said, handing Scruples one of them stubby revolvers. "I'll dispose of this."

"A hundred yards from here at least, Mr. Glan."

The sniper vanished through the rear door, and I heard him clanging down the metal steps. I wondered where he'd put that little gift from Aggie Cork. They didn't have no bunker around, near as I could tell.

Scruples wielded the little popgun. "I do believe this is the property of The Apocalypse," he said. "He's been lamenting its loss."

"I took it from the Pock when he was actin' like he owned me," I said.

"He wouldn't want you calling him Pock, you know."

"Well I don't want you callin' me Cotton Pickens neither, so I guess we're evened up."

"No, not evened up. You deserted us. You had a contract."

"I sure did have an agreement. I was fixin' to spend a few nights with Amanda, like you agreed, but it didn't happen, not even after them miners in the Hermit was cleaned out. So who's busting the agreement? She is!"

Amanda was smiling. "Cotton, dear boy, you come with me. We'll make everything right."

"No, you already done cheated me once, and it ain't gonna happen again!" I said, half afraid I'd back down. About all she had to do was untie that lacy gown, and I'd a been a cooked goose.

Scruples, he was laughing.

Well, she upped and did it. She sort of loosened that

robe a little, and pretty quick I was seein' more and more of her, and my pulse was climbin' through the roof.

"He's not going anywhere. Enjoy yourself, Babydoll," Scruples said. "Glan's outside."

She just smiled at me, and beckoned with her little finger, and all I could do was follow her down that narrow little corridor past them rooms like she had a string tied to me. She pushed open the door, and then we was in that little bedroom of hers, the one with the painting of her lying there in the buff, and I'm thinking at last, at last.

She's just smiling, and filling up a bowl with hot water.

"Honey, you'll want to wash up. I'll be waiting for you."

She handed me that bowl and a towel and steered me toward a little water closet alcove I didn't know was there. So I set to work, scrubbing up. If she wanted me scrubbed up, I'd scrub until my flesh was pink.

I'd sure waited a lifetime for this, and now it was happening. It would sure beat anything I'd ever seen in a parlor house. I could hardly believe my luck, and I hadn't got it all figured out, but that didn't matter. There she was, around the corner. I could see her bare legs lyin' there on the bed, so I scrubbed away, and then I toweled myself dry, and stepped into the room.

She sure was pretty, lying there like that without a stitch on, just smiling and waiting for old Cotton.

I can't hardly explain what happened next, but in my head I seen old Aggie dead, and I seen that miner's wife and boy shot dead, and I just wilted away.

"Come on, Cotton," she said, and for a moment I thought I'd just faint.

But I turned back and got into my duds, while she was lyin' there frowning.

"I'm leaving. Go ahead and shoot if you're gonna do it," I said.

"You're not very bright, Cotton," was all she said.

That made me mad, too. Not bright, was I? Not bright for pullin' out?

She was pouting now, but I didn't care. I opened her bedroom door, headed down the corridor to the rear parlor, and opened that rear door, stepped out to the steel platform, and down the metal steps. I untied Critter from the hitching post and was about to board him when Glan, he showed up.

Glan, he was grinning in the dark. "Amanda, she prefers men who wash up now and then," he said.

That made me so mad I almost decked him, but I figured I'd done enough damage for the night, and I steered Critter down the slope. No one stopped me. But now they had every gun I was carryin', including the Baby Dragoon, and them popguns. I felt sort of naked.

That Amanda, she sure made me mad. I thought she liked me, but she was just usin' me, and was spending her nights with Glan.

I rode down that long slope and headed for Swamp Creek, still trying to sort things out. But the farther I got from the Pullman Palace Car, the better I felt. Amanda had me scrubbing my body, but it wasn't my body needed cleaning. If I'd gone back in with them, I'd of felt dirty down inside of me. That Amanda, she was the sweetest thing I'd ever seen in my life, and she had me wrapped around her little finger. I was about to let my pants rule me, but my head took over, and I got away. But it sure was some lesson. If I hadn't got away when I did, they'd have me in their crew again, jumping claims and shooting anyone in the way.

It was clean mountain air I was riding through, not the perfume air in that bedroom, but clean with pines and sagebrush on it. I'd come closer to jumping into the manure than I ever had, and it was that part of me south of the waist that done it. Even then, as I smelled that pine scent on the night breeze, I was remembering how Amanda looked, waitin' for me on that bed, and I knew I'd never get entirely past this one. But I'd got out. That's all I could say. I'd got out.

I was in a fix. I steered Critter into Swamp Creek, not knowin' what to do, but when I arrived at the Mint Saloon, I thought that was as good a bet as any, so I tied up Critter and Aggie Cork's mule and went in.

It was late, and it turned out that Billy Blew was just shutting down.

"I'll pour a fast one," he said.

"Truth is, Billy, I can't afford it. You need a swamper? I'd trade some swamping for some of them pickled eggs in that there jar. And I'd do some serious cleanin' for a night on the billiard table."

"Bad, is it? Well, you ain't the first. Sure, Cotton. You set to work and I'm going to hit the hay. Them eggs is overdue to get et." He looked me over. "And there's a sack of oats and a feedbag in the back. You put in some time around here and you put the feedbag to those animals."

"I'll do her!"

"What brings you to town so late?"

"My south half almost whipped my north half."

Billy stared at me, and then cackled a little. "Ain't that the truth about all of us. Reckon you was heading for Big Sally's House."

I just grinned, not wantin' to say what really tempted me.

"Lock that front door," he said as he left.

So there I was. I found a broom and began sweeping up that stinkin' sawdust. Boy, it smelled. No one had lifted that sawdust for weeks, and I swear, about half them customers had leaked into it. Billy had him an old scoop shovel, and I swept the sawdust into there and dumped it in the alley, which already stank of piss, so I wasn't doing it no more harm. It took a while, but I got her swept out, and mopped down, and I found a bin of fresh sweet sawdust and sprinkled a load over them planks, and pretty soon the old Mint smelled less like miners and more like a mountain breeze.

I found the old feedbag and the oats and I put in a bait for Critter, and hooked it over his snout.

"I guess you'll like that," I told him, and he sawed his head up and down and tried to kick me.

"You're next," I said to Aggie's mule, but he just stared at me.

I went back in there and headed for the pickled eggs. They was rank, all right, but I was hungry enough so it didn't matter. They had a nice rubbery vinegar feel to them, and I put away three or four before getting vinegared out. Then I fed a bait to Aggie's mule, and eyed the billiard table. It wasn't any cleaner than the floor, so I gave Billy a bonus and swept the table out, too before dropping my bedroll on it. By the time I got all that done, the mule had et up the bait, so I took both animals over to the creek to water, and then tied them up at the rail again.

My last stop was the alley for a leak, but when I started in I kept staring at some dark lump just down a piece, so after I buttoned up I went over there, and that lump was sure enough a body. It was just lyin' there. I couldn't see who it was, so I went to fetch the lamp in the Mint, and headed out there.

I sure wasn't feelin' good about it, but someone had to do it, and I was elected. I got the lantern off the wagon wheel chandelier in the Mint, and edged over to that lump of darkness lyin' in the muck, and the first thing I noticed was that it had been an execution. That fellow's hands had been tied behind his back.

I eased him over, so I could see his face, or what was left of it. A bullet had entered between his eyes. He was dark and slim and had a goatee and was dressed real fine, in a black suit and a string tie and high white collar. This here was murder, not some gunfight. Next door to the Mint was the Miners Exchange, which is where most of them wage miners go after shift. That crowd doesn't visit the Mint, and them wage miners don't even like the independent miners.

Something kept ticklin' my memory, and I finally realized I knew the dead man a little, not from having met but just because most ever'body in town knew who this one was.

He was Armand Argo, a New Orleans gambler who won hisself the Fat Tuesday mine at cards two years earlier. The mine had some other name, but Argo changed it to the Fat Tuesday Mine, in honor of the partyin' they do in New Orleans ever' year. And there he was, just as dead as anyone gets. Argo, he had mostly gave up playing poker, and was runnin' his gold mine, and doing well, too, from what I'd heard. He ran two shifts of eight or ten men, and was makin' good money from the mine. Argo was always quiet and gentlemanly, with a cigarillo danglin' from his lips half the time, and a way of lookin' at you like you were some beef he was gonna buy. But mostly he was just studying on you. He had the gift of knowin' more about you than you knew about yourself. It goes with playin' cards, I guess.

Well, I didn't know what to do. I couldn't just leave him there. And there wasn't enough law in Swamp Creek to call on for help. I realized the body lay behind the Miners Exchange, so I decided I'd better take it in there and let them look after it. The next shift wouldn't be out of the mines until two in the morning, so there wouldn't hardly be no one in there. I hardly set foot in there, because I didn't like to down boilermakers with them clodhoppers.

I worked my arms under Argo, and finally got to lifting him and headed for the alley door. It stank there. Like the Mint, it had no privy and if you wanted to piss, you just stepped into the alley and cut loose.

So I worked my way in there, and there was two barkeeps and two patrons, and just one lamp lit. Them two drinkers turned around and stared at me. I set Argo down on a billiard table. One barkeep reached under the bar and came up with a sawed-off Greener aimed my direction.

"Found him in the alley behind your place here," I said. "It looks to be Argo."

"He was just in here an hour ago," the keep said.

"Guess I better pinch you for murder, Cotton," Johnny Brashear said as he came over from the bar.

Chapter Sixteen

Muggsy Pitt, the barkeep at the Miners Exchange, didn't like that at all.

"Hold it right there, Brashear," he said.

Since Muggsy was the one with the sawed-off scattergun, Brashear got real polite real fast.

"Cotton, tell us," Pitt said.

"I was next door, come out to piss, and there he was, behind here. I brung him in," I said.

"How come next door?"

"I was bedding on the billiard table."

"Argo's hands behind his back like that?"

"Lying facedown in the muck, hands tied like that. That's all I know."

"Likely story," said Brashear.

Muggsy waved the scattergun at him. "You lay off. Maybe you done it yourself. You're the only one went out there last hour or so."

The district mining secretary who carried a deputy badge didn't like that none.

"Brashear, maybe I'll just ride up to Butte and tell the sheriff about this," I said.

The mining district clerk looked real itchy. "No, that's my job. I'll do it," he said.

"Then go do it," Muggsy said.

That's when the whistle blew up at the Fat Tuesday mine. The second shift was done, and in a few minutes most of them miners would be sitting right here, ordering suds and a shot on the side. Maybe that would be a good thing.

Brashear, he looked sort of tentative at Muggsy, and then edged out the door and into the night.

"That outfit in the railroad car, they wanted Argo out," Muggsy said. "And they own Brashear. You can bet that he's taking the news up there."

"Anything happens in the valley, someone's running up to the railroad car to talk about it," I said. "Johnny Brashear's a regular errand boy, looks like."

"I got a body in my saloon, and I want to get it out of here," Muggsy said.

"Anybody know anything about Argo? Like who's his relatives? And who's partners with him in his mine?" I asked.

"Armand Argo, he come in here for almost the first time tonight. Like he was looking for someone, or gonna meet someone here."

"I guess he met someone, all right," I said.

"He came and went. He looked around here, didn't see what he was looking for, and headed out the doors."

"Rear door?"

"Naw, front door. And that was the end of it, until you carried him in here."

"Them off-shift miners are comin'. Maybe we better see what they know," I said.

"I don't like it. I want the boys to have a good time in here."

"Muggsy, there'll be no good time for anyone tonight," I said.

About then, the double doors swung open, and five or six of them Fat Tuesday second-shift men pushed in, laughing and ready for a beer and a shot. It was a hard thing to watch. They crowded in, noticed what was lying on the billiard table, and crowded around it, dead silent.

"It's the boss," one said.

"Argo, yes. In the alley. We brought him in," Muggsy said, starting to fill some mugs from his tap.

That sure was a quiet crowd. Three more came in, caught the silence, and gathered at the table. Not a one of 'em said a thing.

"What?" asked a big one with a flowing beard.

"Found him in the alley behind here, just a few minutes ago," I said.

"Executed. Hands tied!" the miner said.

"You know why?" I asked.

"Hell, yes, we all know why," the bearded one said.

"Who are you?" I asked.

"Card Penrose," he said. "I'm the shift foreman." He sighed, ran a big grimy hand through his locks. "We all knew it would come, sooner or later."

"Scruples?"

The foreman nodded. "Can't be no other. They told him to sell out or get out and gave him a deadline. I think it was yesterday. Sell out for a cheap price or face the music."

"Threatened him?"

"Argo, he just laughed, and said they wouldn't dare."

"Looks like they dared," I said.

"Argo, he always carried a piece," Penrose said.

I nodded at him, and he reluctantly opened Argo's coat and felt around the chest, and then shook his head.

"Not now," he said.

"You know if he had partners? Or family? Or heirs? Who owns this mine?"

"He had a little office at the mine," one of them said.

"Where'd he live?"

"He had him a place above the Moulin Rouge."

That was a gamblin' parlor and maybe a little more, down the block. Rumor had it that he owned the gamblin' franchise there, but not the bar. Kept his hand in his business, which was cards and dice.

I sure didn't know what to do. I just come to Swamp Creek to get me a meal and a flop. But no one around there was doin' much.

"I guess we'd better see what we can see at the Fat Tuesday office and maybe in his rooms," I said.

"I'll see what's in his rooms," Muggsy Pitt said. "Anyone needs a refill, pour it yourself and put it in the till."

"I'll go with you, Muggsy," one of them miners said. That was a good idea.

"Penrose, let's you and me see what's in that mine office," I said. "I got a feeling we ought to get there and make sure things are proper."

The rest, they didn't want to know, seems like, and crowded the bar with their back to their late boss. But no one was sayin' much.

We stepped into the chill night. Swamp Creek was plain black at this hour, but for a couple of saloons catering to the last shift. I remembered I didn't have no gun. Them Transactions people had got ever' gun I owned, and I was nakkid as a jaybird. Seein' as how there wasn't no law to speak of, a man in Swamp Creek without an iron is sure gonna invite every mugger around.

"You work long for Argo?" I asked Penrose.

"Come over from Cornwall 'twas two years past and this was just starting up, and I thought it's a good place in the New World for a old tin miner, so I hired on. That was before Argo won the place in a game of cards. Now that gravels me Methodist heart, it does, betting cards on a mine."

"Were his miners happy with him?"

Penrose didn't reply at first. "About average, I'd say. He wasn't doin' his miners any favors, and that mine needs more air. But so do the rest."

"Someone plain kilt him."

"And there's no heirs neither," he said. "I had a few talks with old Armand. His whole family died of yellow fever down there in New Orleans."

"Who's gonna get this mine?"

"I'd guess it's already gotten," Penrose said.

We trailed up a sharp grade. The mine head was located well above the town. But it was already dark up there, lamps out and all.

"I can't see nothing," I said.

"I know my way around," he said.

He put a hand on my shoulder and guided me off to the side, where some dark buildings loomed. I'd never been to the Fat Tuesday, and was sort of wonderin' how I got mixed up in all this stuff. But there I was.

Penrose, he steered me toward a dark building off to the side, and gently tried the door. It wasn't locked, so he pushed her open and we stepped in.

"The office," Penrose said. "Probably some records here."

A wooden floor creaked under us, and then a match flared. It blinded me a moment, and when I got past the surprise, there was The Apocalypse standin' there, one of his stubby little pot-shooters aimed square at me, and next to him was Arnold.

"Well, well," said The Apocalypse, waving his stubby revolver in my direction. "Fancy finding you here."

Arnold lit a lamp, and sure enough, there was four of us in that office. It wasn't no grubby office neither, but one with red wallpaper and real nice furniture.

This was getting tiresome, me without a gun since everything got took by them nice folks in the railroad car. I always say, if you don't have a gun, go git one, so I sprang straight at The Apocalypse. Only he was ready for me this time, and cracked a shot that burned across my upper arm, but then I landed on the little fart and knocked him over 'bout the time the next shot cracked right next to my ear. I was scuffling with him hard; for a little guy he was mean, but I figured I'd just better win or he'd put my lights out, so I got one of them popguns loose from him, and was goin' for the other when the whole world went black, and I knew Arnold had landed a good one on me and I might wake up in a week or two.

Well, that was something all right. I wasn't out long, and when I woke up I didn't even had no headache. Arnold was an expert. He just thunked me in some way as to douse my lights. I lay there on the floor with them two Scruples men a-watching me, and old Penrose standing there. He had a lump on his head, so I knew that Arnold had knocked him loose of a few teeth, too. And The Apocalypse was smirky.

"Thought you could get away with it, did you, Cotton?" he asked.

He was armed with both of his popguns again, but didn't even have one in hand. All he needed was Arnold to keep me on the floor. I didn't argue with that none. That Arnold, he was a man with talents, and it took nothing more than a boot to keep me real quiet there on that polished wood.

There was one other thing I was just discoverin', and that is that my hands were tied behind my back, real tight. That was a little unsettling, given the local history during the last hour or two, but there wasn't nothing to do about it. The Apocalypse was watching and smirking, and seeing me wiggle my fingers a little just to try them out. He laughed softly.

"Out like a light," he said.

"Well, I suppose you got some reason for being here in this office," I said.

"Trespassers," the little gunman replied. "Mr. Scruples frowns on trespassers."

"Let me guess. The Fat Tuesday now belongs to Transactions, Incorporated, right?"

"Your wisdom is remarkable," the twerp said.

"And let me guess. You're here because you heard Armand Argo's no longer the owner, right?"

"Poor devil had an accident, it seems," The Apocalypse said.

"I reckon he did," I said. "And I suppose you're of a mind to cause a few more accidents."

He sighed. "I wish I could, Cotton, but Amanda, she wants you all for herself. She says you and she have unfinished business she's going to finish, even if you got your hands tied behind your back."

"She said that, did she?" I asked stupidly. "How'd she know where to find me?"

"I sent word that you were expected here, Cotton. You're lucky. You'll spend the night with Amanda."

This was getting plumb entertaining.

"To hell with Amanda. I ain't going," I said. "Tell her no, I ain't a-going up there. And here's what you're gonna do. You're gonna get a bandage on my arm. You're gonna tell her she owes me a shirt, and I want a good shirt right now. You're gonna cut me loose and I'm going back to Swamp Creek. Me and Penrose here, we're going down to town."

The Apocalypse sighed softly.

"Amanda wouldn't like it," he said.

"That's just too bad. You fix up my arm and cut me loose now."

The little gunman smiled sadly and nodded to Arnold.

Next I knew, my lights went out again. That Arnold, he had skills I never seen before. When I did wake up, I knew exactly where I was. There was that oil painting of Amanda hanging above the bed, and there was Amanda, dressed just like in the painting. My arm was bound up real nice, but that's all I was wearing.

"Hello, Cotton," she said. "You sure are hard to get."

Chapter Seventeen

There she was, just eyeing me and smiling, and I didn't mind lookin' back neither.

"Amanda," I said, "I've got me a headache."

She pouted some, and I thought maybe she was gonna ignore me.

"That Arnold, he whonked me twice tonight, and now I got me a king-size headache, and there's nothing you or me can do."

She sighed, mighty unhappy, but it was all her fault. She had Arnold whonk me and then she had Arnold carry me up to the Pullman Palace Car, so she could only blame herself.

"Some other time then," she said. "You won't escape for long."

That was a puzzler, too. "How come you're always after me?" I asked.

"It's just a personal whim," she said. "You don't count in the larger scheme of things. Carter and I have the whole Swamp Creek District almost wrapped up, and there's nothing you or anyone else can do about it."

"Then why am I here?" I asked.

"Cotton, you could fit your brains in a thimble, but your south half makes up for it."

Now that was the damndest thing any woman ever said to me in all my life, and it riled me some.

"Well, if that's how you feel about me, I'll be gettin' out of here."

"Your headache'll go away, Cotton. Just spend the night."

"You just added to my headache," I said.

I got out of that feather bed, and hunted around for my britches, and had a hard time finding them. She just lay there smiling sweetly. I hunted high and low, and here and there, and I couldn't find nothing of mine. This Transactions outfit had transacted my clothing from me, along with everything else. The only thing I wore was that bandage on my arm.

Well, that done it. "I'm gittin' out," I said.

It was plumb dark out, and two or three in the morning, and I knew where to get some spare duds. So I just quit her lamp-lit bedroom, while she lay there pouting, and made my way along that dark corridor in the car, and finally out the rear door, plumb nakkid, but I didn't care. If this Transactions outfit wanted my old stuff, they could have it.

It was a chilly night, and so dark I couldn't see where I was going, which was hard on my feet because I kept stepping on sticks and stubbing my toes, but then I stepped in some nice warm horse apples, and that made my feet feel just fine. Pretty soon I was down the slope, and walkin' the valley road, and thinkin' what to say to any preacher's wife comin' along, but there wasn't none.

Swamp Creek sure was dark. Them second-shifters had all gone to their cabins, and the saloons was shut down. But Critter and the mule was tied to the hitching post. I scared Critter half to death; he never done see me butt-ass bare before, but he got used to the horrible sight. I untied my kit from behind the cantle and dug in there until I got my spares, and slid into my union suit, and my old worn Levi Strauss jeans, and an old flannel shirt with the elbows busted out, and finally the pair of moccasins I kept in there, and then I was fixed up good. I worked around behind the Mint and let myself in, and there were my blankets still lyin' on the pool table, so I knew I'd get a couple hours of sleep anyhow, before I got wakened up by some joker or other.

But no sooner was I sawin' wood than there's a banging on the rear door. I got to wonderin' whether the Mint was doing some sort of business I didn't know about, and what old Billy Blew was peddling out the rear door. But I yawned and lowered my feet over the billiard table and got myself to the rear door, and opened her a crack.

"Cotton, it's me, Muggsy," said a voice.

That would be Muggsy Pitt, the barman from the Miners Exchange, and he had someone with him.

"Yeah, come in, and I've got a headache, so make it quick," I said.

Truth was, my head still throbbed. That Arnold sure knew how to dent a skull, but someday I'd dent his soon as I figured out how.

I got a lamp lit, and there was Muggsy with a girl. She was raven-haired, curvy in the right places, pouty-lipped, and maybe was half growed up. She also was carrying a little lady's revolver, and not bein' careful where the business end of it was pointing.

"This here is Celia Argo," Muggsy said. "She's Argo's widow lady."

"You mean daughter," I said.

"Married tight to Armand," she said. "And I don't do incest."

"Just a minute. Argo had him a little wifey?" I asked.

"He was man enough for two wives, but I'm woman enough for three Armands," she said.

"That's what comes from owning a gold mine," Muggsy said.

"I'm going to shoot the sonofabitch killed Armand," she said.

"How old are you?" I asked. "They got a reform school going over in Twin Bridges, I think, just in case you shoot someone dead."

"Sixteen and one half," she said.

"And how old was Armand Argo?" I asked, just curious.

"Old enough to keep me happy," she retorted.

"She was up there in Argo's rooms," Muggsy said. "She yelled a little when she heard about Armand."

"I imagine you was plumb sad," I said.

"I hardly knew him, so why should I be sad?"

"You hardly knew him?"

"We was so busy messing around, we hardly met."

"You hardly met Armand Argo?"

"Oh, we were getting around to it. He got introduced to all of me except my mind. He never got that far. And I never got to know what was in his head."

"And you're the proper widow?"

"Far as I know."

"The Fat Tuesday's your mine now. Leastwise, until the claim-jumpers get it, and they already have. It'd help if you had some paper saying you and him got hitched before a preacher."

"It was a justice of the peace in Louisiana."

"Then the Fat Tuesday's yours if you can keep it."

"Well, that's what I'm going to do. Do you know who killed Armand?"

"I got a good idea, but I can't prove it."

"Well, I'll hire you to go kill them."

"Whoa up, Celia. I didn't say I know for sure. I just got me an idea, is all."

"Who? I'll kill them myself if you're too chicken."

"It ain't a matter of chicken. It's getting it right. You can't go makin' mistakes in the killing business."

"Well, I wouldn't mind a mistake or two if I get to keep my gold mine. Armand bet me against the Fat Tuesday, and won the Fat Tuesday and I got to stay with Armand."

"He bet you?"

She smiled. "And I'm worth it, too. But that other player, Godfrey Gore, he was just an old fart and it would take ten of him to keep me happy, so it all worked out. But if Godfrey won me and kept his mine, he'd a died of a heart seizure after a few nights."

"Well, you ain't got the mine," I said. "Them claim-jumpers have got two men in the office, and they're not letting anyone near the mine."

"And they're the ones that tied up Armand and shot him," she said. She squinted at me, but I was squinting at her. She sure was cute and curvy. "I'll hire you," she said.

"You can have me for free," I replied, "but I've got a headache now."

Muggsy, he thought that was pretty good.

"I mean, I need someone who's good with his gun," she said.

"Sounds like me," I said, "but they took my guns and ever' time I lay hands on one, they get it, too."

"Come with me," she said.

So I followed her and Muggsy into the night, and she took me over to Armand's rooms down the street, and when we got up there, she smiled at me like she meant it, and disappeared for a moment. When she returned, she had a black gunbelt in hand, with a shining black Peacemaker in its holster.

That sure was a nice outfit. She sort of smiled and wrapped that leather around my waist and buckled on the belt, and I felt the weight at my hip, and I would have felt a lot more, but she backed off.

"You're hired," she said.

"Just a minute, Celia, I ain't seen an offer yet."

"You get the Fat Tuesday back, and you get half of it."

"I gotta eat meanwhile."

"You can munch on me."

I liked the way she was talking, but munching on her wasn't going to keep me in groceries.

"A hundred a month," I said, naming wages so high I knew she'd turn me down.

But she didn't bat an eye.

"All right. Now go take over my mine and find out who shot Armand."

"You sure don't waste no time. What I'm gonna do is try to get some sleep. Then we'll see."

"No, you'll get that mine back. You can sleep next week," she said.

I knowed then that I was workin' for a she-cat.

"What happened? What did Argo tell you?"

"Armand sure got talky in bed," she said. "He couldn't keep a secret from me if he tried, long as we were horizontal."

"I need to know everything you know," I said.

"That district secretary, Johnny Brashear, a week ago he came to Armand and said his claim was faulty. The Fat Tuesday wasn't even inside the lines. And he was gonna auction it off, according to the district rules. Armand, he told Brashear to go to hell."

That sounded familiar.

"Then Carter Scruples, he said he'd bought the Fat Tuesday at a public auction, so Armand had to vacate in twenty-four hours. Armand laughed at him. That went on three or four days, back and forth, and then Scruples told him there'd be trouble unless he got out. He told me he was staying armed. He's been around. He thought he could handle those thugs, and he was staying alert for trouble." She took a breath. "And now this."

"Getting the Fat Tuesday back won't be easy, Celia."

"I thought you'd be man enough."

That sure started me percolating, I'll tell you. "I ain't any more man than anyone else around here," I said.

She looked kinda pouty, but I'd made my point. Them slicks Scruples hired was tougher and meaner than me, and I respected them.

"You tellin' me you're gonna fail?"

"Failin's not what I have in mind. Getting himself kilt was not what Armand Argo had in mind neither. I'm saying you'll get the best from me I got, and not just you neither. This Transactions outfit up in the railroad car, it's overrun pretty near everyone here, and if no one stops it now, no one ever will. They scattered the small-timers, drove off others, and now they have just one more to go, the Big Mother. Cletus Carboy runs that. It earns ten times what all the rest around here earn. That's the prize. Get that, and they'll be millionaires. They're gonna sell the whole district and get out. I got that straight from them up in the Pullman car. So, it's me against the whole lot, and the odds are good, but I'm crazy that way," I said.

She wasn't smiling when she absorbed all that.

"And there's somethin' else, Celia. If I'm getting into this, it ain't just for you. It's for all them people that got kilt or driven off. It's for that mother and boy got kilt at the Hermit Mine. It's for my friend Aggie Cork. It's for all of you."

"Maybe I'll join you," she said. "Where are you going next?"

Chapter Eighteen

I thought maybe to start with the mining district secretary, Johnny Brashear, seeing as how it was about three in the morning and a good time to have a friendly conversation.

Me and Celia, we hiked down them dark streets of Swamp Creek to the two-story board-and-batten building that housed the offices of the mining district on the first floor and Brashear's rooms upstairs. You had to go up an outside stairway to get to them digs.

"This oughta be interestin'," I told her.

She sort of giggled. I didn't know what to make of her yet, but she kept Argo happy, and that was in her favor.

I steered her up them wooden stairs behind the building. It stank back there, but it stank behind most every building in Swamp Creek. There was only a few real outhouses in town, and them was all square over the creek.

"He didn't aim good," she said. "I can aim better than that."

I sure agreed with her.

We got up there and just to be on the safe side, I pulled that iron, and then knocked.

Nothing happened for a while, while the moon dipped behind some stringer clouds, and then I knocked again. Three in the morning was a pretty good time, I thought. We finally heard some hollerin' in there somewhere, and finally the door creaks open a piece.

"What?" Brashear asks.

I pushed hard, and then we were in the doorway and he couldn't slam her shut. He was wearing one of them nightshirts. I'd heard tell of such things, baggy cotton dresses, but I'd never seen one live on a body.

"Time for you to do some explaining, Brashear," I said.

"What are you talking about? Get outa here."

"You're gonna open up that office down there and we're gonna look at some records and you're gonna tell us how come you took the Fat Tuesday mine and gave it to Carter Scruples."

"Come back in the morning," he said, trying to shut the door.

But he wasn't getting nowhere 'cause I was in the middle of it.

That's when Celia Argo, she sort of got right into it.

"You crook," she said. "You're gonna come downstairs and show us the books." She was wavin' that little lady gun at him. "Know what'll happen next? I'm gonna shoot you in the crotch. And after that, I'll shoot your fingers and hands off. You want to go through the rest of your life getting fed because you can't hold a spoon? You want the friendly fellow next door to wipe your butt with a corncob because you can't?"

He wasn't paying her no attention, so she sent a shot sizzling past his ear. That sort of got his attention. Then she pointed her lady gun straight at his family jewels, and he got the message. I had to hand it to Celia. She was a match for Armand Argo, all right, and most ever'body else come around. And she didn't neglect to pull that spent brass and shove another in there, ready to perforate the minin' camp secretary.

"I'm going to haul you to Butte," he managed to say. "I'm a deputy."

"I'm thinking maybe we'll haul you to Butte," I said. "Haul you up and lock you in there and tell that sheriff what you're doing around here."

He looked mighty sullen, but she waggled that lady gun and aimed straight at his jewels, and he got the message that time.

I followed him in there whiles he got his skeleton key, and it was mighty close in there. In fact, it plain smelled bad. But so did Brashear. We followed him down them stairs. I knew he wanted to stop for a leak, but I was in no mood, and Celia would have shot anything that came to view, so we just shoved him down, and he barefooted around the building and opened up the door.

"There's nothing to see," he said.

"There's records, and they been fixed to make Carter Scruples look legal, even if he ain't."

Brashear, he didn't say nothing.

"How'd you steal the mine from me and Armand?" she asked.

"It was all perfectly up and up," he muttered.

"Show me," she said, waving that little lady revolver right at his crotch.

"Don't," he said, placing a limp white hand between that lady gun and his jewels.

Real slow, he lit a lamp and pulled a big ledger book off a shelf.

"Look for yourself," he said, plainly not wantin' to go any deeper into it.

"You show us," I said.

"All I do is keep track of who owns what," he said.

"Where's the Fat Tuesday?" Celia asked.

"That's claim number forty-seven," he said.

He thumbed through the ledger. Each claim was on a separate page. When he got to Number 47, he paused. At the top was a description: "From claim cairn, 600 feet west to staked corner, then 1500 feet north to corner, then 600 east to corner, then 1500 feet south to cairn."

"They're all like that," Brashear said.

Beneath was simply a record of the original claimant and transfers of ownership. The Fat Tuesday had gone from Willis Bank to Armand Argo to Transactions, Incorporated. That transfer was dated a week earlier, which sure interested me.

"Who come here to record the new ownership?" I asked.

"Carter Scruples, he came with a bill of sale from Argo, so I recorded it proper," he replied.

"What bill of sale?" Celia asked.

"Proper bill of sale, signed by your man," he said.

"Show it to me."

"That's in Scruples' possession."

"How much was paid for the claim?" she asked.

"How should I know? Me, I just keep the books is all."

"Show me the Hermit Mine," I said.

"That'd be claim number 122. That was one of the last ones filed," Brashear said.

He paged through and found it.

"That was filed on by six men, as you can see, standard

600-by-1500-foot claim, and transferred to Transactions, let's see, two months ago."

"And he showed you a bill of sale?"

"Yep. That's how I keep the books."

"And did you challenge it?"

"Scruples had a proper bill. That's all that's needed. I'm just the recording secretary, keeping a legal record."

"This stinks."

Celia waved her little lady gun at his privates. "Stop making it look right. You show me the true bill now, or I'll blow your balls off."

That little widow lady sure was determined. All of us knew that Armand Argo hadn't sold his mine to anyone, but there it was on the books, lookin' legal and proper. Me, I ain't got the brains to figure it out. Crooks are a lot smarter than me, which is why they're crooks. There's crooks, and the rest of us are just ordinary dumb folks trying to do the right thing.

Next I knew, Celia was counting. "I pull the trigger at three," she said. "One, two . . ."

"All right, all right," Brashear howled.

He reached for another gray ledger book on the shelf, this one smaller. It had a label on it that said "Assessments."

"District assesses every mine every year," he said. "That's sort of a tax to keep this office going and settle disputes and write out deeds and claims. If a mine falls behind on the assessments, it can be auctioned off, and that's how Scruples buys them up."

"Auctioned off?" she asked.

"I hold auctions one minute past midnight on the announced day. And Scruples, he's the only one shows up."

I started laughin'. "You turd, what's he paying you?"

Brashear cooled down. "You accusing me of something?"

"I'll shoot your pecker off," Celia said.

"This district is run up and up," he said.

Celia put a bullet between his legs, right through that nightshirt. I didn't see no blood gushing down his leg, so I guessed she spared his privates.

"My Gawd," he whispered.

"I don't know how your crooked game works, but here's what you're gonna do," she said. "You're gonna write me a deed that says that Armand Argo or his heirs owns the Fat Tuesday. Then you're gonna write the same thing for every other claim that Scruples took over."

"He'd kill me."

"Then get out of town. Now start writing," she said. "'Cause if you don't, you won't have any fingers left, and that's just the beginning of the parts you'll lose."

I sure had to hand it to her.

Brashear, he hunkers down at his desk, dips the nib into the ink pot, and begins scribbling out deeds and recording them in his ledgers. She's lookin' over his shoulder, too, making sure he's doing it proper. I never seen such a woman. She knew more words than I'd thought there were. She taken each deed, compared it to the original, and tucked it under her arm.

I didn't know if all this paperwork did much good, not with that army Scruples had roaming around out there, but at least it was something to hand them miners, them that hadn't fled the district. If Scruples was gonna get this Swamp Creek District, it'd be straight shooting-iron theft, and not a lot of stealing only a law clerk could figure out.

But then I remembered something that Carter Scruples told me when I was tied up with that bunch. He said he didn't know a thing about mining, and he was gonna sell the whole Swamp Creek District, once he got his hands on the mines, and get out. So that was why he needed all that paper. He had to prove to any buyer that he owned all them mines. Him and Amanda weren't gonna get far without those deeds, or claims, or whatever. I never did know all the proper words, but it didn't matter none. They needed good paper to sell out, and that's why they was putting the screws to the district secretary.

Old Brashear, he sat there in his nightshirt, sweating, lookin' into that muzzle of Celia's little lady pistol now and then, but he kept scratching, and she kept eyeing the result and comparing it with the ledgers. It took an hour, and it wasn't long until dawn when he finally finished up.

"Open that safe," she said.

I'd hardly noticed the safe. It had pink cupids painted on black enamel.

"No, what's in there's mine," Brashear said.

"Open it before I blow off your fingers one by one."

"Then you'll never get it open," he said.

"And anything else dangling around," she added.

He got religion, all right, and began spinning that dial, and pretty soon he creaked that heavy door open and we got a look in there. It was just a little safe, after you got past them thick walls, but it was stuffed with flannel bags, and they sure was heavy.

"How much gold is that?" Celia asked.

"That's my personal money," Brashear said.

"That's what Carter Scruples paid you, and we're taking it to the sheriff in Butte," she said.

I sure marveled at that girl.

"But that's mine!"

"We'll let him get it straightened out," she said. "Now, you gonna get out of town before Scruples comes hunting you?"

He didn't say yes or no. He just sort of deflated, like gas leaving a gasbag, and then he walked wearily around the building and up them smelly steps, with Celia right behind, not giving him a chance to do her harm.

Well, the deal was, he got himself dressed and packed, and we followed him over to Bunsen's Livery, where he woked up the proprietor and got himself a buggy and a trotter, and tossed his stuff in there and headed toward Virginia City, just about the time dawn was breaking.

"Don't know whether we'll see him again," Celia said as we watched that old crook slap reins over the trotter and take off.

"Guess we'd better take this loot up to that there sheriff in Butte, before Scruples get ahold of it," I said.

"Lotta gold in there," she said. "Maybe we could just bury it."

"No, we're gonna do it right," I said. It sure was funny what gold did to good people. "It don't belong to us."

Chapter Nineteen

Well, I had second thoughts about that. I didn't know that there sheriff in Butte. For all I knew, he was Brashear's kid brother and twice as crooked. I got to thinkin' maybe we'd better sort this out ourselves.

But I sure didn't know what to do with all that stuff.

"You or Armand got a trunk?" I asked Celia.

"Yes, there's an old leather one with straps in our rooms."

"Well, let's get this stuff into it. I want ever'thing. Them ledgers, that seal, the stamp, the blank forms Brashear used, all that stuff, and the bag of gold, too."

I had in mind getting every record and form from the mining district out of there, and hiding it so Scruples couldn't get his mitts on any of it. That would slow him down when it come to sellin' off the whole Swamp Creek Mining District, like he was plannin' to do.

So Celia, she got her an armful of stuff, the ledgers and blank forms and all, and I got the seal and some stamps and the little bag of double eagles, and when we emptied that little safe and all, I shut her tight. It was gettin' toward dawn and I didn't want nobody to see us, so

I looked real sharp around that quiet little mining camp, and then we slid out, and cut along the creek instead of the streets, and pretty quick we got into them rooms Armand and Celia had.

She dug out the old trunk, which looked like a little casket of leather, and even had an ancient lock on it. We opened it up, found it was empty, and pretty quick we loaded the mining camp ledgers and papers in there, and put the little bag of gold on top, and then some of Armand's duds to sort of cover the whole thing, and then we closed the lid. I turned the lock and gave Celia the skeleton key to keep. The whole thing didn't weigh a lot, maybe thirty pounds.

I had a pretty good idea what to do with it. I didn't want it out in the open country, or at some abandoned mine site, where someone like Glan would find it. I wanted it hid in plain sight, and that meant the Wells Fargo office, where they stored trunks on a shelf for pickup by customers.

"Celia, can you run down to the Wells Fargo and get a tag for the trunk? And see who's laying about?"

She nodded and took off into the gray dawn. Swamp Creek was still mighty quiet. She come back with a tie-on tag.

"I didn't see anyone," she said. "The clerk, he just handed the tag to me."

I'm no good at writing, and it's all I can do to print letters. I never did figure out how to write that script. So I let her do the job.

"Choose a simple name," I said.

"Philippe Desiree?"

"That's simple? I guess you think so. Make it to him."

She wrote the name on the tag.

"I gotta look like someone else," I said. "Armand got a hat?"

She found two, one of them a black silk stovepipe, and the other a white straw Panama. I thought the stovepipe might do just fine, so I left my own slouch hat there, and screwed the stovepipe down. She found a string tie and helped me wrap that thing around my neck, since I didn't know nothing, and then I hefted that old trunk, and we headed out the door.

We got that trunk down to the Wells Fargo office and shelved before the town began to stir, and I thought we'd done a good job. That clerk, he didn't know me from Adam's off ox, and when I was done, he said, "thanks beaucoup, Mr. Desiree."

So the keys to the kingdom were sitting there in Wells Fargo, and maybe that'd slow Scruples down a little.

"I guess we'd better see if old Billy Blew's got his saloon open," I said.

We slipped over there, and he was up and around, all right.

"Where were you? I took your blankets off the pool table," he said.

"Busy night," I replied.

He looked Celia over but didn't say nothing. She was too young to be hanging around in a saloon, but nobody paid no mind to that in Swamp Creek.

"Billy, I need your help. But you'd have to be real quiet. These here are deeds to all them mines out there. They're good, signed by Brashear. I want you to hand them real quiet to the owners of the mines when they come in here. Like if those boys from the Hermit Mine show up, just give 'em this," I said. I pawed through the pile and found the one for that mine and showed it to Billy.

He sort of cocked an eyebrow. "I thought Transactions got all the paper on those mines."

"Well, Billy, someone sort of persuaded Johnny Brashear that it would be healthy for him if he fixed up these deeds."

"You?"

"Nope, not me," I said. "But I didn't mind it at all."

He glanced briefly at Celia, not crediting her with anything, and that was fine with me.

"Yeah, I'll do it," he said. "But some of them boys, they've packed up and left the country."

"Well, do what you can, and guard those deeds real good," I said. "They're good as gold. Leastwise, that's how I understand it. Those boys have got their mines back—if they can keep Scruples out."

"That's a big if," Billy said.

I didn't argue it. I didn't know if that paper would do them any good at all. But at least it would make it harder for Carter Scruples to steal them mines.

Billy turned to Celia. "Have we met?" he asked.

"No," she said.

"I'm Billy," he said.

"Pleased to meet you," she said, and let it stay like that.

Billy was a little miffed at not getting a handle on her, but he tried not to show it.

"Guess we'd better go," I said to her.

Billy, he studied on us as we walked out of there. He sure wanted to put a name to her, but if she didn't feel like telling him one, that was her choice.

Swamp Creek was stirring now, and shops were opened up.

"Guess we'd better ride up to your mine," I said. "If there's guards, then we've still got trouble."

She nodded. I tightened the cinch on Critter, who didn't like it. He preferred to see me roll under his belly because I didn't cinch the saddle down good.

Celia, she said she'd walk and lead the mule. It was Aggie's mule and I sure didn't know what to do with it. But we started anyway, me riding, Celia leading that four-footed beast, and when we got to shouting distance of the Fat Tuesday, I hollered, half expecting the muzzle of a gun to poke from a window somewhere. But nothing happened.

When we finally pulled into the mine yard, there were a few miners standing at the shaft, watching us ride up.

"You fellows waiting to do your shift?" I asked.

"Who are you?" one big one in bib overalls asked.

"Most people call me Cotton."

"Who you work for?"

"Right now, I'm working for her. She owns this mine."

They stared at Celia, not quite believing.

"This sign says the mine's closed, and owned by Trans-actions. That you?"

"No," Celia said. "I'm Armand Argo's widow, and this mine belongs to me. I have the papers."

"I guess you owe us some shift money. We been work-ing four days. If this here mine's shut, then pay us off."

Celia didn't even hesitate. "You go one over to the Miners Exchange Saloon and put in your claim for day wage, and I'll see that Muggsy Pitt pays you. And later, when we open up, I'll want you back. The mine's been stolen by those people in the Pullman car, but I'm going to get it back."

"We're all three-dollar-a-day men," the big one said. "That's twelve dollars for all of us. I don't know what we'll live on now. You gotta open fast or we'll be gone."

"Give me a week," she said. "I'll add something to your pay to tide you over."

"Can't make promises," he said.

"Neither can I," she replied. "You tell the others to get back wages from Muggsy."

She walked over to the place where the Transactions sign was nailed to a beam, and ripped it off. But she kept it, and I wondered what she'd do with it.

We left the miners there. I was real impressed with that girl.

"You got money to pay them?" I asked.

"Armand was a gambler. He had a bank."

We headed into Swamp Creek and the Miners Exchange, and found Muggsy swamping the floor. In short order, Muggsy agreed to record the wage claims and pay out cash she would provide, and keep some records.

We went back to Argo's rooms. "You stay outside," she said.

I did, and she returned with some half eagles, which we took to the saloon. She was all business, and I could see that Muggsy respected her.

"Give me a list of who got paid what," she said.

"I'll get it done," he said.

"If you don't, your life isn't worth beans," she said.

He laughed uneasily. Celia sure had a way about her.

When we stepped outside, it was still morning. But a cloud sort of come along just then. It was Lugar himself, Scruples' straw boss, walkin' down the main drag with a big old revolver hanging off his waist. He sure was ugly. I hardly never seen anyone so much like a cloud covering the sun.

"Looking for you," he said, walking right up.

"I'm not looking for you," I replied.

"Carter wants to talk to you."

"I got nothing to say to him."

"Oh, I think you do, Cotton. You come along. Bring her, too."

He stood there, ugly as a dill pickle, so I finally agreed.

We hiked through town and up that long grade to the Pullman Palace Car, past a few new guards I never seen before, and pretty soon I got off Critter and they let us in to that parlor at the back of the car. There was old Scruples himself, wearing some sort of red velvet robe and puffing on a pipe.

"Ah, there you are, Monsieur Desiree," he said. "Welcome to our humble home."

That's when I knew all hell had busted loose.

I stood there sort of leaning on one foot and the other, waiting for the rest.

"We have snitches all over town, Cotton. Nothing transpires in Swamp Creek without my knowing of it in minutes. The Wells Fargo expressman earns a silver dollar from me now and then. I knew about the trunk about five minutes after you had deposited it. You see? There it is."

He waved toward the old trunk, sitting on top of his writing table.

"I'm glad everything's there. You missed nothing. You've even returned the gold I'd paid to Brashear. And you did me a real favor, getting rid of him. Now that I own nearly all the mines, I'm voting myself the next mining district secretary. This is a fine new turn of events, and I wish to thank you for it. I've already reissued the claim papers to the company. I suppose that black stovepipe hat was Argo's. Poor fellow. He was trespassing, you know. All we can do is warn people off of our property."

I pretty near jumped on that swine, but he had a

couple of his goons hoverin' right there. I think maybe Celia was fixing to shoot some of them, but I didn't see no profit in it.

"I'm quite able to read your intentions," Scruples said. "They are always very simple, because you are a simple man. But of course, the first person to be hurt would be the young widow here, and the second person to be hurt would be you, and that would be rather foolish, wouldn't it?"

I could see how things stood in that there Palace Car, so I just stood real quiet.

"You're done for, Cotton. I'm giving you until sundown to leave the district. If you're still around tonight, you might walk into flying lead." He turned to Celia. "I would hate to see the young lady suffer the same fate," he said.

There sure wasn't no sense in arguing with the man, with a few of his thugs lounging around there. I thought I saw Arnold in the corridor, and I suppose The Apocalypse had sat his dainty ass in some little chair around there.

Scruples smiled. "We might even let Critter out there survive," he said. "I'm always charitable toward innocent animals."

Chapter Twenty

What happened was, I got mad. I got so mad I couldn't see straight. So I done what I did. I plowed into Scruples and landed one whopper on him, and saw him topple backward, but that's the last thing I saw. Old Arnold come out of nowhere and all went black on me.

Next I knew, I was lyin' on the grass somewheres, my head hurting bad and a few of them miners lookin' down on me. It took me a while to get a handle on where I was. I didn't even know why I was there at first. My head, it throbbed bad, and the rest of me hurt bad, too. I peered up at them, and they was lookin' worried.

"You all right?" one miner asked.

I didn't feel all right. So I just lay there.

"This your horse?" asked one.

Sure enough, there was Critter. And we were on the Swamp Creek Road outside of town. That's where they put me.

"You got something stuck in your shirt pocket," one said.

I reached for it, and my fingers clawed a small piece of paper. I couldn't see well yet, with my head all fogged up, but I got the message. It was a bull's-eye penciled in. Someone had gone to some trouble to draw them black and white circles.

"It's a bull's-eye," I mumbled.

"Guess someone doesn't like you," the miner said.

"That's about half of it," I said.

I sat up, and they helped me up. I stood real shaky. Celia was nowhere in sight, and I wondered what they done with her. I almost didn't want to know.

"Guess I fell off my nag," I said to the miners.

I don't think a one of them believed it, but they was being polite.

"I'm all right now," I said, and took a step or two and landed on my ass.

"Guess I'm not quite all right yet," I said. "But I'll get there."

I stood up again, and got me over to Critter, who snapped at me for being so dumb, and then Critter let me get on board.

My hat sat on a knot on my head. I lifted it and thanked the miners. "They changed my name to Target. You call me Target," I said.

"You sure you're all right, Target?"

"You ain't seen a girl around here, have you?"

"No, no girl. We was just walking along the road and there you were."

"Well, I'll find her," I said.

I put heels to Critter, which made my head ache, and I headed toward town. It was mid-afternoon. I had until sundown. The only thought in my head was finding Celia.

Critter sure was mean. Every time he stepped, my head hammered. Then he lifted into a trot and my head

couldn't believe it. He was gettin' even with me for all
the times he stood around waiting for me to sober up.

I got to laughin' even though I hurt bad. I'd given old
Carter Scruples a good whonk. Last I knew, he was
flyin' backward in that little railroad car parlor, lookin'
so surprised he couldn't believe what was happenin'.
That made it worth it. The sight of him going ass over
heels backward done my heart good. So I drove Critter
on into town, hurting and howlin' and making a fuss as
I steered down the main drag. I didn't much care.

I thought maybe to fire a few shots in the air, but decided I'd need them bullets for the future. I still was mad,
and now I was gonna take on that whole lot of killers and
crooks old Scruples got together, and I wasn't gonna quit
until I drove the whole bunch out of Swamp Creek, and
blowed up that railroad car into scrap metal. All Scruples
done was made me real determined and bullheaded.
Right then I was so bullheaded and pain-headed that I
knew nothing was gonna slow me down.

I turned off to the alley where I'd park Critter while I
was fetching Celia, and let myself down to the ground.
That hurt, too. It didn't matter what I did. When I was
riding, it hurt my head. When I was walking, it hurt my
head. When I was singin' or talkin', it hurt my head.
That Arnold, he was something, but I knew a trick or
two myself, and there'd come a time when he wished he
didn't have balls.

I lurched up them stairs to the Argo rooms and
knocked, but there wasn't no answer, so I knocked again,
and finally tried the door. I shouldn't have let myself in
like that, but I was worried and wanted to make sure she
was all right. Well, all I found was a lot of nothin'. I
didn't see her, and there was no sign that she'd ever come

back from up on the hill. That was plumb worrisome to me. Maybe they was keepin' her hostage. She'd sure caused them some trouble, and she was just a slip of a girl in her growin' up years, but she was also Mrs. Argo, and that was bad news. That Transactions crowd might just have some use or other for the widder of the owner of the Fat Tuesday Mine. I sure didn't like it none.

I vowed then and there I'd get her freed. I was making a heap of vows just then. I'd get that whole outfit out of Swamp Creek. I'd take on the worst of them, Rudolph Glan, The Apocalypse, Arnold the street fighter, and the rest. They scared me plenty. I'm not one to pretend I don't get mighty scared. Only, I was determined to do whatever damage I could, and if they finished me off, it would be at a high price. Someone had to take them on, and I just appointed myself. I also owed it to Celia, since I was still on her payroll.

I thought my first business was to find Celia and make sure she was safe. Old Scruples, he knew it, too. And if I was still in town at sundown, lookin' for her, they'd start sniping from any alley or rooftop they chose. I'd been warned. I sure ain't bright, but I could see that the jaws of that bear trap were wide open. At least I still had me a little time till sundown.

I needed to hide Critter first. If they saw Critter, they'd know the whole story. I didn't have Aggie's mule with me. That one disappeared. Maybe Celia had him if she was around. There's no good way to hide a horse, especially one as noisy as Critter, but then I got me an idea that wasn't half bad. I'd put Critter in Celia's up-stairs rooms if I could get that ornery cuss up the stairs with no one lookin' and get a few baits of hay from the livery barn. That sort of settled it for me. I wandered outside, got Critter, and walked around to the creek side of the building where there wasn't no traffic except for people taking a leak, and then I tugged him up. He didn't like it none, and took one step at a time, snappin' and snarling at me like I was a lunatic, but I got him up the stairs without them busting under him, and into Celia Argo's rooms. I didn't have no shovel to clean up after him, but I couldn't help that. I got Critter a bucket of water, and then went over to the livery barn and got a bait of hay, and finally got it all together in Celia's rooms. If she came in, she might not like to sleep with a horse in her parlor, but I couldn't help that. Once I got Critter settled up there, I'd be all right, and I could slip around Swamp Creek in the dark pretty good. I didn't count on when Critter started stompin' up there, or pawin' wood, so maybe that saloon man downstairs would wonder what was going on. But he probably would think Celia was just bein' frisky, as usual.

I sure needed a plan, but I ain't one to do much plannin'. I knew what I wanted to do, and that would have to do for me. Find Celia. Get her mine back to her. Get them other mines back to their owners. Keep Scruples from claim-jumping the one big mine left, the Big Mother. And drive them gunmen and thugs out of the valley, along with them two in the Pullman car. I could count on one sidearm lent me by Celia, and a little of my usual bullheaded determination. That wasn't much, but it would have to do.

I slipped down them stairs and into the night. I could hear Swamp Creek flowing alongside the town. It was a dark night, and the darkness would be my friend. I waited a bit so my eyes would get used to the dark, and then headed toward the saloon row in the middle of town. There wasn't much light even there. The pale light from a few kerosene lamps tumbled from small and dirty windows. Glass was scarce in all the West, and there sure wasn't much of it in Swamp Creek. When a window got busted, it was usually boarded up since glass was hard to come by and cost a lot. But now that suited me fine. I eased under the dark gallery of the hardware emporium, where I could see what moved and what didn't and who was leanin' against what. This was a drinkin' town and often as not, there'd be a few schnockered miners stretched out in the muck, waiting for the rats that came with every known mining town to eat on them or someone to steal their brogans.

I didn't see nobody at all. But just to make sure, I glided along the darker side of the street, and checked all them alleys between the buildings. One feller, he was cutting loose of some beer, but he buttoned up and went back into the Ponderosa House. I slid over to the saloon side, after checkin' second-story windows, and then began peering into them drinkin' parlors just to see who was bellying up to the bar. I was keeping an eye out for Celia, too. In one of them places, I spotted them three thugs of Scruples that had been around a while and wouldn't give me a proper name. There were Garfield, Arthur, and Cleveland leaning into the bar, nursing mugs of beer. Well, that was something anyway. I continued my tour, wanting to know what Scruples men were hanging around.

I didn't know what to do with them worthless slugs neither, but I'd think of something that would be persuasive. I wouldn't have minded shooting the lot and tossing them into the creek. But they were just the foot soldiers, the buck privates in that outfit. No sense wasting energy on them.

I slipped along the boardwalk, and peered into the

Deuce Saloon, which was a low dive full of people who'd rather shoot than talk. Sittin' in there drinkin' amber stuff was Lugar, and beside him was Rudolph Costello Glan.

Big stuff. So Scruples was making sure I left town, and he'd put his whole bunch in here to enforce it. That meant that The Apocalypse and Arnold were floating around, too. Carter Scruples was never one to go halfway. Suddenly, the dark didn't seem so friendly around there. I peered around, looking for that deadly little killer and the hulking eye-gouger who hung around with him. I hardly dared move, for fear movement would show me. And I could no longer risk even a peep through a lit window. I gradually ghosted back between a couple of log buildings, and listened real sharp. Sometimes, ears were better than eyes in thick dark.

Sure enough, I thought I heard some silky sound, so I ghosted along a log wall until I got to the creek bottoms beside town, and stood there in deep shade, in a corner so dark that no one would see me. I stood there so long I got itchy, but it paid off. Movin' real quiet along the valley was the long and short of Scruples' army. It made my head start hurtin' again just to see Arnold out there. I still had some aches from the last time he knocked me out. Them two was quietly inspecting every alley and space between buildings, very businesslike. I drew my Peacemaker, knowin' I'd aim at that smooth little killer first, and Arnold second. But mostly I didn't do nothing.

They missed me. I was shadowed up pretty good. That's all that saved me. I guess they figured I was in town. Maybe they saw me get a bait of hay or something. Scruples had his whole army out, checking for me.

And where was Celia? Probably still up at the Pullman.

There'd be more guards there, new ones I'd not had the pleasure meeting. Scruples was hiring whatever army he could hire, and it wasn't hard to get a few more hardcases.

But if his old hands were here in town, chances were Celia was being kept up there. And being bullheaded and all that, it looked like a good time to spring her if I could. I waited for The Apocalypse and his pal to get to the end of the row of buildings, and then I slipped straight across the creek, using one of them outhouses built over the flow to do it. I didn't know what I'd find over there, but I knew I had a chance to fetch Celia if the mob was all in town. It was an easy trip through piney woods and then up a forested grade to the place where the Pullman car and its outbuildings sat. The moon was cracking over the horizon, which meant I'd be seen by anyone with good night eyes. But I was determined to snatch Celia if I could, so I eased toward the bunkhouse first, to take a quick look. I ended up walkin' right in. She wasn't there.

Some joker was lyin' in a bunk there.

"Where'd she go?" I asked.

"She's tied up in the barn."

"I got orders to get her," I said.

"Yeah, that Scruples, he's had an eye on her," the man said.

I thought I'd gotten there just in time.

Chapter Twenty-one

She wasn't in the barn. I couldn't see nothing, but I sure poked around. I even tried callin' softly. But she wasn't there. It still was plenty dark, so I sort of poked around. Celia Argo was somewhere nearby; I just had to find her.

Then I noticed something peculiar. That outhouse was tied shut. The door was closed and rope wrapped around the whole crapper. I edged up and tried the door a little.

I heard a muffled sound.

"It's Cotton. You in there?"

More noise. That did it. I found the knots at the back of the crapper, worked them loose, and got the door open. Man, it stank in there. That one didn't even have a quarter moon sawed in it for a vent. She was sitting there, legs tied, arms tied behind, and a gag on her. I got her out of there fast. If you ask me, that was a fate worse than death, and far worse than any other fate worse than death. I got her untied and ungagged. She had the sense not to say nothin', since we didn't know who or what was around there. But I could tell she was almighty pleased to get out of the crapper. She wiped her hands on grass and shook her skirt, and then I took her real gentle by the arm and we slid through shadows. We didn't know when that crowd was going to come back to the bunkhouse after enjoying a few shots of booze in Swamp Creek.

I swore a few times that someone was watching, but we made it into the pine forest and only then did we whisper a little.

"What happened?" I asked.

"Scruples wanted to spend the night with me. But I told him I'd turn him into a soprano if he did. That cooled his ardor some. He was still hurting from the fist you landed. He's got a big black and blue spot coming up on his jaw."

"Then they put you out there?"

"They didn't know what to do with me. They thought I'm a lady friend of yours."

"That explains why they didn't just bury you somewhere."

She eyed me silently. A quarter moon was rising.

"I don't ever want to be locked in an outhouse again."

I led her to a rill I knew of, and she knelt beside it and washed herself, cupping her hands in the cold water and rubbing every inch of flesh she could.

"My clothes stink," she said. "I'd like to go to my rooms and change."

"Well, there might be a little surprise in there."

She eyed me, waiting for an explanation.

"Critter's in your parlor."

"Say that again?"

"I had to hide him. They was all in town lookin' for me, and lookin' for Critter, and I knew if they found Critter, my goose was cooked. So I got him up to your rooms."

"Up those wooden stairs?"

"Yep. He didn't like it none, but I told him he'd get

some oats soon. So I got him in your parlor. I pulled that rug aside, so I can clean up the apples."

"And what happens if he hoses that floor? It's just plank, Cotton."

"I guess them fellers down there at the bar'll get their beer improved."

She smiled, and darned if she didn't give me a hug. I hardly ever got hugged before, except for my mother and she did it about twice. But there Celia was, huggin' away, so I hugged back just as enthusiastic as I could. I took to huggin' like I was born to it.

We filtered through them piney slopes toward town. It sure was late, and the town had quieted down, at least until the shift miners from Big Mother hit it. There was only a lamp or two glowing, and I thought probably them toughs from Scruples' outfit had gone home. But I had Celia to look after, and I wasn't sure of nothing, so I parked us in the woods across the creek and waited. There was a bit of moon now, so anything moving would have a little white light falling on him.

It was a good thing I waited, because big Arnold and his deadly little sidekick, they were patrolling, and came drifting by, The Apocalpyse in black, looking like a moving shadow, and that slab of meat Arnold twice his size. They made a pair, all right.

So we just settled down in the grass since we couldn't get into town. It sure was a long wait, but maybe an hour before dawn, them two finally gave up and drifted toward the Palace Car on the hill. I eased down real cautious to one of them outhouses that spanned the creek, and crossed over to the town side, and had me a look around. The next shift of miners was about due to tumble out of the Big Mother, and then Swamp Creek would come alive again, with them miners downing boilermakers until they fried their brains.

I kind of beckoned Celia, and she come across and we slipped up them wooden stairs and into her rooms. Critter, he butted me so hard I toppled back, but after some cussing, Critter and I got peaceable. Celia, she lit a lamp and looked around. Everything was all right until she got to her bedroom, when she started cussing with words I didn't even know sixteen-year-olds knew.

I walked in there, and saw the trouble right away. There was a pile of horse apples on her bed. It sort of stained the coverlet.

"I'll fix it," I said.

"No, you're going to get that animal out of here and keep him out of here." She paused a little. "Thanks for cutting me loose. If you can get the mine back, I'll find some way to thank you. But you and Critter can't stay here."

I was sort of disappointed. I thought maybe me and her and Critter could make a threesome up there in her rooms, but she wasn't having no part of that.

"All right, I'll get him out," I said.

That wasn't easy. Critter, he pretty near had a conniption fit when I started to lead him down them wooden steps. They sort of creaked and gave under him, and he knew it, and if he'd blown up and starting kicking every slat and plank, the whole stair would have tumbled down, and Critter would have been ruined, along with me.

"You quit that or I'll punch you in the nose," I said to him, and he sort of sighed, cut loose with a mighty fart, and stepped down one stair at a time, being real careful. Soon as we hit bottom, I saw Celia up there shaking the horse apples out of that coverlet and cussing away. There went my dreams.

I was about to ride off when a voice stopped me.

"You owe me," someone said.

I turned and found the barkeep from below standing there.

"My saloon's a mess," he said. "You ruint it. That horse got a bladder bigger than a fire barrel, and it all come down on my customers."

I didn't know what to do, but I remembered that eagle in my pocket.

"Here, this'll fix it," I said, and handed it to him.

"Fix about half of it," he grumbled, but he was gettin' more than he figured on, so he wasn't grumbling too bad.

"You can fix me a sandwich, and I'll be gone," I said.

He did it. I went in there and he cut me a slab of beef rustled from some ranch, and laid it between two slabs of sourdough bread and handed her to me. It sure tasted fine.

"See ya," I said.

"You're Cotton, ain't you?"

I nodded.

"Them thugs was lookin' hard."

"I'll be lookin' hard for them, soon as I figure what to do."

He just shook his head. I'd seen that sort of head shake before. It's how sane people dismiss crazy people. They just shake their heads, and we all know what they're thinkin'.

I peered around real sharp, but there was nothing around, and some few clouds was chasing the moon, so I climbed onto Critter and forded the creek and headed into the woods. I sure didn't know where I would go. A hunted man ain't got many choices.

It wasn't far from dawn.

"Critter, take me where you will," I said.

Critter snapped at me and turned downstream, away

from the mines, and settled into a cheerful jog. He was plumb happy to get out of that upstairs jail.

We were jogging along when we got to the big place owned by Cletus Carboy, owner and proprietor of the Big Mother gold mine. And that blasted Critter turned in then and there, and followed a graveled road toward the man's house. Well, I thought, that wasn't a bad idea. It might be the safest place for me in the county, the one place that Scruples didn't control. So we jogged in there at a fine time when dew was on the grass and all the world was hushed and peaceful.

Then a Chinese fellow, he sort of appeared out of nowhere. He smiled and pointed toward the house, and said something I couldn't quite figure out, but his gestures said I should tie Critter to the hitch rail and meet the boss. Least that's how I took it.

So I tied old Critter and looked around. It sure was quiet and dewy there.

"Good morning, Mr. Cotton. I've been expecting you," a man said.

He was standing in the deep dark of the veranda, and I'd missed him. I looked around, trying to make sense of it.

"In a few minutes there will be light enough. I'm Cletus Carboy," the voice said. "This was the right place to come. Now that Scruples' men have turned you into a bull's-eye, and Mrs. Argo has evicted you and your horse from her rooms, and you have turned down Amanda Trouville's advances, and that thug Arnold has knocked you senseless a few more times than you appreciate, I imagine you would enjoy a haven."

"How'd you know all that?"

"Snitches, Mr. Cotton. I have ten times more snitches than Scruples, and I pay them well. I even have snitches in Scruples' own little army. I have snitches in every saloon. Not much escapes me. I've known most everything that has happened to you for some while. But by all means, come join me here on the veranda. I am awaiting the sunrise."

Indeed, a streak of soft blue in the east was heralding the new day. I stepped up to the veranda, which stretched around three sides of his house, and discovered something I could hardly imagine. This man was dressed in a swallowtail black tuxedo with a boiled white shirt and a black bowtie. His dark hair had been slicked back real nice, and he held a little white stick in his hand. He had a little white pointy beard, and a gold ring on his finger.

"Have a seat," he said, pointing to some porch furniture.

"I was sort of looking for a place to stay," I said.

"My baton," he said, waving that ivory stick. "As soon as the light quickens a little, I shall conduct the bird chorus. It is my delight. From the first soft note, tentative on the morning breeze, to the full symphony of cheeping and trilling and whistling and singing, we shall have our morning symphony. The meadowlarks and jays and crows and robins all have their own way of celebrating the new day. I like to think they take direction from me as I conduct their serenade. This is the perfect dawn, the best of the year. No breeze. A clear heaven. A soft dew on the meadows. A bold and brassy sun even now gathering itself to burst over the eastern horizon, and when it does my whole orchestra will play."

Well, I thought, I had nothing to lose.

Chapter Twenty-two

Even as the light quickened, the birds started chirping. There was a slow peep, and then a chirp, and finally even the doves were cooing. Cletus Carboy, he listened with a little smile lifting his lips, and an ear cocked toward the trees, and then he waved that ivory stick, and a few more birds began tweeting, and pretty soon it built up into a bunch of birds all bursting their hearts out, greeting the sun as it got strength and began rolling toward the horizon. I never seen nothing like it.

Carboy, he looked like a band director, only he was all dressed up in one of them swallowtails, and every time he twitched that there ivory stick, another bird joined the crowd. He knew just where them birds was sitting, and he'd look at a big old cottonwood, and next I knew, them birds up there would start a full-throated melody, chirpin' like there was no tomorrow. Carboy knew where ever' last bird was hiding, and knew when every last sparrow would start whistling and twittering. He knew them meadowlarks and he knew when the crows would start cawing and the jays would start rattling like snare drums and the pigeons would start wooing. He stood there on the veranda on the balls of his feet mostly, his arms a-flailing away, as the music got rolling. Me, I sat behind him in deep shadow, watching the sun bust over the eastern side of the world, and watched that sun start to turn him yellow, like he was wearin' gold.

And then off yonder near the creek, I saw the sun glint off of metal, and I didn't think none, I just dove for Carboy and slammed into him and toppled him even as a shot chopped away the serenade, and struck the house just behind where he was standing.

He looked outraged. "How dare you!" he snarled as he started up from the porch planks, but I landed on him again until he quit the struggling, and I pointed at that there bullet hole, big as a fist, in the window frame behind him, and he quieted some.

"Crawl in there and get a gun," I said. "I'm going after the bastard."

He shook a little. "Rudolph Costello Glan," he muttered. "I've been expecting it."

If he was expecting it, why was he standing on that porch as the sun came up? I was going to have a little talk with that one.

"Stay covered," I said.

I didn't see sunlight on that rifle no more, but that didn't mean nothing. I began dodging this way and that, zigzag, straight for the woods along the creek, finding cover here and there, but never quitting. I pulled my revolver out and was plain ready to unload every shell in it if I got close enough. My heart was sure hammering, but it didn't matter. I came right at that place, and plowed through brush and trees, never giving him a chance to aim, and finally I got to the place and he was gone. I couldn't even say someone had been there. I didn't even find no brass. He'd picked up the spent shell. I didn't trust nothing, so I circled around, this way and that, ready to blow that swine to kingdom come. But he'd plain disappeared, and there was no sayin' where he'd gone. I hunted along the creek, and thought maybe I saw a place he had used to cross to the other side, but he'd vanished.

"Glan, I'm coming for you," I yelled. "I'll get you. You ain't gonna kill again."

But all I got for that was silence.

I made my way slow and careful back to the big old house that Carboy had put up there, near the creek, on an open flat. I didn't like crossing that open meadow the last hundred yards, so I dodged this way and that, never giving Glan time to fire, and then I reached the porch.

The door opened smoothly, and Carboy, standing in deep shadow, motioned me in. He was holding a small revolver.

"You saved my life," he said.

"For the moment," I replied. "He vamoosed."

"The birds are quiet," he said. "The symphony stopped."

He was right. There wasn't one chirp. It was like a dawn funeral around there.

He sighed. "Settle yourself in the parlor whilst I abandon my swallowtail," he said. "Tea?"

"Ah, I ain't never tried it."

"It's time for you to try it," he said. "A most vigorous beverage."

I nodded. I hardly knew what a vigorous beverage was.

"Excuse me for a moment," he said.

He vanished somewhere, and I looked around that parlor of his. It had wallpaper on the walls. I hardly never seen it before, but I heard tell of it. There was them oil paintings of nature scenes, and stuffed furniture, and shiny cabinets, and fancy carpets, and everything smelled nice. I never been in such a place. The man spent a lot of money for a place out in the middle of nowhere.

Pretty soon, a Chinese woman, she come in with a tray with a sort of blue teapot on it and cups and saucers. She smiled, poured some tea, and held up the sugar bowl.

"I guess I'll just try her raw," I said.

She nodded and handed me that blue cup, and left the tea tray on a little table there.

I sipped the stuff, and it were pretty meek compared to coffee, but I didn't see nothing wrong with it. Just meek is all. Some people live life meek, but not me.

So I sipped away, and sort of liked it, except it was too meek, and waited. It sure was a fine sunny morning, and them birds had started up again. You'd hardly know that a little earlier someone had tried to kill Carboy.

I just sat there. I noticed they'd taken Critter to a pen and given him a bait of hay, which was mighty kind, and got him out of rifle range of someone shootin' at Carboy. Critter was back there, protected by the barn and some other stuff, chomping like he was enjoying some good chow.

Me, I just waited, and pretty soon, old Carboy come into the room, dressed more casual, sort of like a king would out in the country, with an open shirt and a wool jacket on, and shoes with a little black on them, all clean and nice.

"I'm glad you came by, for more reasons than one. And I'm indebted to you," he said, pouring some of that tea. "Do you like the tea? It's summer Darjeeling."

"I sort of swill her around and down her," I said.

"It's an acquired taste. Coffee's an acquired taste, too."

"I ain't acquired it yet," I said.

"You know, sir, I don't really know your name. Is Cotton your surname?"

"Well, it ain't rightly no name. I just got stuck with her."

"It's neither then."

"This here's making me plumb uncomfortable, Mr. Carboy."

He laughed softly and sipped his tea.

"I can well understand it, sir. I'll call you whatever you wish, or just sir if you'd prefer. The truth is, I was born under a name that has visited me with grief and disgust."

I sort of thought he might not like that name of his.

"Cletus, sir, is not a name I would wish upon anyone. The question was, what to do about it. I could live with it and suffer, or I could change my name, but I chose another course. I decided I would triumph over my name. I gradually transformed myself into a person quite the opposite of Cletus Carboy. Now, when the sun rises, I conduct symphonies, and I support myself with one of the finest gold mines in the territory, and live in comfort and elegance. I have servants I pay well and who enjoy being here. I pay my men at the Big Mother—that was the name of the mine when I bought it, not a name I would have chosen—an extra two bits a day, and also give them a shorter shift. The result, sir, is that I earn more, not less. I do not suffer from turnover. They work hard. They remove more tons of ore per man than any other mine in the area. We share in the benefits. I've given them year-end favors also, if the mine has yielded good fruit."

I sort of got the drift of this. He didn't like his name none, so he licked it. I envied him. I wish I coulda licked my name, but I hardly gave it a thought. I just buried it and hope no one will never know. Cotton ain't my name and Pickens ain't either, and I'd rather die dead than confess how I got named.

He eyed me with a faint smile on his face. "More tea?" he asked.

"It ain't got character," I said.

"How shall I address you?" he asked. "If you object to Cotton, how about boll weevil?"

He was funning me, and I didn't like it.

"Or Gin? Eli Whitney invented the cotton gin, which spun the seeds out of the cotton, and made it much more usable."

He was still funning me, and I was about set to high-tail outa there.

"I suppose I'll call you Cotton Gin, a most honorable invention and one you can take pride in."

"I guess I'd better git a move on. Thanks for tea and that bait of hay for Critter."

"I'll have My Ling bring you some brownies," he said.

I hadn't had brownies since my ma baked some, so I settled into that stuffed furniture.

He rang a little silver bell and instructed the Chinese lady to bring that stuff. This sure was working out to be a strange morning.

"I have plans for you," he said. "Since you don't have plans for yourself, mine will substitute."

I didn't think I liked this dude at all.

"I've given some thought to Transactions, Incorporated. An interesting and nefarious operation," he said.

Them big words were comin' fast at me, and I itched to vamoose.

"They are superficially a legitimate mining company,

making deals for mining properties, but in reality they are killers and thugs. They've been perfectly clear about their intentions. Mr. Scruples and Madam Trouville don't know beans about mining, but they know a lot about buying and selling properties. To sell this whole Swamp Creek District, they need good and valid titles to everything, including my mine. That's why Carter Scruples was so happy to relieve you of the stuff you had tried to hide from him at Wells Fargo. Now he can manufacture deeds and titles and validated claims at will, since you chased Johnny Brashear out of town."

I was sort of half listening, but then old Carboy got my attention.

"I would like you to engage in a heist," he said.

"A what?"

"A heist. A robbery, burglary, theft. I wish to engage you to lift everything liftable in that Pullman car. Every deed, every title, every claim, along with the forms and seals and records. In short, I want you to clean them out so thoroughly that they can't make a sale to anyone because they haven't the slightest evidence of ownership."

Now that was an interesting proposition. Once I cut through all them big words, I got the gist of it all right. Get all them titles and Transactions, Incorporated's got nothing to sell. Not a thing for all its troubles.

The pretty Chinese woman returned with a plate of brownies, and I plunged right in, collecting three, one for my mouth and one for each hand. I took a good look at her, and she sure was pretty. In fact, she was the best-lookin' lady I seen in a long time.

"My Ling is a beautiful woman, is she not?" he said. "I am thinking I might make it a union one of these days. She doesn't mind my name at all, you see. I've encountered dozens, maybe hundreds, of attractive women, but not a one of them wished to become Mrs. Cletus Carboy. But My Ling thinks it's a cheerful name, which she rolls around in her mouth. Yes, it's looking very promising."

I hadn't asked him. All I'd done was take a long look at that beautiful Chinese woman, and all of a sudden there was Carboy sensing what I was wondering about and giving me the what-for of it. I really was getting to like this feller, even if he was drinking that weak tea stuff.

I nibbled on them brownies for a while. Carboy, he rose, pushed up a window sash, and let all the birdsong into his parlor. Them birds weren't giving up, just tweeting and tooting away out there. I wondered if he'd drugged them all stupid.

"The heist," he said. "This was a most propitious moment, you showing up this morning, just when I was thinking about what had to be done."

I didn't know what propitious was, but if it was like eating brownies, I'd go along with it.

"Here's what I want you to do. Either alone or with a crew of your choosing, I want you to break in to that Pullman Palace Car and clean out the safe. Everything's in there. I have a snitch who knows. Right there in Scruples' private office, the compartment just behind the rear parlor in the Palace Car, are the keys to the kingdom. Now that safe's bolted to the steel floor of the railroad car, and it's got a combination on the lock known only to Carter Scruples, and that office door is locked all the time. Amanda can get into the office, but not into the safe. Inside that safe, my friend, lies the salvation of us all. And I will be pleased to pay you a pretty penny—far more than the hundred dollars a month Celia Argo's paying you—to clean out that safe and bring those papers and forms and seals to me. And if you can't bring them to me, at least to burn every last title and deed and claim and form, so that nothing but ash is in Scruples' hands. Are you interested, Cotton Gin?"

Chapter Twenty-three

That's what comes from readin' books. Carboy gets shot at and is going to get shot at again, but he's thinkin' about snatching a bunch of papers. It didn't make no sense. It was just the sort of thinkin' you'd expect from some dude that sat around thinkin' and reading all them big words.

"You're crazy," I said.

He set down his teacup and sort of cocked his head, waiting.

I went on. "That outfit, it ain't gonna sit around. And it don't worry much about havin' good paper. If all that paper got burned, they'd still have them mines they stole. And they could hire smart men to do the mining. Meanwhile, they're shooting at you, and they're fixing to drive you out of the Big Mother any time now."

"I am offering you a job," he said, not budging an inch.

"What kind of job? I ain't a safecracker. I don't even know how to spin them dials. I never opened a safe in my life."

"If you can get the safe to me, I'll take care of the rest."

"You're getting shot at and you worry about this?"

"Have you a better plan, Cotton?"

The only plan I had was to string up Glan and then string up The Apocalypse and Arnold with him, and maybe that would tone down Scruples a little. I had a hunch if I caught the three and turned them over to the law up in Butte, they'd be back in business the next day.

"No, I don't got no plan at all. But I'm workin' on one," I said.

"Your plan no doubt involves dealing lethally with Glan and some of the rest. How would that be any easier than snatching the safe?"

"A lot easier," I said, but I didn't believe it none. Those gents was pretty tough customers, and I'd almost rather try to get into that Pullman car and bust open that safe.

"Maybe you're right," he said.

Now in all my life I hardly heard someone say that. Most people I knew, they just thought they were right and no one else was right, and here was Carboy saying this. It made me wonder if he was some sort of weakling, caving in like that. Now if it was me, I'd be shouting and stomping and telling him he was all wet.

"It's not an easy thing to do, getting a safe out of a guarded place," he said. "But it's worth thinking about. I think that once Scruples and his lady know they can't sell those mines, even if they have taken them over, they'll give up."

"All right, I've got a question for you," I said. "What are you doing to keep them from jumping your mine? They've moved in on every other mine in the district. You've got the last one they don't control. And you can bet they're ready to pounce."

"I've put some thought to it," Carboy said. "Those toughs can't even get near the mine. I've men with shotguns guarding it nonstop. They are protected by guardhouses. I've let it be known that if any harm comes to my miners, coming on or off shift, the criminals will be in for serious trouble of a sort I will not divulge."

He eyed me. "I have another little task for you, if you should want it. That attempt to kill me must not go unanswered. I would like you to answer it. The task is quite simple. On the next ridge from the Pullman car is a fine vantage point. I have a superb rifle I will lend you. Go up there, carefully, of course, and pump a few shots into the windows of the Pullman car. I don't want to kill, or wound anyone. I'm not in the business of shooting people. Two wrongs don't make a right. I don't want you to kill, but I do want you to persuade them to give up, and to consider the danger to themselves if they persist on their lawless ways. From now on, every time Mr. Glan pulls his trigger, a round or two or three will pierce the railroad car . . . if you are willing, of course."

"I'm willing," I said.

"Fine. I've strolled the neighboring areas, and it's actually an easy shot. But perhaps they've thrown up a perimeter recently. You'll wish to do this at night, of course. If your wish is to avoid killing, which I trust it is, nighttime will let you see who's where in the railroad car, and aim to shatter a window but hit no one. I think it might be instructive if you were to shatter every window in the car. Don't you?"

I was sorta liking that idea. It would send a few messages.

"I'll do her," I said.

He nodded, rose, vanished into some other part of his big house, and returned carrying a good-looking rifle and a couple boxes of shells. "It's a Browning," he said.

He showed me its operation and handed it to me. It sure was a fine-looking piece of hardware.

"Your safety lies in darkness," he said. "With the first shot, you can expect Scruples' thugs to swarm up the neighboring hills after you."

"I got the idea," I said, hefting that rifle. "I sure hope this piece shoots as good as it looks."

He stared intently at me. "I will not stoop to their level. I don't want you to. I want your promise that nothing you do will violate moral law or the law of the land."

I hardly knew what he was yakkin' about, but I got the gist of it.

"I ain't gonna kill nobody with this," I said.

"That's what I want to hear. I hope also to hear that you've given them an idea of the true cost of their conduct. They've killed, or at least their gang has killed, and the same punishment awaits them. It is their bridge to cross. If they continue, I might change my mind about a lot of things."

"Mr. Carboy, let me give it a shot."

He nodded slightly. "Return the rifle when you've completed your mission. And think about the heist. Meanwhile, there's some bunks in the shed behind the barn, and you and Critter can make yourself at home. My man Harbinger knows you'll be camping with us."

He rose, letting me know the meeting was over.

I headed over to the barn and found the bunks in a lean-to shed off one side. I had the place to myself. I hefted that rifle, sighted down the barrel, felt its comfortable weight in my hand. There was something wrong with Carboy's plan, but I didn't let on that I knew what. Them two in the Pullman car, they drew down heavy shades from rollers at night, blocking the view. If them shades were down, I didn't know what I'd hit. I ain't in the sniping and killing business. I wasn't even sure this was a good idea. My pa, he used to tell me don't draw a gun unless you plan to use it. Trying to scare people with a few near misses didn't make no sense to me, but I could see what Carboy was after. He was hoping a little flyin' lead would get them two crooks to back off and maybe quit. That's book learning for ya. What a few bullets into the Pullman car would actually do is make them mad as hornets and eager to git it over and done with, and that meant killing Cletus Carboy fast and grabbing the Big Mother even before they got the man buried proper. But no one ever paid no attention to me, so I just thought I'd do what was asked and wait and see. Maybe old Carboy knew a thing or two that I sure didn't know.

I checked on Critter, who was munching fresh alfalfa, and he let me know of his undying friendship by trying to kick me, but he missed. I'd leave him there this night. It was only a mile to the town and another half mile to that ridge where I'd get a potshot at the railroad car. I'd do better without a horse anywhere in sight.

I hung around there in that little bunkhouse until dark, mostly looking over my kit, which sure wasn't much of anything anymore. But I had a little of Celia's gold in my britches, so I could get me some new stuff. I wanted a long-handled union suit most of all, with a good trapdoor. Them things are real comforts.

I looked over that Browning. It was sure a smooth-built piece, and seemed to slide open with a quiet click. It had a good heft to it, and I thought I sure could get used to a piece like that. But I hardly knew what I'd do with it.

I slipped out of there at full dark and made my way toward town, which I skirted wide, and then on up toward that ridge overlooking the Pullman Palace Car. I went slow and easy, moving like ink through the night, and waiting now and then with my ears wide open, just in case someone was floating around and about.

I finally reached that ridge, and could look down a long grade toward the railroad car, lit by little more than starlight now, with a lamp glowing only in the rear parlor. From that distance, I could hardly see them other windows, and couldn't tell whether them shades was drawn or not. It was a long shot, too far for comfort. Aim at a window from that distance and you wouldn't know what you was putting lead into. I'd need to get closer if I was to loose a pop. I knew them thugs would patrol, and I knew I'd have to retreat over that bare ridge, and if the moon was up I wouldn't have much of an escape route. But old Carboy thought it'd all work out, and I was game enough.

I needed to get a lot closer. That little square of light from the rear parlor didn't tell me nothing. I worked my way another hundred yards toward that car, and still couldn't make out who or what was in there. By now, I was getting deep into their turf and was lookin' out for them thugs patrolling the slopes. But it was plenty dark and I didn't spot nothing.

I tried another fifty yards. That car was pretty close now, but I was on the back side, not the valley side. The shade was open, but there was some gauzy stuff so I couldn't see in none, and that's when I got to feelin' bad. My pa used to say, don't pull the trigger unless you know what you're shooting at. I lay down in the grass and lifted that Browning and sighted down the barrel, but truth to tell, I couldn't see nothing except some light. I thought about pumping lead into them other windows, where there was no light, but I didn't like that either. I am just not a sniper like Rudolph Costello Glan, coldly killin' and not caring. A fair fight's one thing, but squeezing the trigger on someone minding his own business is something else. I knew I wouldn't do it. I didn't mind Carboy's idea of scaring them outta their plans to take over the valley, but I wasn't gonna do it this way. So, that settled, I begun to back away from there. I'd have to tell Carboy I refused to put a bullet in there blind. Scarin's one thing; killin's another.

I got myself halfway back toward that ridge when one of them thugs come out of the dark and jumped me. It sure was a surprise. It was one of them jokers who was calling themselves the names of presidents. Maybe Arthur, looked like. But I didn't have time. He'd been stalking me when I was sighting down that Browning, and now he come in a rush. But even as he about slammed into me, I swung the barrel of that Browning and cracked him good. He howled and staggered and then come at me again, fending off my rifle like it was a feather, and come on in at me, knocking me slantwise in the dirt. I twisted before he landed on me, his big fists hammering at my ribs, and I elbowed him good and then chopped my fist into his gut. He let air go like a gas balloon, and I wrenched free, kicked him in his privates, and dodged what he thought was a killer blow. I stepped back, found the Browning, and clobbered him with it, cracking his skull bone until he lay there whining. I thought he'd earned himself that headache. Me, I was panting some, and hurting in my ribs and a few other places, but I had a few moments to get out of there. That or kill him. I took the middle course, kicked him hard in the shin, told him to leave the country or he'd get worse, and then left. He lay there whining and holding his head, but he didn't have enough brains in there to spill out and all I'd whacked was solid bone.

I thought maybe the barrel of that Browning got itself bent, but it was in a good cause. So I got out of there and headed back to Carboy's estate over on the other side of Swamp Creek and got myself nerved up to tell him I was gonna quit.

Chapter Twenty-four

Well, old Carboy threw me for a loop.

"I don't accept your resignation," he said.

"What do ya mean? I quit."

"I don't accept it."

"You're crazy. I just done quit. I'm outa here."

Carboy, he just smiled. "It wasn't a good idea, trying to scare off Scruples and Miss Trouville. My apologies. You did the right thing. We mustn't turn ourselves into casual killers like Glan. My original idea was better: we need to clean them out of every paper that makes them look legitimate."

"I'm getting Critter and moving to Mexico City," I said.

"Fine, but wait a bit. When the day shift leaves the Big Mother, Scruples' gang is going to jump the mine. They'll be dressed as miners and look like they're the night shift. And once they get past the guardhouses they're going to take over."

"You got this from your snitch, right?"

Carboy smiled and said nothing.

"So what do you want me to do?"

"Snatch the safe from the Pullman car."

"What? What's this?"

"They're sending in every hood they've collected. We're planning on sucking them into the Big Mother and trapping them in there. Only one man will be guarding the railroad car, your old friend Lugar, and of course Carter and Amanda, who'll be waiting in it for word from the Big Mother."

He smiled broadly, waiting for my response.

"I'm heading for San Diego," I said.

A faint flash of annoyance showed up, and then his blandness reappeared. "Ah, well, I thought you might enjoy the heist."

I always liked to get into as much trouble as possible, so I stood there and let him say what he was going to say.

"I imagine you'd have two or three hours. You'd need to disarm Lugar and bust into the railroad car, barricade Scruples and his doxy in a room, and unbolt the safe and skid it to a wagon. Unless you can persuade Carter to open it up." He cocked an eyebrow.

"All alone? Who's driving the wagon? Who's gonna help me drag a five-hundred-pound chunk of steel? Who's gonna get under the car with a wrench and find out how to pull the nuts off them bolts?"

Carboy sighed. "How would you do it?"

Danged if I knew what he was jabbering about. Never work for someone that reads books, that's my motto. They're all nuts. Carboy sure was one of a kind. Instead of bossing me around, he was always real polite. Instead of insisting he knew how to do things, he was always backing off, saying he was mistaken. I don't know how he bossed the Big Mother mine; that's a tough bunch of miners, but there he was, halfway apologizin' and backin' off all the time.

"Do you have a better plan?" he asked.

Well, that's the first time in my life someone asked me that. I stared at him like he was just plain loco. I ain't known for having a better plan.

"I got to think on her," I said.

"Do that," he said.

He sure was something else. I thought I'd at least give it some thought before saddling Critter and vamoosing from there.

"Now what's gonna happen at the mine?" I asked.

"My day shift is done at four. They change out of their duds and head for the saloons. The night shift starts at five. Scruples' men are going to mix in with them, get past the guards. Then they're going to rush the office and take over. They'll shoot any guard who resists."

"How do you know this?"

"I have ears where I need them, Mr. Cotton."

"And what'll you do to stop this?"

"Nothing. There won't even be guards in the guard-houses."

"I ain't following you too good."

"My guards will be here, protecting me. You see, grabbing the Big Mother's not enough for Scruples. They need to extinguish any resistance, which means rushing this home. Never underestimate Carter Scruples, my friend. Taking over the Big Mother's a diversion intended to draw me out of here. I think that by four this afternoon Rudolph Glan will be set up outside this house somewhere, and there'll be a few thugs ready to rush us."

"So you want me to help you here?"

"Oh, no, I want you to head for the railroad car and do whatever it takes."

"But how'll you keep yourself alive here? They could burn you out."

"I suppose they could, but I have a few resources."

He sure was calm, just settin' there in his parlor, playing this mental chess with Carter Scruples. I wasn't very sure I'd be seeing him ever again, at last not alive. For Carboy, war was outwitting the enemy.

"I tell you what, Cotton. This is a conflict of opportunity. Why don't you just go looking for some?"

I thought Carboy was plumb crazy.

"You sure you don't want me here?"

"Go," he said.

I did like he told me. But first I put Critter into his barn and fed him good, because I didn't want no stray lead hitting him, and for that matter I didn't want them Transactions thugs to know he was there. Then I sort of ghosted my way to town through woods, keeping a sharp eye for Glan. I sure didn't know what to do, and whether I was trying to help a crazy man.

I come into Swamp Creek from the woods, crossed the creek, keepin' an eye out, and climbed them stairs to Celia's rooms. I thought that was as good a place as any to watch the show, since I wasn't gonna be part of it. And maybe Celia would need some protectin', too. I knocked, but she heard me on them wooden stairs and opened right up.

"Oh, Cotton," she said, and drew me in, and then durned if she didn't hug me tight. I liked it well enough, but she wasn't bein' very widderly if you ask me, hugging me like that just a few days after she'd planted Armand Argo. But some widders were merry, and maybe she was a merry one. So I hugged right back for a while and things was getting pretty good when she sort of wiggled out. Her eyes, they was very bright. I could see what Armand Argo liked about her, all right. But there wasn't nothing I could do about it except suffer.

"I just come from a crazy man," I said. "He might own a gold mine but he's got no iron in his spine." I told her the whole thing about Cletus Carboy and how he was full of book notions and didn't know what end was up.

She listened with a little smile on her puss. "Don't you underestimate Cletus," she said. "He's tougher than you think. Cletus and Armand used to get together a lot, the two owning the biggest mines and all, and I sure got an earful. Cletus, he wants to make a name for himself. He's been reading up on new books about how to run things, and he's trying them all out. He's real tough and he could flatten you in about two seconds, I bet, and he can do it to his miners, but he kept telling Armand that doesn't make them miners work better or harder or brighter. So he sort of tries to inspire them, make them find their own ways to do better. His secret is, he wants everyone to be his own boss, so he doesn't have to boss."

That sure was a new way of looking at Cletus Carboy, seemed to me. How could he not be the boss? There's workers that need flattening regular or they just mess everything up and loaf. I didn't think much of Carboy, for sure. My idea of running a mine is to pound hell out of anyone messes up, or fire them quick. Miners ain't much good unless someone's pounding on 'em.

"He wants me to figure out my own way of getting that Transactions crowd out of Swamp Creek," I said.

"And did you find a way yet?"

"Nope. I ain't known for smarts, Celia."

"You're known for a few other things, Cotton," she said, and I got all flustered up again. I swear, it was so bad, I was gonna get down them stairs before I got into real bad trouble. So I changed the subject real fast.

"There's gonna be a lot of trouble this afternoon, Celia," I said. "Them thugs are going to take over the Big Mother Mine between shifts. But that's not all. They's gonna hit on Cletus, too. They're gonna try to get him out where they can kill him. But he's wise to it, and got his guards at his place. And he's got some plan or other to catch all the thugs inside his mine."

She absorbed all that. "What does he want you to do?"

"Go hit the railroad car," I said.

She stared blankly.

"Bust open that safe and get all them papers, deeds, claims, forms out of it, so Scruples don't have a leg to stand on."

"How?" she asked.

"That's where Cletus Carboy's full of book learnin' and don't know nothing."

"It'll be guarded," she said.

"They're leaving Lugar there to keep watch. The rest of them thugs will be raiding the Big Mother."

She smiled suddenly. "Let's do it."

"Sure, we'll just get past Lugar, get past Scruples, and maybe Amanda. They ain't going to be holding licorice sticks in their paws, Celia. Then we bust open a safe and grab the stuff Cletus wants."

"Can you take out Lugar? That's all we need."

"I can give her a try."

She smiled at me, like maybe there'd be a reward if we got this here heist done right, and I smiled right back. I was ready for rewards, and thought I'd reward the widder lady, too, if I could.

Well, the afternoon took a long time spending itself.

We couldn't move until all them thugs was gone from Transactions and over to the Big Mother Mine. I looked out the window overlooking the main drag of Swamp Creek. I don't know if it ever got a name. And the whole street was chock full of teams. There was a twenty-mule-team beer wagon stocking up the local saloons. There was a couple of long ox teams, maybe ten or twelve span, dragging in some mining equipment. Those teams went slow, but they could sure drag in some heavy stuff. These were all parked along the street while the teamsters wet their whistles. There'd be a lot of grunting and hauling later. One of them ox teams looked to be hauling a new stamp for the stamp mill, where the ore got the hell beat out of it so chemicals could get the gold out of the rock.

Me, I didn't fret none. I didn't have no plan. I thought I had to get the job done before them thugs all come back from the Big Mother. I didn't know how to open that safe neither, but maybe a gun aimed at Scruples' left ear might persuade him to spin that dial.

Long about four, we saw them thugs all dressed up as miners, in brogans and bib overalls and all, stomping through town just like all the other three-dollar-a-day men working in the stopes and drifts. They didn't look like miners, though. I don't know why. They looked like thugs dressed as miners, just the way a cop looks like a cop even when he's not wearing his blue uniform. People sure have a look about them, all right. I saw Arnold all dressed up in denim, and I saw his sidekick The Apocalypse trotting along with a shovel. Mines don't hire runts like that, but it didn't bother him none. I didn't see Glan, and I figured he was with the other bunch, aiming to polish off Carboy.

So the party was on. Carboy's information was correct. Scruples was making his move this afternoon.

After all them thugs drifted by, going to jump the Big Mother, Celia and I slipped out the rear door and headed toward the Pullman Palace Car. I sure didn't know what to expect. But if I could get Lugar out of the way, I thought we might come up with something pretty good. In fact, I got to thinking a little, and maybe we could get Scruples and Amanda out of that Pullman car like rats quitting a sinking ship.

Chapter Twenty-five

Me and Celia sort of ghosted through Swamp Creek. I was remembering that Scruples had warned me to git out or face a lead pill. So when I thought I saw one of them thugs in the shadows, I steered her into the Mint real fast.

Billy Blew raised his eyebrows at her bein' in there, but he didn't say nothing.

"Need a little corner to lay low for a bit, Billy."

"You got it."

"You gettin' much trade?"

"Look for yourself."

"I sure don't see no one in here."

"Most of my customers is gone. This was the watering hole for the small-time mine owners, and Scruples chased 'em off."

"Even that bunch from the Hermit Mine?"

"Haven't seen them in days. Truth is, Cotton, Scruples has got himself most every little mine in the area. There's only the Big Mother left. And the Big Mother owns the stamp mill, so Scruples got to get both to own the whole kit and caboodle. Ain't much good jumping all the mines and not owning the mill."

I hadn't thought of that. Scruples still had two big operations to pull off. Maybe three, if he intended to bust old Carboy out of his house.

"I'd like a drink," said Celia.

Billy looked her over pretty close. "Sarsaparilla?" he asked.

"Sarsaparilla? Hell, a double red-eye."

Billy was lookin' right nervous. "I ain't supposed to serve women, especially ones about your size and age."

She dug into her coin purse and slapped a silver dollar down.

"Well, there ain't anyone around anyway," Billy said.

"I'll have sarsaparilla," I said.

He stared at me like I was loco, but I didn't want no booze in my veins if it come to shooting it out.

He served us and got the change back to Celia.

"How come Scruples is going after the stamp mill last?" I asked.

"He can't monkey with the deed. That mill's not sitting on a mining claim. It's not even listed in the books kept by Brashear. It's not part of the Swamp Creek District, waiting for government deeds. The mill's on township land, and the land under that mill is deeded to Carboy, and that deed's on file in Butte. So Scruples can't just barge in there and say it's his. It's gonna take some doing."

I hadn't known any of that. It was just sitting on the edge of town, hammering away day and night, ten stamps driven by a steam boiler, crushing ore from all the local mines on a consignment basis, pounding that ore so fine that the chemicals in the vats could leach the gold out of it. I didn't know the whole deal, but I knew that ore had to be pounded to powder or them nasty chemicals couldn't get a handle on the gold.

"Maybe Scruples don't need the mill," I said.

Billy, he just snorted, as if I was dumber than an ox.

Celia sort of snickered, and had another sip. For a sixteen-year-old girl, she wasn't having no trouble skimming that red-eye down her gullet.

"Cotton, you got a lot to learn, if you don't mind my saying so," Billy said. "This here mill controls the whole district. They charge whatever they feel like charging. They can make or break any mine. You want to know what a mine owner does if he can't do business with that mill? He loads his ore in freight wagons and hauls the stuff to Anaconda, forty miles distant. And you know what that means? All his black ink turns red. This is good ore here, but not so good it can be milled forty miles away by ox team and come out profitable. You follow me?"

"Sure do, Billy."

"All right, here's the skinny of it. Every mine, big and little, in the Swamp Creek District needs that mill. Without that mill, none of these mines is worth much. Whoever holds that mill, he's got the aces in his hand. If Scruples owns every mine in the Swamp Creek District, and Cletus Carboy says he's not gonna mill that ore, then Scruples is plumb outta luck, ain't he?"

This sure was stuff I knew nothing about. "So what's Scruples gonna do? He's gotta have that mill, don't he? Especially if he's plannin' on making a killing selling the whole district to some deep-pockets man?"

"Yep, he does, Cotton. I figure Scruples didn't know enough about mining to figure that out before he got into this racket, and now he's trying to get that mill."

"What's he gonna do, Billy?"

The barkeep shrugged. "Kill Carboy maybe. No

heirs. Then, in the confusion, take over the mill and hang on to it legal or illegal."

It bothered me that Carboy hadn't said a word to me about the mill. Or why it was so important to the whole district. Without it, none of them mines would be profitable. But Carboy was a man who kept most of his plans to himself, and let you find out only what he wanted you to know.

Celia had downed the double and was grinning crookedly at me. I don't care if a woman's sixteen or sixty, a double red-eye's gonna give her a crooked grin.

"Maybe I'll marry you, Cotton. I'm feeling the need," she said.

I was sippin' sarsparilla and feeling itchy.

"I'm thinkin' you ought to go to your rooms and rest up a little, Celia."

"Hell, no," she said. "You're stuck with me."

I didn't mind that, but she was a little on the young side to get stuck with.

"I'm heading for the stamp mill," I said. "It'll give you a headache."

"The red-eye already did that, Cotton."

"It's a dangerous place, Celia."

"I've sat at card tables beside Armand holding a derringer and ready to use it on some lout," she said.

She sure had lived a lot for a little girl. I gave up, and studied the street some, not wanting to run into them toughs filtering in. It was a good hour before four, when all the stuff was supposed to begin, and I knew they was getting ready. But I slipped out the rear door, with Celia tailing behind me, and started for the mill uptown a piece, along the alley.

"This town needs outhouses," she said. "Why can't men stay buttoned?"

"That there's a question you shouldn't be asking," I said.

It was bright afternoon, and I worried about getting caught by a bunch of them thugs sitting in the saloons, and maybe Celia getting bad hurt, but we sort of ghosted along until we got to the edge of the main street, and the stamp mill was maybe a quarter mile away, through a lot of slag and waste. It wasn't bad cover, all that dead rock piled up around there. Mining towns sure ain't pretty, and mining can take a sweet little valley like Swamp Creek and turn her into a hellhole that poisons everything in sight. I could see all them forests dying, just because the mill was pumping a lot of bad stuff into the ground and the air. It was a wonder we didn't all croak in that stunk-up valley.

The closer we got to that thing, the more the earth trembled under our feet. That sure was something, those ten stamps hammering down on the ore running through. Them stamps, someone told me once, was three quarters of a ton of iron each, and they was all coming down on rock, smashing it to bits. They operated in some sort of succession, so the stamps was lifted up by steam power and then cut loose to hammer that rock. It got so I could hardly talk to Celia, and it made me wonder how them mill men could work in a place like that without going stone deaf. But they were around, often pushing rock and ore around, ignoring that hammering. I never saw the like, the way them stamps powdered rock so the metal could be got out. There was a bunch of vats where that powdered rock was mixed with some sort of stinkin' chemicals to get the gold out. And another bunch was lookin' after all that. Over to the side was the steam plant, with a big firebox below it, and there was a bunch of men doin' nothing but shoving wood in there to make that steam. I never knew it took so much work and machinery and chemicals just to get a little gold outta some rock.

And that wasn't the end of it neither, because there was half a dozen wagons of wood waiting to be unloaded. Woodcutters were whacking down the forests to keep that old boiler going, and it looked like every day that boiler crew went through several cords of wood that was supplied by all them woodcutters. Them boys was independent, and went off into the forests and chopped down trees and let them dry some and then whacked off the limbs and cut them into lengths. They were a bunch, all right, with arms as thick as fence posts and shoulders wide as an ox.

"It sure is scary," Celia said. "I never saw it before. In town, it's just a lot of steady noise a long ways away."

"It's a monster, all right. But every ounce of gold coming out of this here valley is milled right there. See all them wagons? Some are woodcutters, but others are from the Big Mother Mine, the only one still running, and all that ore in them wagons is shoveled out and run through here. You wonder how anyone makes a dime mining gold."

It sure was getting bad around there, and I was getting itchy. That slamming never stopped as them big stamps came down on that rock. But I had to see how it might be shut down by Scruples, or anyone else for that matter.

"If you was to shut this down, how'd you do it?" I asked Celia.

I was thinkin' of how to take over the office and all, but Celia, she's a lot smarter than I'll ever be.

"Don't let them get any firewood," she said.

"Holy cats, Celia," I replied.

That old mill could be shut down cold if it didn't have no fuel for its boiler. If a body wanted to shut her cold, he'd scare off the woodcutters. There wasn't enough backup wood for more than three, four days piled up in there, so that mill was working pretty close to the bone.

"You got her," I said.

"Got what?"

"The way to do it," I said.

But she'd seen some big guy with muscles like a bull standing there without his shirt, and she wasn't listening to me at all. I didn't like that none. Them miners and mill men made me look like a midget.

"Gotta get outa here," I said, steering Celia away.

She came right along. I headed for the wood yard, where a bunch of them wood choppers was waiting in their wagons to unload and get paid. Maybe half a dozen wagons, with two-horse teams, big draft animals, was waiting to get unloaded. Most of them wagons had two men on board.

So we angled over there, and I went right up to the first. "You sell that wood to the mill?" I asked. "What do you get for it?"

"Him and me each clear about two dollars a day, but it's getting harder now," the driver said.

"Longer drive?" I asked.

"Yep, more'n an hour each way now. That mill eats about two square miles of wood a year, and that makes the hauling worse every trip."

"You work in pairs?"

"Mostly. He's a Bohunk off the boat and can't talk

English yet, but we get along fine. And he's good with an ax."

"You knock down live trees and dry them?"

"We knock them down but they don't get dried much. That mill wants all it can get, so it's burning a lot of green wood."

"How many wood cutters are there?" I asked.

"Oh, hell, how should I know. Hell of a bunch if you ask me. Just think a little. This whole mining district, it'd shut down fast if we quit 'em. Maybe they should pay us more, eh?"

"You get paid on delivery?"

"You bet. We get cash or we don't unload."

"How many days of wood does the mill have backed up?"

"Oh, sometimes they run out. Take a rainy spell or a lot of snow, and that old mill, she just shuts down because there's no way we can feed them boilers."

"Looks like enough here for a few days," I said.

"Sure, late summer like this. It's easy to haul. Roads ain't a quagmire. Sun dries the wood fast."

"You men live in town?"

"Nah, we make camps and live in them. Maybe in the winter we come in. Lots of times in the winter the mill ain't running, and the ore just gets stockpiled until we can bring in wood. There's no coal around here, so wood's all they got."

"That's what I wanted to know," I said. "You fellers are mighty important."

Chapter Twenty-six

The four o'clock whistle blew, sending a mournful howl over Swamp Creek, and scarin' up a few crows. That meant the show was about to begin. And if I was gonna bust into the railroad car, I'd better get packing.

"Celia, I got some business now," I said.

"I'm coming with you."

"I mean, real bad, dangerous business."

She just grinned and started hiking along through all them slag piles around the mill. It sure was an ugly place, all that black waste full of chemicals I didn't even want to know about. I didn't see nothing livin' in there, so I figured it wasn't a place for living folks like Celia and me, so I hurried through. The only good of all that stuff was that it hid our progress. I had to get up to the road headin' up the valley and then up to the Pullman Palace Car. It sure was lonely out there; most everyone was in town this here afternoon.

No sooner did we skirt the last of them piles of slag than I spotted that ebony carriage headin' toward town. I pushed back and so did Celia, and we watched Carter Scruples and Amanda Trouville trot by. Last time I seen them driving that rig, they was on hand when Aggie Cork's mine was being jumped. They was right there in the woods, keepin' an eye on the whole show. And here they were, driving into town. They'd get there right about when the day shift was done comin' out of that black hole, and the night shift would be going into that place where the sun never shone. I guess they was fixin' to see the biggest prize of all fall into their paws. Get the Big Mother, and it'd be over most likely. Them two would have just about every mine and glory hole in the Swamp Creek District.

We waited until they was past, and I steered us toward the railroad car on the hill, wondering who was still around there guardin' the place. I figured, since we was a man and woman, we'd get farther walkin' right in. They wouldn't pay no attention to a couple like us.

So we hiked up that grade toward the Pullman and the barn and bunkhouse and pens and all, and no one jumped out of the woodwork. We finally got up to the yard and I hallooed around, and no one come runnin'. They was all down in town, fixing to take over the Big Mother and celebrate. Old Scruples, he was getting mighty close to where he wanted to be, controlling every mine in the district. He and Amanda might soon be rich, maybe even getting half a million out of it all. A man can live like a king on a lot less.

Well, we hallooed around and no one answered, so I poked my head in the bunkhouse and no one was there, and I checked the barn, too, and it was plain empty except for some nice-lookin' horses staring at me like old friends. I felt like feedin' them some of that good alfalfa there, but I didn't. Instead, I steered Celia toward the Palace Car, climbed up them little steps falling away from that rear observation platform, and next thing I knew, we were walkin' right in. It sure was pleasant in there, and silent as could be.

"I want you to keep a sharp lookout. Not just on that drive coming up here but in all directions, like someone comin' down from them foothills to check on us."

"Do your stuff," she said.

She sure was a firecracker, all right. Armand Argo had had himself a pistol.

It felt kinda funny walking in there like some burglars, but I remembered that old Scruples had not only wandered onto property he didn't have no right to, he'd caused a few of them owners to be killed. If that's how him and Amanda wanted it, then their Palace Car was fair game.

Celia, she'd bounce from window to window checkin' things, and then explore the car. When she got to Amanda's boudoir, she opened the door and then started to giggle.

"No wonder she tells Carter what to do," she said, eyeing that oil painting of her.

"How can anyone compete with that?"

I didn't want to look in there. I didn't want memories. I made my way to the office and walked right in. It wasn't big; nothing in that train car was big. But sure enough, there was that safe with the dial on it. That thing was lacquered black and had some little pink cupids messing around it. But it wasn't no fairies that was inside of there. I tried to budge it, but it wouldn't budge. I don't think Scruples would have left the place unguarded if he thought that safe could be gotten out. I yanked at the door, and it was shut tight, and studied on it. The safe was bolted down, but them bolts had rounded tops that no wrench could loosen. I tried giving that door another yank, and moving the dial a notch or two, but it was tight.

I was getting a little worried. "You keepin' an eye out?" I asked.

I got sort of a muffled response from her, so I slid out and looked through all them windows myself. It was quiet out there, sunny and silent. From here you could barely hear the stamp mill, but I knew that when the windows were open, them ten stamps could be heard thumping away here and even farther up the valley. I didn't see no one. I headed outside and looked under the car where that safe would be bolted down, but there was a double bottom to the car and no bolts visible under there. It was just the usual stuff there, steam lines, compressors, and all. I never did know much about railroads. The car sat on its regular trucks, the wheels on that mining rail they laid there. The tracks didn't go nowhere and were just to hold up the car.

I heard tell they dragged the car all the way from Butte, going where no railroad car ever went, but they had the car on a special flatbed carriage with wagon wheels, which made it much easier.

I gave up any hope that I could nip them papers from the safe then and there. It would take a blacksmith a month to chew into that safe. But maybe there was some other way, like getting Scruples to open up while I was waving a revolver in his direction. Fat chance, I thought. If Scruples was smart, he would laugh at me. He was the only one knew the combination, and a dead Scruples wouldn't help me none.

Carboy, he was full of book learning, but he sure didn't know nothing about the real world. I'd probably have to tell him that it'd take half the infantry in the territory to get that safe open and get Scruples thrown behind bars. And by then, he'd have his Pullman car back on the rails and off somewheres else.

"Let's go. This was a bad idea," I said.

I was also getting nervous that maybe them thugs would drift back up to the place. We stepped out into the sun and quietness, and I sure didn't see hide nor hair of anyone, and I thought maybe we'd better steer clear of Swamp Creek, with all them thugs in town and me with a bull's-eye sort of hanging from my chest. I steered Celia back toward the stamp mill, that being the best place I could think of to hide out. A man could sure be invisible out in them slag heaps where no one ever went.

"I'm gonna wait out in the slag, but maybe you should go on in and stick close to your rooms," I said.

She eyed me. "Where'll you be?"

"I got to get over to Carboy, and if he is still alive, I'll tell him I done no good."

"I'm glad you're not quitting."

"I never said I would! I just can't do this Carboy's way. I gotta figure out my own way."

She reached out and took me in her arms and kissed me good, right in the middle of them slag heaps, and kissed me again, and I thought that was mighty widderly of her, so I kissed back a few times, and was just thinkin' them slag piles were a real private place when she busted loose and laughed and took off, the wind whipping her skirts, and that was the last I saw of her.

There I was, out in the middle of the slag, nowhere to go, unable to do the job that I'd been asked to do. I didn't feel so good. Swamp Creek belonged to Scruples. If he took over the Big Mother Mine, he'd probably be celebrating at one of them watering holes, along with most of his hooligans. I thought maybe I'd detour around town. I didn't mind meeting up with one or two or three of them toughs, but the odds weren't good that I'd live to tell about running into four or five.

Them stamps was thundering so loud I couldn't hear much, and that noise was making me itchy. I didn't know how them mill men stood it. I'm a cowboy at heart, and all I want from life is the peace of the big open country, with a few clouds chasing the sun. But I was hiding near the stamps, and hadn't any idea what was happening in Swamp Creek because them thumping stamps blotted everything out.

I was just about to get out of there when I saw that lacquered black carriage and them trotters come prancing along the road, so I peered over the slag to get a good view. That outfit was coming straight toward the stamp mill, and pretty soon I could see it had three people in it. There was Scruples and Amanda, but I couldn't make out the other one. But they came straight on, though the trotters didn't like the noise of them stamps and kept sawin' their heads and acting unhappy, but then the carriage pulled up at the mill office, and I got a good view at last. That third person was Cletus Carboy. I couldn't hardly figure that one out, but that's who it was for sure, him the enemy of the whole Transactions crowd. Scruples got out of that carriage and put down a carriage weight and hooked the lines to it, and then helped Amanda down. She stood dusting her skirts while Carboy climbed out, and them three went into the office. I couldn't hardly believe it.

It didn't take long for them to come out again, along with the mill manager, some gent named Wally Wilde, who was supposed to be related to that fruity poet over in England, but Wally was all man. So I just kept right on watching from the slag, keeping low so none of them could see me, and pretty quick Wilde takes Scruples and Amanda out to the mill men and they jabber a little, though the noise is so bad no one seems to hear nothing, and then Wilde takes them over to the woodpile and all of them talk to them woodcutters who're lined up to unload the cordwood for the boiler. And then they're done. Carter Scruples loads Amanda back into the carriage, and Carboy gets in, and the three of them start for Swamp Creek, and them trotters are mighty glad to get out of there and dance right along.

Pretty quick they're gone, and Wilde is back in his office, and I'm itching to learn what's happening. My best bet is to slide over to them woodcutters and have a palaver. So I get over there to the woodpiles, where the woodcutters in the wagons are waiting their turn to get credited for the wood and unload. I sort of selected a couple of them down the line some, who weren't busy.

"You mind telling me what that was all about?" I asked a feller in a gray slouch hat.

"You mean them new owners?"

"Well, that's what I want to find out."

"Transactions has got the mill, they said. They was telling us it's business as usual, only now it's a different company that's running the mill. That was the former owner, feller named Carboy, and the new owners, the two that camp up there in the railroad car. The new owners, they say just to keep on going, hit's all the same to them, same pay, same deal, only new company."

"Carboy sold?"

"I reckon so. He didn't look very happy about it. Fact is, he was angry-looking."

"Did they say anything else? Like who's the owner of the Big Mother Mine?"

"Sure did. Mr. Scruples said it was his now. They got the whole son-of-a-bitching mining district all to their lonesome selves."

"And Cletus Carboy was going right along?"

"Looked that way to me, friend. You got any objections to it?"

"I guess maybe I do," I said.

Chapter Twenty-seven

I slipped over to Carboy's fancy estate after dark, glad for the cover of night. I sure didn't know what was going on, and I needed to know. So I plain walked up and knocked. Cletus Carboy himself answered.

"I was expecting you. Come in, Cotton."

That feller was always knowing where I would be before I knew it, and it sure made me itchy. But I followed him in there, and pretty quick they brought some of that tea to me, and I thought I'd manage to swallow some of that dishwater, but it didn't taste half bad.

"It's oolong," he said.

"Well, not too long for me."

He sort of snorted at that, but I'm used to it.

"I'd better tell you I don't have no way to get that safe open," I began.

"You tried?"

"Spun that dial and looked for ways to pry her loose."

Carboy smiled. "They didn't guard the place?"

"Didn't need to. It'd take a few sticks of DuPont to pry her out of there. Now you tell me your side of this."

"Defeat, Cotton. Utter defeat. Scruples outmaneuvered

me and achieved a bloodless coup. They actually moved in about noon, before I had men posted. The four o'clock takeover was a ruse. He now controls the mine and the mill. And everything else in the mining district. And without firing a shot."

"Every blamed thing?"

"Everything," Carboy said sadly. He lit his dead pipe and sucked until he could get some smoke going. "It turned out that Carter Scruples has his own snitches, including my head groundsman, Gerd Thimblestiff. They knew my plans, knew my intent to trap them in the shaft of the Big Mother, and knew how I intended to defend myself here in the event that their thugs planned to invade, and worked out a way to get around my guards. They put a man on the roof. Gerd was well paid, and of course no longer works for me."

"They taken the mill, too?"

"Oh, yes, Cotton. I signed a deed with a forty-five-caliber bullet aimed at me. I'm not the hero of fiction. When I had a forty-five-caliber revolver pointing at my ear, with a bullet forty-five-hundredths of an inch waiting to pierce one side of my brain and exit the other, and listened to instructions to write a bill of sale, I proceeded quite cheerfully. I weighed the possibility of refusing, and decided not to be the dead hero. So it was all done under duress, and might technically be invalid, but that won't stop Scruples. He got what he wanted."

"You quitting?"

"Oh, no, not at all, Cotton. I survived, you see, and to survive is to hope, and to hope is to plan. I lived to fight another day." He eyed me levelly. "By the way, thanks to Thimblestiff, they know you're here and never left Swamp Creek. They know your nag's in the barn. But

Scruples doesn't care. He told me he didn't care about that riffraff, meaning you. He's got what he wants."

"That's another of them big words I never heard of," I said.

"Riffraff? Trash. Rabble. Rubbish."

That got me mad. "Trash, am I. I'll show that Scruples what trash is," I said. I was plumb heated up. No one ever called me riffraff in my life, and I was getting steamed up real good.

"Scruples, he called me that? Not Amanda?"

"I think she agreed with him. She didn't object."

"I thought she liked me," I said.

"You going to saddle up Critter and ride into the sunset?" he asked.

"Then I'd be trash, Carboy. If he called me riffraff, then I'm gonna show that whole outfit what riffraff is. Only, I ain't got a plan yet."

"Time's running out for both of us, I'm afraid." He sipped some of that oolong.

"What's he gonna do next?" I asked.

Carboy shrugged. "Keep on mining my ore and milling my ore while he tries to line up a sale of the whole district. He got what he set out to get, which was every mine and claim in the Swamp Creek District, and he snatched the mill too."

"I can shut down the mill, I think, and maybe the Big Mother, too, if it's got a boiler. Would shuttin' it all down do any good?"

"Well, it'd keep the gold in the ground. A mine is a diminishing asset. Some mines last just a little while. None last forever. One of the games is to tie up a mine in litigation. After years of fighting in courts, someone gets the mine—which by then is depleted. In other words, Cotton—control is everything. And Scruples controls everything."

"You got a little cash I could use?"

"For what?"

"Getting all them woodcutters to take a vacation. They was tellin' me that without cordwood, the whole shebang shuts down real quick."

Carboy rose, paced the study, puffed deeply on his pipe, and then disappeared. When he returned, he had a stack of eagles in hand.

"There's about twenty woodcutters supplying the mines and mill. See whether an eagle apiece would persuade them to take a vacation for a month."

"Only ten bucks for a month?"

"Cutting wood is hard and heavy work, Cotton. Ten bucks will look good."

"What does that get you?"

"Time, Cotton, time."

Well, twenty eagles was two hundred dollars, and I never had so much cash in my hand in all my life. I thought two dollars was pretty hot stuff. And there I was with twenty of them little gold pieces, light as can be even though gold's heavy metal.

"I'll give her a try," I said.

"Oh, and Cotton, find out if you can whether Scruples is putting the whole district up for sale. He's got to start somewhere, an advertisement, or hiring a broker, or wiring someone. I have a notion that if we can find out who's the buyer, we can maybe talk to the gentleman about a few facts of life."

"Seems that'd make him all the more eager to move in here," I said.

Carboy scowled at me. "It's called due diligence. You want to know what you're getting into."

"Not me," I said. "I'll just take a chance on whatever looks real good."

He smiled bleakly at me. I think maybe I didn't do so good with him, but I couldn't help it. I'm just me, Cotton, and don't know how to be some other feller.

I headed out to the pens to saddle up Critter. He greeted me with a friendly bite and a butt.

"You and me are gonna travel, Critter," I said.

He clamped his yellow teeth into my shoulder.

"Quit that," I said. "I bite back."

He dropped some apples and let me saddle up. I rode out of there and skirted wide of Swamp Creek, thinkin' maybe some of them toughs might want to clean out twenty eagles tied up in an old handkerchief of Carboy's. I knew about where them woodcutters worked and let Critter run a little, since he was getting barn sour. This Swamp Creek was same as all the rest of the mining camps. Half of them start in the middle of woods, and as the town grows, the forests get cut away for firewood and boiler wood and planks and timbers. New camps, they got woods close by; old camps, you got to ride a heap to get to any forest that ain't cut down. Swamp Creek was showing some age, with hardly a tree left standing close in. The bigger the town, the more woodcutters is needed, and sometimes there's more of them than there is miners. It takes a lot of timber to run a mine, more to run a mill, still more to nail up all those stories and shanties and houses.

Critter farted some to let me know he was enjoying life. He could sound like a cathedral pipe organ if he was of a mind. And after a while, we reached one of them woodcutters' camps, with a few wagons around and a few wall-tents where them cutters can live halfway comfortable for a season.

I stepped off the hurricane deck and waited for them woodcutters to gather around. They was a rough lot, and half couldn't speak English, but neither could I so it didn't matter none.

"I suppose you heard that Scruples, he took over the mill and the Big Mother," I said. "That Scruples, he sort of weaseled around Carboy and got a lot of armed men into them places and kicked out the managers and took over."

"We heard a thing or two," said one.

"Then I'll get right to it. Carboy, he wants his mill and mine back, and 'bout the only way to do that is to shut 'em down tight."

I sort of waited, but no one volunteered nothing.

"I mean, no more wood."

Now I saw a mess of frowns. I was talkin' pay and makin' a living.

"If he can get near all of you fellers to take a month vacation with pay, he'd do it. He'd shell out for you to take a while off, and not deliver a stick of wood to the mill or the Big Mother. No cordwood, no planks, no mine timbers."

That sure got their attention, all right, but they wasn't lookin' like they'd go along with it.

"How many woodcutters is working around the district?"

"Hardly know from day to day," one said.

"Twenty maybe?"

"More'n dat."

"Well, I'm supposed to tell you he'll pay you each

an eagle to shut down for a month. But only if you are all in it."

That sure sank like a rock in a pond.

Finally, one said, "We ain't all one crowd. Some of the others, if we took eagles to shut down, they'd just work harder and get better pay. We lay off a month, maybe we don't get back into the wood line at the mill."

"You're afeared of losing business?"

None of them answered. This was going to be harder than I thought. "Where are them other camps? I'll go talk."

They were pointing in several directions. But I finally got her straightened away. There were three more camps, several men in each, which made work easier for all. None was very far off. They all wanted to stay as close to the mill as they could get to save haulin'.

"I'll just ride Critter here to where they is and do a little talkin'. I'll get back soon as I hear from them."

They eyed me suspiciously, and I put foot in stirrup and clambered up. Critter snorted, bucked once or twice, and settled down.

"He don't like it here," I said.

We headed for two of them camps that was up the valley a little, but not far. I rode in there about when they was scrubbing the pots after eating some elk stew, and they heard me out, but with the same look on their faces. They was mostly saying, yeah, we'll take a month off for an eagle, but what about them others? They didn't much care who owned the mill, or who paid them for each load of cordwood, just so long as they got some hard cash out of it. Like most ever'one else, they wanted to get along, and for men straight off the immigrant trains and boats, cuttin' wood wasn't a bad way to get going.

So I wasn't making much headway there neither. I finally climbed onto Critter, who humped his back up just to let me know I was abusing him and he wanted time off, and we took off for the next camp, which I thought was maybe half a mile up.

It was getting along toward dusk now, pretty gray, and that's what saved my life.

That old rifle shot clipped my slouch hat right off my head. I felt the hat rip away before I even heard the shot. I bailed off of Critter, hit the ground hard, lots of sticks and stuff there which didn't do me no good, and was up, my borrowed hogleg in hand, and runnin' straight toward that son of a bitch Rudolph Costello Glan.

Chapter Twenty-eight

I bulled right through that brush and stuff, working up toward a ridge I knew was the place where Glan took a potshot at me. I don't know if that was smart or not. I just was goin' after him and plowing through all that scrub growth on the slope, dodging this way and that.

Maybe he was up there takin' aim, maybe not. It was getting too dark to see anything. Maybe me going after him like that was the last thing he expected, straight into the sights of his rifle. I didn't much care, and it sure beat laying on the ground waiting for him to slide down and finish me off.

"Riffraff, am I?" I snapped. "I'll show you some riffraff."

That word still graveled me. Calling me trash, that did it. "I'll riffraff you off that ridge, Glan."

But there wasn't any reply, and I think maybe Rudy Glan, he decided to get the hell out of there while he could, because he had a mad bull dodging through that brush and he couldn't swing a rifle fast enough to know where the target was.

The last part of that hogback was pretty steep, but I

thumped along, my heart banging in my chest, ready to shoot anything that moved. When I finally got up there, it was pretty dark, but I made sure to crouch low and not silhouette myself against the night sky. Darkness is a friend, but you gotta know how to use it right.

He was gone. I couldn't even find any brass. But I knew who done it, and I knew I'd be settling accounts one of these days. I also knew Scruples wasn't ignoring me at all, and was still stalking me. I crouched around there, lookin' for brass, and then lookin' for a place some horse stood a while, but I didn't find nothing.

I started toward Critter real careful, knowing Glan might be there waiting. It was going to be a bad time, collecting Critter. But I had a thing or two up my sleeve, and when I finally got to a protected little park on the slope, I gave Critter the old whistle. I didn't hear a thing, and whistled again, and pretty soon old Critter, he comes snorting up. I peer around sharply, and lead him under a big cottonwood where it's dark as pitch and there's no sky, and got on board.

We was some distance from the valley road, and I sat real quiet, listening, and finally gave Critter a loose rein, and he pussyfooted down that slope, only snapping sticks once in a while. I was still a target. Anyone crouched along that valley road could have ambushed me, even in that dark.

I wasn't doing so good with the woodcutters. I wondered how come Glan knew where I was heading. Maybe he was paying for information, like everyone else around there. It were the strangest thing, everyone spying on everyone else. He must have been paying a few of them woodcutters to let him know anything interesting. So Glan had snitches and Carboy had snitches and Scruples had snitches, and about the only one I met around there that didn't was Celia. I thought maybe I'd head into town and pay her a visit, long as them woodcutters was not interested in doing business. I thought I could park Critter on the other side of the creek and we'd be all right. I tiptoed up them wooden stairs to get to her rooms, and knocked.

It took a while, but pretty soon she opened up, wearin' a white cotton sleeping gown and carrying that little revolver in her hand.

"Oh, it's you," she said.

"Want company?"

"Not tonight, Cotton. If I let you in, you'd have your way with me."

"Well, that's not a bad idear."

"I'm still grieving for Armand, Cotton. But try me in a day or two."

"That's when you quit grieving?"

"No, that's when I'm gonna have my way with you."

She smiled. Them girls pushing seventeen sure had notions.

"Well, guess I'll have to hold out. Don't know whether I can last that long," I said.

"Go home," she said.

"I ain't got one."

She reached forward, kissed me on the lips while that little lady revolver was pressed to my belly, and then shut the door. I stood there, half loony. You ever been kissed by a near-seventeen-year-old widow lady who also has a gun pushed into your gut? It's an experience.

I slipped down them wooden stairs real quiet, not wanting to wake up half of Swamp Creek, and got aboard

Critter, and rode into the night. It'd be Carboy's bunkhouse again, which wasn't bad but didn't hold a candle to Celia.

I got Critter corralled and hayed and watered and brushed, and then staggered into the bunkhouse. There was someone bunking in there, but I paid no never mind and pulled off my boots and britches. I got down to my union suit, which I was thinkin' I oughta wash in the next week or two, on a nice day, and crawled into my bunk and started to doze off.

Next I knew, there's this feller sitting on the edge of my bunk.

"How you doing, big fella?" he asked in a soft voice.

I'm outta that bunk so fast I hardly took time to get my britches back on, and about the time I'm stabbin' feet into boots, I hear this female laughter. I turn around just when a match flares and a lamp gets lit, and sure enough, it's a woman, and one I know, too, and she isn't wearing more than a little white thingamabob.

"Amanda," I said, sort of repentant.

"Want some company, Cotton?"

I always want company, but I sure wanted to learn a thing or two first. "What are you doing half naked in Carboy's bunkhouse?"

"I came to see you," she said.

"Well, now you have," I said, because I couldn't think of nothing else to say. This last sixty seconds or so set a record for something or other, though I don't know what. "Maybe you should pull a blanket over you."

I don't know why I said that neither. Most of me didn't want no blanket pulled over her at all. But here was the source of half my torment, the woman whose hired man Glan had tried to kill me a few hours earlier, sitting in her unmentionables in the bunkhouse of a man who didn't much care for her.

"Why you here?" I asked.

"To see you, Cotton. I couldn't get you out of my head."

This here business was taking a bad turn. "I'm sparking someone else," I said, real desperate.

"Celia Argo," she said unhappily. "Look, Cotton, I want to talk to you."

"You already are," I said. I sure was feeling put out.

She rose, slipped into a white robe she had, and sat on the bunk across from mine. "There's a lot you don't know," she said.

"That's what I'm learnin'."

"I'm trapped. I don't like the company. I don't like Carter Scruples. I'm a prisoner in a way. He's got signed contracts making me a partner, and equally responsible for all that happens, including . . . anything bad."

"Well, too bad. You shouldn't have got into it."

She eyed me levelly. "Cletus Carboy has a spy inside the railroad car. It's me. I've been telling him what's going to happen."

"You?"

"Carter Scruples dragged me into it. I didn't know it was going to be crooked. I didn't know people would die. I didn't know he'd hire killers. He talked about his business ideas, working out agreements, transactions, and sticking to them. It's all a jumble in my mind. He was always talking about contracts and integrity and at the same time he was stealing mines, scaring people off, and using force. He's rotten, but he's got this surface idealism, I guess you'd say, this . . . talk that hides who is he and what he does. He talks like some Yale graduate. I got roped in. I'm not smart enough to see through him entirely, but I know I'm in trouble. If the law comes down on him, it comes down on me, too. He made me a partner, even if I don't know about his decisions. Like having Glan shoot you."

"What's Yale?" I asked.

"It's like Harvard."

"Never heard of it. But there's cows called Herefords."

She eyed me quietly. "It doesn't matter. Here's what matters. He talked me into something bad. He talked about new ways to do business, and that fooled me. I'm trapped and I need you now. I'm sorry I'm half dressed this way. I thought the only way to get help was . . . well . . . you know."

"Transactions," I said. That sure was some word, all right.

She nodded.

"You want me to get you out of it."

"I don't know what I want, Cotton. I want to escape. Take me to Butte, and the railroad."

She was lookin' at me so soft, I almost went for it.

"Onliest way I know of to get out of it is to give back what's been took. There's nothing you can do to bring good men like Aggie Cork back, but there's miners all around here got squeezed out, and you can't escape until you've done what you could. I could put you on a nag and take you to Butte right now, and you could catch a train out, but you wouldn't escape nothing. All that stuff, it'd still be on your shoulders."

She looked so desolate that I thought maybe I'd been meaner than a skunk.

I wasn't inclined to take her away from there and leave the whole mess she caused behind her.

But I relented a little. "You been helpin' Cletus Carboy, and that's something. He still got his mine took from him, and now his mill took from him. Carter Scruples had a snitch here, so Cletus didn't have a chance, even with what you was tellin' him. You want a transaction? I'll make one with you. We got to turn this whole thing around, and get them mines back to their proper owners, the ones still livin', and find some way to stop Scruples cold. You willin'?"

"I was hoping you'd just take me away from here."

"How long have you knowed about what he was up to?"

She stared into the kerosene lamp sadly. "From the beginning. I went along with it until innocent people . . . you know. I wanted money, lots of money."

"You think Scruples knows about you?"

"He knows someone's talking. He knows I'm not happy with any of this. He spends hours talking about contracts and how we've got to meet our contracts and how I agreed to this and that, and he agreed to this and that, and we've got to uphold everything."

That went clear past me, so I got down to the bone of it. "He finds out you're talking, he gonna kill you?"

She stared bleakly at me and finally looked out the window, into the night. "That's why I need to go to Butte and catch a train," she said.

"You think you were followed over here?"

She looked frightened. "I don't know. I come and go as I please."

"I think maybe we had oughta douse that lamp, and you should get away from the window."

"Cotton—do you really think?"

"Carter Scruples is a lot smarter than I am," I said.

I turned down the wick, and the light blued out. "I'm going out for a look. Maybe you should get back into whatever you was wearing."

She began to shuffle around in the dark. Very little starlight drifted in, but that's how I wanted it. I creaked open the door, listened hard, and stepped into the night.

I didn't get far. That thug Arnold, he landed a whack on me that sent me into the manure. I knew it was Arnold. And that meant The Apocalypse was around there somewheres, and things weren't lookin' so good as I tried to get out of the muck.

Chapter Twenty-nine

I rose up mad. That Arnold, he knew all the tricks, but he didn't ever meet a man growed up in the West. He come from someplace I never heard of, New York or somewhere, and I wasn't gonna let him and his tricks take me down. So I went after him like a longhorn bull, all horns. And I was ready for the knee to my groin and the chops at my knees and the whacks to my temple that could knock me senseless.

I just gone after him like a bull moose, whacking back at that punk, and I landed some good ones, too, and got a hand on his arm and twisted it good until he yowled and bit me. I was so steamed up I didn't even feel his whacks. They was just bouncing off me like raindrops. I was so mad that I was kicking and hammering, and he was starting to weaken a little. He was doing stuff I never seen, hooking his leg around to drop me, punching right under my ribs to take the breath out of me, and it didn't make no difference. I was hot, worse'n I ever been before, and I wouldn't take no for an answer. So I was evening up the odds with Arnold at last, and whatever he was landin' on me wasn't doing him any good.

Then I lowered down and thumped into him and sent him sprawling in that cow muck, and I was on him and whacking his face to pulp. I could feel that jaw crack and feel his head bouncing around and I knew I'd finally got the best of Arnold, and high time, too.

Then I heard the click. There's no mistakin' that click. Anyone who's been around some knows the click of a revolver being cocked, and I was hearing that click square in my ear, so I quit working on Arnold to see what was clickin', and it was The Apocalpse, all in black, smiley as he saw me quiet real fast.

"Get off Arnold. Stand up. Once false move and you've bought the ranch."

Bought the ranch, he says. That sounded just like The Apocalypse, always fancying with words. I got up real slow. Arnold, he thumped my kneecap as I did, and I lurched, but a bullet didn't plow into my skull, so I got the rest of the way up.

There was Amanda, pale and afraid, in the moonlight. The Apocalypse was keeping an eye on her.

"Cotton, you're privileged. You get to witness what happens when a contract is broken. You get to see the enforcement of a transaction. An agreement ought to be honored, right? And if it's not, then it needs to be enforced."

I didn't know what the hell he was talking about, but Amanda did, and began shaking. Arnold got up and scraped muck off his tweeds, and grabbed Amanda's arm and led her behind the barn, to a place not visible from the Carboy's darkened ranch house.

Then The Apocalypse pressed his popgun to her ear and shot her. She collapsed into a heap, staring at the night sky.

"A completed transaction," that little killer said. "She was squealing. She was Carboy's snitch. So of course Mr. Scruples was forced to act."

I stared at the woman lying in the dirt, who had found herself and found purpose only a short time before, and I felt bad.

"Carry her to the veranda. She's a gift to Carboy. And don't make any noise or the next shot will go through your own thick skull."

She sure weighed a lot. She was a medium-sized woman, and she weighed about ten tons. I was pretty sure I'd be next. We'd get to the veranda and I'd lower her and then I'd join her. But after I lowered her before Carboy's darkened door, the little killer waved me away. Seemed I'd live a few minutes more anyway. Arnold waited until we got back to the barn and then chopped me one with his balled-up fist, and I tumbled in a heap. Nice fellow, that Arnold. I got up slow, and he cracked my kneecap, and I went down again and stayed down until The Apocalypse told me to get up.

I hurt so much I couldn't think of nothing else, except Amanda.

"Mr. Scruples wishes to entertain you," the natty little killer said. "We'll walk."

So I started limping through the moonlight, which lay white and ghostly over the valley and the town and the hills beyond. Pretty soon we got to the hill with that Pullman Palace Car perched on top, and from there we could see down the slope to the great marsh that gave Swamp Creek its name. It was quiet around there. That enameled railroad car had a lamp in the rear window, the only light shining for miles around there. It looked bright and welcoming, but I knew I wouldn't get no welcome up there, and it might be the last light I'd ever see.

A prod from The Apocalypse sent me up them iron stairs at the rear of the car, and Scruples opened the door. He was in that red satin smoking robe, or whatever they call them things, and his hand was in the pocket where he probably kept a little bit of safety.

"Why, come in, Mr. Cotton," he said.

He eyed us all. "I think I'll ask you to stand, rather than sit," he said. "The furniture might be stained."

He eyed Arnold. "You're a little the worse for wear," he said. "That is something I will take into consideration."

He eyed The Apocalypse. "Perfectly groomed as usual. You may sit."

The little gunslinger settled in a chair, but his hand still had that popgun in it, and that popgun was aimed at my heart.

Scruples turned to The Apocalypse. "Was the transaction completed?"

"Perfectly, Mr. Scruples."

"It's a pity, but people must learn to abide by their agreements." He turned to me. "The poor dear decided not to fulfill her obligations. Just like you," he said.

That didn't set well with me. "I quit you. So what?"

"You welshed on your agreement with us," he said.

I wasn't going to get into this all over again, especially with Amanda lying dead on the porch of Cletus Carboy. So I just shut up and thought of ways to take out Scruples with my last breath if they was thinking of another execution.

"I'm going to give you a new agreement. You will do exactly as I tell you, on your part, and on my part I will let you live, if you conduct yourself as required."

I just kept my big old mouth shut. Some deal.

He smiled. "You're wise to listen carefully. This transaction I am making with you will be renewed at sundown each day, or canceled if you fail to meet your obligations. I'm sure you'd not like to be . . . canceled."

I didn't say nothing. Why bother?

"I'm now in the final phase of completing this transaction," he said. "The entire Swamp Creek District is for sale, being advertised in Eastern papers and financial journals. I have excellent brokers. Within a short time, I believe, we will have a contract. After that, I may or may not retire. It will depend on whim. But I will have approximately a million dollars, give or take some commissions." He stared into the night. "It was well worth the effort, in spite of a few difficulties."

I sure didn't know what this had to do with me.

"Financiers and deep-pockets men are cautious with their funds, and want to know everything there is to know. They want a history of the mines, an estimate of ore remaining, a detailed accounting of the mill and how much refined gold was shipped from the district. They will want titles and deeds and claims. They will check with the territory. They will, in short, examine every possible facet of the business, which of course they should. I'm ready for them. In my safe are deeds and claims, and a few mineral patents. Bills of sale. All that sort of thing. When they send their accountants and lawyers and mining engineers and geologists to look it over, I will be well prepared. It should all go smoothly, save for one thing. I don't know what Cletus Carboy will do, other than lick his wounds. If he entertains visions of getting it all back, or simply plans to be a spoiler, raising questions, spreading gossip and lies, then I will have to deal with it. He's well guarded, of course, and his sudden departure would be embarrassing just at this moment."

He eyed me cheerfully.

"That's where you come in, Cotton. You are going to be my informant. Oh, forgive me, that's too long a word for you. My snitch."

"Doin' what?"

"Extracting information. Every iota of it. What Carboy's up to. His plans. What he wants you to do. Who he is talking to." He eyed me again. "And if you spill the beans, Arnold here will pull your fingernails out, and cut your privates off, and flay the flesh off your body before your contract . . . expires."

Well, that was putting it right on the dotted line, I thought.

He smiled. "Of course, that's up to you. Actually, you're a bit smarter than I'd thought. That gambit with the woodcutters was clever, Cotton. It almost got by me. Shutting down the mine and the mill. Very good. I had to deal harshly with it. My excellent man Rudolph Glan made it clear to all the woodcutters that they had a contract with us, and we wouldn't let them out of the contract. Not now. I don't care what happens after I've sold out. But until then, they're going to cut wood, each day, every day, cord by cord, and bring it into Swamp Creek. And if they don't keep up, they'll . . . shall we say, disappear. Glan is first-rate at making people disappear. They simply vanish from the earth, and are soon forgotten. Wilderness is a marvelous thing, Cotton."

So the sniper would be busy with any woodcutter not producing wood, I thought. You had to hand it to Scruples. He could turn life into a contract you never knew you signed. Sort of a handshake contract.

"Are we clear?" Scruples asked.

"'Bout what?"

"About your duties and your rewards. Oh, yes, the reports. At sundown each day, you will appear in the Miner's Rest Saloon, and if I choose, I will have you report in person. If not, you'll have a word with The Apocalypse—what a fine name, eh? He has a keen mind and will convey to me exactly what you tell him; a daily report on everything—everything. If you should fail to report any single thing, Cotton, our agreement will come to an abrupt end."

"I didn't know I agreed to anything."

He smiled. "You're agreeing right now."

"You sure you want to cut a deal with riffraff?"

"Oh, you've learned a new word, Cotton. You're making progress."

I sort of wanted to strangle the son of a bitch.

"Mr. Apocalypse will show you to the door. Until tomorrow evening then."

That there train car door got opened and I got eased out, and I got to walkin' down that hill wondering what the hell to do with myself, since I wasn't gonna snitch on Cletus Carboy. Maybe I could just get onto Critter and flee the country, start somewhere else, get out before a bullet went in one ear and out the other.

I hardly got to the bottom of the hill, in the quiet of the night, when I knew there was something that needed doin'. I headed back to Carboy's place on the creek below town, wishing I didn't have to do what had to be done. But there wasn't no one else to do it. I knew where a spade was in Carboy's barn, and I knew where I could find an old blanket to wrap her in. There wasn't no one else to bury Amanda proper, so it was up to me. I thought maybe it'd be good to get her off that porch before dawn, and spare Cletus Carboy the sight of her when he got up in the morning or someone else found her.

So I hiked back there, thinkin' how I'd miss Amanda. She'd come around to being a different person, or maybe it was just a way of growin' some, but she was a fine woman by the time her life got taken away. If there was one thing for me to do, after burying her, it would be to get that two-bit murderer and give him back his own medicine. But that was for later. For now, there was just one thing workin' in me, and that was to carry Amanda's body away into the slopes somewhere, and put her to rest proper. It'd be a blanket around her, not wood, but it was the best I could do. It wasn't any job I wanted, but someone needed to do it, and that meant me.

So I walked all the way back there, and got a blanket and some rope, and a spade, and then went to fetch Amanda, dreading every step. Only one thing was wrong with the whole idea. She wasn't there.

Chapter Thirty

I turned away, but a voice stopped me.

"Come in, Cotton."

Carboy was standing in the dark doorway. I slipped in, and discovered he had a revolver in hand. He led me to his dining room and lit a lamp.

Stretched out on the table was Amanda carefully wrapped in a winding sheet.

"She came here to tell me she was looking for a way to leave Scruples," Carboy said. "Then she left. Later, I heard a shot, and lit no lamps, for safety. Then I saw them drop her on my porch and lead you away."

I stared at Amanda.

"We wrapped her in linen, the traditional cloth for a burial sheet," Carboy said. "I happened to have a coverlet. My people washed her carefully and then we wrapped her and tied the sheet tight. When it's light, we'll bury her. I've set aside a family plot, even if there's no one in it now. I planned to stay after the mines were exhausted. This is one of the most beautiful corners of the world, this cheerful valley. It would be a good place for Amanda to lie in eternity."

I couldn't think of nothing to say, not then. All I could think of was Carboy, making this place his home, and Scruples, perched in a railroad car ready to be hauled away the minute he sold out.

"Amanda found me in the bunkhouse," I said, leaving out a few details. "She wanted to go, and she hoped I would help her. I said I would. Then them two, Arnold and the little one with the big name, they come in, beat me, and take her off. They made me watch it, and I guess watching them shoot her is never gonna leave my mind."

"They took you with them?"

"Up there to the railroad car. Scruples himself, well, he laid it out for me." I hesitated a moment and then made my decision. "He offered me a deal. My life if I snitch on you, death if I don't, torture and death if I tell you about it. It wasn't pretty-sounding, talkin' about cutting me up piece by piece."

He stared at me quietly. "You've crossed the bridge."

"Guess I had to."

"I'm the only thing in his way now."

"That's what he said. He said the whole district's up for sale, the brokers have it, and there's been lots of advertising, and he thinks he'll make a fortune real fast. He said the only trouble might come from Doo Diligence, and I thought that was some kind of shooter you'd hired somewhere, but he said it wasn't nothing like that, it was bein' careful."

"Due diligence is the process of making sure a property is up and up," Carboy said. "And if a buyer were to check with me, he might learn some things that Scruples isn't talking about."

"He come after you yet?"

"So far, no. He's got Glan keeping the woodcutters in

line, and the others haven't had much of a chance at me because my own people are alert."

"I wouldn't be so sure he's got Glan on them woodcutters. You're his target."

"That's good advice, Cotton. Thank you."

"Like at the buryin'."

We stared at that wrapped form, so silent and sad. I was wonderin' how we'd even get her into the ground, with Scruples' wolves circling around out there. I wanted Amanda to have a fine funeral, a funeral that said she was a fine lady that come far with her life.

"It'll take my people most of a day to dig the grave," Carboy said. "I was thinking of twilight. That's a fitting time, isn't it?"

"I'm going up after him," I said. "Ain't no other way. There's usually some good spot, some place to shoot from, and I'm going to find it."

"You sure you want to?"

"I never been so sure of anything. And the deal is, I want to get up there now, while it's still dark, and that means leavin' real quick. If your people could put some food together for me, I'd like to head out and start prowlin' and stay out all day, and maybe if Glan shows up, have a little surprise for him."

Carboy nodded. He vanished into a darkened kitchen and returned. "You'll have something in a moment."

"I'm gonna do this on foot, not with Critter. With him around, that'd be like announcing the show. Hope you can have a man hay and water him."

"Consider it done, Cotton."

"Where's the burial plot?" I asked.

He took me to a window opening on the night. "Back

there, at the base of the foothills, maybe a quarter of a mile. It's a fenced half acre."

"Who knows about it?"

"Amanda did. That means Scruples probably does. And if Glan is now stalking me, chances are he does."

"I'll start there."

"Cotton—go with God."

No one ever said stuff like that to me before. I nodded.

That Chinese lady, My Ling, she gave me some grub in a sack, and I slid into the night. I wasn't sure how to get to that burial plot, but I could make out the foothills, and just headed that way through a whispering night with a cool breeze lifting my hair. I made sure Celia Argo's revolver snugged into the holster at my waist. I could handle long guns all right, but felt better with a short one, even if I had to get in closer. Maybe, if me and Glan were both out there, we'd see who was who and what was what.

I respected him. He was a ghost, and a killer, and an ambusher, and I knew he had a lot more experience, and he could easily get the best of me. So I just glided along, making myself aware of the soft noises of the night. When there's trouble in the night, those soft noises disappear, and there's a strange silence, like something waiting, and all the rhythms of nature just shut down. If I had any chance at all with him, it'd be because I wasn't no city feller who didn't know what peaceful night was like. I knew, and now I was counting on that to keep me outta trouble.

So I just pushed away from the creek, heading toward the foothills where Glan would be patiently waiting and watching. I found the cemetery plot all right, or it found me. I ran plumb into the wire. I found the gate and looked it over. There wasn't nothing. The diggers wouldn't even start until daylight. But what I wanted was to see the ridges, and there was just enough of a moon to show them to me. Glan didn't need to get close, not with that fancy artillery of his, so he could be well back and still do his job.

It was a good place, that plot. Carboy was planning to stay there, and begin a family, and this is where they would rest. I studied it close and then headed for the foothills, ghosting along, not really knowing where I was going. I just wanted some height so I could see how the land lay when the sun rose. Maybe this was all just nonsense. Maybe Glan was somewhere else. But I had some sort of feelin' that him and me, we'd meet this day, and someone would get hurt bad. That didn't quiet me any.

So I climbed them hills, and now and then I could see the peaks and ridges of the mountain high country up above, but I wasn't interested in that. I just wanted to find a place overlooking the plot. I finally reached a little flat and realized I was far beyond a rifle shot to the cemetery plot, but it was a good place to hunker down. I dug into the sack and found some boiled eggs and a beef sandwich, which suited me fine. It'd been a long time since I ate, and the stuff tasted real good. That My Ling, she was a talented lady.

Then I sat down and waited for the dawn, which wasn't long coming. I was grateful, since I get bored fast, but pretty soon the sky blued up in the east and I could start makin' out things off a way. There hardly was light on the land when I saw a pair of grave diggers set to work down there, cutting through the sod with a spade and then digging down. It takes a heap of work to dig a grave, and if a rock stops you, then you either got to bust it up with a pike or start over. But they took turns, and pretty soon were down a couple feet. By the time the sun took hold and lit the valley, they were knee-high in that hole.

I took to studying the country, but I didn't see nothing. Glan, he had himself a good spyglass and could see some ant crawling over a rock a hundred yards away, but I didn't have nothing. I did quietly move to an aspen grove where I'd be concealed, and settled there in the middle of a lot of sticks. Them aspen drop leaves and sticks all over, real sloppy. But it was a good place, and I was down in deep shadow but could look out and around, checking for movement in most every direction.

But I'm not patient, and I itched to get my legs moving. It was a battle between my itchy legs and my mind, telling me to stay quiet. At least I could see them grave diggers at work, and about the time they got down to their chests, they quit. It wasn't even noon yet, but immediately there was a procession coming out from Carboy's place, and they carried Amanda's wrapped body on a handcart. They was going to do her real quick, which seemed a good idea, and soon they was all gathered at that fresh grave, and Carboy was standing at the head, fixing to read something or other down there.

I looked around sharp, and didn't see anything, and thought it'd go well enough. I checked the ridges above me, and there wasn't nothing, and no crows flapping around or magpies jabbering like they were disturbed, so I thought it'd be pretty good, and they'd get Amanda proper buried.

But then I glanced off to one side, and halfway down the slope was Glan behind a big old log, where no one would look for him, and he was fixing to shoot that long rifle. There wasn't no time at all, and I was out of good range for a revolver. Glan was lying easy on the ground, that rifle resting on an old log, taking his time.

I reckoned it was an awful long shot for a revolver, but I couldn't get closer in time. Down below, they were slowly lowering Amanda into that grave, and Carboy was standing at the head, waiting for them to put her into her last resting place. But that didn't matter now; all that mattered was me stopping Glan from assassinating Cletus Carboy. I found a dead aspen log and laid my revolver barrel over it to make a rest, and sighted down it, and raised it some because I knew that lead pill was going to drop a lot at that distance, so I aimed a foot or so above Glan, and squeezed. The revolver went off, and not much happened far as I could see. Glan heard it, though, and turned around, swinging that long barrel at me. He spotted me all right, just as I tried again, a little lower this time, right at his head. I felt it buck in my hand, and this time I hit him good. He flipped up and settled down, looking surprised, and then he got a shot off at me. I tried again, and nicked him in the shoulder, but he'd taken the measure of me and fired that Sharps of his, and that big chunk of lead lifted my slouch hat clear off my head.

I'd fired three and had two more and a blank chamber, so I tried again. This time I missed, or at least didn't see him move. The shots rolled on down to the funeral party, and now they was scrambling for cover behind that cart or wherever, and there was a couple of Carboy's men coming fast toward us, revolvers out.

Glan didn't fire and I rested that barrel on the log and aimed a little high, and squeezed, and felt it buck, and Glan took it somewhere. I don't know where. His arms flailed out, and he dropped that rifle and lay on the grass dying slow and hard. I opened the cylinder and dropped the brass and reloaded from belt loops and shut her up again and waited some. But Glan was lying flat on his back, studying the midday sky. So I stood slow and waved at them two men of Carboy's and they waved back, and we all reached Glan about the same time.

Glan had three holes in him, but my bullets had gone so far they hardly done damage. It was the last one, right into his teeth, that did him.

"Let's get Amanda buried proper," I said.

the territory here now and then on business. It was plain that Scruples' brokers had lured him to take a look.

Next I knew, that bunch of bigwigs had toured the valley, stopping at each property, where the geologist took ore samples and looked over the mine. They were being real thorough, and took a long look at Aggie Cork's old mine as well as Bob Brass's Lola Montez Tunnel Mine and all the rest, all the while guarded real good by Scruples' thugs. I seen old Lugar sort of commanding the whole lot of them. There was a lot of firepower riding along with them buyers.

I couldn't do nothing about anything, and neither could Carboy. Scruples pretty much owned the town of Swamp Creek, and the whole district, and controlled a lot of the people around there. You couldn't even get near that hotel without facing a few thugs ready to say no.

I decided late one afternoon to go see Celia, since it'd been a while. So I did my usual routine of comin' around behind, crossing the creek, and climbing her stairway, making sure no one saw me. I knocked, and she asked who it was.

"Me," I said.

"Alone?"

"Yep."

She opened a crack and studied me, and then let me in. She had that little lady revolver in hand.

"Town's full of crooks," she said.

"Ain't that the truth."

She was looking a little drawn, like she hadn't been out for a while. She led me into the parlor, but didn't put down that revolver.

"I'm glad you came," she said. "Cotton, I'm in trouble."

"What kind of trouble?"

"Those people looking to buy up the district, they asked if they could talk to me about the Fat Tuesday, and why Armand sold it to Scruples. If they'd come by, I would have told them that Armand was killed and the mine was stolen and belongs to me. So, well, you can imagine. I've had those thugs standing around this building. You know what would happen if I went out? I'd be kidnapped and killed somewhere. If one of those buyers came calling, there'd be big trouble. I don't know what, but I probably wouldn't live through it. So I stay here, keep my door barred, and keep this revolver ready. I'd shoot anyone who tried to push in, and I'd keep right on shooting, too."

"Looks like a word from you could blow Scruples' deal."

"A word from me, or a word from your friend Carboy."

"And they've got you penned up in here, short of killing you, and they've got Carboy penned up at his house."

"But they're going to find out, sooner or later. Someone's going to tell those buyers all about Swamp Creek."

"Some of those toughs decide to bust in here and silence you, Celia, there's no stopping them with that five-shot revolver."

"I told you I'm in trouble," she said, some irritation in her voice. "I don't dare leave here. I've been here three days without going out. My, well, chamber pot's full, and I'm running out of food, and I'm real glad you came."

"This ain't good," I said. I slipped aside a drape a little so I could look out of one of them upstairs windows.

"There's always a man watching here," she said.

I couldn't pick one out, but that didn't mean nothing. A man could be over to Ma's Dining across the street, keeping an eye peeled.

Scruples had her boxed in here. He had Carboy boxed

in to his house. He simply wanted them out of sight and out of the way while he did his deal. Carboy had some mine guards protecting him. It was enough to keep the crooks out of his house, but he couldn't go nowhere, and neither could Celia. The town belonged to Scruples now, and he had snitches posted in every saloon and probably the livery barn, too. You want to know everything going on, you pay a snitch in the livery barn.

But Celia was flat in trouble. She was down to a few pinto beans, and the flat was getting pretty rank.

"We're gettin' out and I'm takin' you to Carboy's place," I said.

We had to wait until it was dark, which took a while, but she packed up some spare clothing and when it was dark enough, I slid out first and looked around. It looked peaceful enough, except a lot of lamps was burning over in the hotel, and them buyers was floating in and out, past some of the thugs standin' around on the street. That was fine with me; it kept people lookin' that direction.

"All right, Celia, let's vamoose."

We slid out of there, down them rear stairs, and waded across the creek. She was game, and didn't mind getting her skirts wet, but pretty quick I got her into the scrub trees, untied Critter, put her on the horse, who thanked me with a nip on the arm, and then I led her out of there real quiet. There was something of a moon to help us, but also reveal us, so I hugged the moon shadow and we made our way down to Carboy's.

"I guess you'll stay in the bunkhouse with me," I said.

She laughed suddenly. "I knew you'd find a way," she said, and I got all heated in the face, and was glad she couldn't see it.

"Carboy's got two mine guards at his house, and

there's some groundsmen in cottages around here, all armed. He don't have a bunch of killers. That's not his way. But at least he can defend himself. I'm sayin' this because you could stay up to the big house if you want."

She sighed. "I just don't understand you, Cotton. First you capture me and take me to your lair, and then you want to pass me along to someone else. What's a lady to think? Don't you like me?"

Danged if I could figure myself out. I thought I was being real proper, but I should of knowed Celia wasn't a proper woman. She was a gambler's widow, and that's a breed unto itself. Truth is, sometimes I'm dumb as a stump.

"Guess we'd better let Carboy know you're around here," I said, diggin' my grave deeper.

She sure eyed me like she'd been rescued by the village idiot. But then she nodded, and we made our way across the moonlit lawn. There was lamps lit in the big house, but the drapes was drawn so no one could see nothing. We got to the porch and a voice told us to wait, so we waited, and pretty soon Carboy came and invited us in.

It sure was a nice house in there.

"How about some tea, Cotton?" he asked. "And you, Mrs. Argo?"

I can mostly hardly swaller the stuff but I gave it another try.

While we was waiting for the tea to be fermented, I told him that I'd rescued Celia. She was boxed in to her rooms, pretty much like everyone around here was boxed in, because Scruples had a mess of shooters loose in town.

Carboy poured that tea when it arrived in a pot made of some dishwatery blue he called Wedgwood, and handed it out. I imagined if I tried hard enough I could get her down, all right.

"Actually, all of Scruples' sales efforts came to nothing," Carboy said. "Oh, I still have a few informants in town, and they get the news out to me. Marcus and his people will be leaving in the morning, and there's little chance of a sale. He told a few people he doesn't like the smell of it. He senses something's quite wrong, even if he never talked to Celia about the Fat Tuesday, or me about the Big Mother Mine. You have to give Marcus credit, you know. He's got a good nose and he uses it."

"They're leavin'?"

"Tomorrow. The Swamp Creek mines remain in Scruples' hands."

"You know what happened? Why they're not gonna buy?"

"Marcus's geologist, Sam Pike, wandered into the Mint for a drink and got to talking with the barkeep there, Billy Blew, and got an earful. Before he had one red-eye down him, Pike learned about how Scruples got the Fat Tuesday, and before he finished another red-eye he got the story of how most of the independent miners vanished or were killed, and how Scruples got Johnny Brashear's papers, including all the blank forms. That's all it took."

"I could go back to town then," Celia said.

"I'd advise against it, Mrs. Argo. There's something you should know. Billy Blew was dragged into the alley behind the Mint and killed."

That sure slapped me harder than a bullwhip. Not Billy. Just for telling the truth. My friend Billy Blew messed up Scruples' deal and paid the price for it. This valley sure had a lot of grief in it. I knew at once who done it: The Apocalypse.

"Oh," Celia said, growing real silent.

"You're welcome here. I've a spare bedroom you may occupy. I think your life would be in grave danger just now, and Swamp Creek is no place for you. You simply know too much. Just as I know too much. There's not much we can do against an army of killers, except lay low for the moment. Our moment will come. I've not been idle, I assure you."

I sipped some of that tea, which tasted like swamp water, and eyed Celia, who was hesitatin', not because she worried about danger, but because she'd be stuck in the big house with Carboy, and living real proper, instead of having her way with me in the bunkhouse.

But then she surrendered. "All right," she said. "I guess you know what's what."

I guess I'm about the unluckiest man ever lived, I thought, knowin' where she'd be staying. But I was a piece luckier than Billy Blew.

Chapter Thirty-two

I took to having a beer at the Miners Exchange now that the Mint was shut down. I sure missed Billy Blew, but Muggsy Pitt at the Exchange was a good barkeep, too. I knew I still had a bull's-eye painted to my chest, and any of Scruples' thugs might try me some time, but I didn't much care. I wasn't gonna let them scare me off.

So I bought my nightly mug of beer from Muggsy and listened to the talk of all them hard-rock miners, good men who worked hard for their wage and liked a shot or a mug at the end of the shift. With the Mint boarded up, the prospectors and independent men, the few left in Swamp Creek, came in, too, and the Exchange was usually full up.

Once in a while, one of them Scruples men came in, Lugar once, and some of them other thugs, and I was ready for trouble, but trouble never came. They'd look me over and buy a drink and suck beer at their own table, and leave. Maybe Scruples was just wanting to keep an eye on me since I was the only one left around there who could maybe give him some trouble.

Swamp Creek looked the same, but it seemed to be

waiting for something. The miners still came up at the end of the shift and went down at the start, and still drifted to their cabins after a boilermaker or two, and the mill kept stamping ore, and the woodcutters still drove in with cordwood, but it was different. It was like life had quit moving forward. Over at Carboy's place out of town, Celia and Carboy were safe enough, with guards keeping an eye on things, but nothing much was happening there neither. Scruples won. He owned Swamp Creek, the mines and mill and all the rest. And he would sit on it until he got himself a buyer.

Then one day, a stranger rode in on a chestnut saddle horse, a fine-lookin' animal. And the stranger was no stranger to money, anyone could see that. He wore a gray woolen suit of clothes, with a starched white shirt and black bow tie, and shined-up black boots, and a pearl-gray wide-brimmed hat. He looked like a prosperous businessman, maybe in his forties or early fifties, just a bit of gray beginning. He had him a square face, with a lot of jaw, and observant gray eyes.

Anyway, he came into the Miners Exchange, and ordered a whiskey neat from Muggsy, and that sort of interested everyone. There wasn't another man with a suit in there. Everyone wore working duds, not fancy clothing, but there was this stranger, sipping red-eye, observing the rest of us openly. We sure were curious about him, but he seemed just to be passing by, and after a drink or two he'd mount up and ride that fancy chestnut away somewheres and we'd never see him again. The West was like that. Lots of people coming through, minding their own business.

Only something was different.

He finished his drink and waited a while, and when

the whistle blew over at the mine, he sort of perked up, and when the crowd off shift come tumbling in and ordering up their brews and shots, he studied them all. I sure was curious, but it wasn't no business of mine, so I just kept an eye out. Once or twice, the stranger eyed me, noting the revolver that I'd gotten from Celia, and then his eyes glanced elsewhere, like he was making notes on just about everyone in the whole saloon.

Then, when the whole off-shift bunch got settled into some serious drinkin', he leaned over to Muggsy and asked if the barkeep would quiet the place for a minute.

So Muggsy, he rapped a spoon against a bottle and pretty soon got the whole Exchange to quiet.

"This here stranger wants to say something," Muggsy said. "So I'll give him thirty seconds."

The stranger set down his shot glass and eyed the silent miners.

"I'm Mike Gilligan from the Four Leaf Clover over at Suicide Gulch. We've hit it big. We've got two exploration shafts started and a mill's arrived on wagons. There's claims being filed daily. The quartz ore's assaying at five hundred a ton. I just hired your woodcutters at two-fifty a day, and I'd like to hire all of you at three a day. We've got a tent city going up, and we'll have lots and cabins for miners going up by the time you arrive. The sooner you get there, the better your chances of getting a good lot. Any questions?"

It took no more than thirty seconds, all right. Gilligan, he dropped a few chunks of that quartz ore on the bar, and anyone could see gold threading through it. Them miners took one look and passed it along.

Suicide Gulch lay about ten miles south, up in a hanging valley. It'd been around for a few years, not doing much, a few halfway profitable little digs, and a store or two. But now they'd hit bonanza gold, and wanted men to work it, and that's why Gilligan was here. Now there'd be a rush, and Swamp Creek would empty out in a day or two. Even the storekeepers would pull up stakes, head for the new camp, and leave Swamp Creek rotting away like it was yesterday, not tomorrow.

The miners did have a question or two.

"You got two shafts going?"

"We do. There are two quartz seams, and it's easiest to get at them with two. We've got woodcutters bringing us timber."

"Three dollars is one more than we're getting here."

"You're worth it to us."

"Who's us?"

"The partners who own the Four Leaf Clover."

"You hiring only Irish?"

Gilligan smiled. "If you're lucky," he said.

There was a deal more of that, and I listened real hard. Then I slipped out, got on Critter, and rode out to Carboy with the news.

Him and Celia were sittin' in the parlor there when the guard let me in.

"There's a rush over to Suicide Gulch. Man named Gilligan come in to the Miners Exchange and hired pretty near the whole town of Swamp Creek," I said.

"Good. We need the men," Carboy said.

"Now just a minute here, say that again."

"I'm one of the partners at the Four Leaf Clover."

This here was getting over my head real fast.

Celia, she just smiled really pretty.

"As you now know, I've been busy, even if Scruples

has me cooped up here," Carboy said. "Everything's going according to plan."

It sure took me some to get that figured out. "You got a piece of that mine?"

"I have investments in many places."

"You gonna move to Suicide Gulch?"

"This is a beautiful valley, Cotton. I've made it home, and soon we'll have the Big Mother mine producing again. And that railroad car and its occupant will vanish. Now, tomorrow I'd like you to spend time in Swamp Creek and report to me what's happening."

"I'll do her," I said.

Like I was asked, I drifted on in to Swamp Creek in the morning, and sure enough there was a rush. People was packing up, loading wagons and mules, and heading for Suicide Gulch. I watched Arnold try to bully them miners into staying, but it didn't make no sense to crack heads, bust kneecaps, and break the fingers of the work force, so pretty soon no one paid him attention, or bothered with The Apocalypse, who was hovering around there looking real dangerous but not killing anyone at the moment. Them miners was heading for better pay, along with the woodcutters and some of the town's merchants. I saw a whole wagonload of scarlet women in furs and feathers take off for the new digs, and then a wagon of pimps following along.

Of course, not everyone was ditching Swamp Creek. There was them merchants that figured the mines in town were still full of ore and things would settle down pretty quick. The livery barn hostler was staying put, and so was the town blacksmith, at least for now. But some of the saloons looked like they was folding, including the Ponderosa House. Swamp Creek was sure slimming down to a quarter of what it had been, and was getting real quiet.

And the whole bunch was headed for what was mostly a tent town, but would quick enough throw up buildings. Suicide Gulch was in a hanging valley higher up, and it was sheer suicide to drive a wagon up that last hundred-yard grade, which is how it got its handle. It was nothing more than a huddle of log buildings until now, but that would change real fast.

I was about to head back to Carboy and tell him that Swamp Creek had mostly died away that morning, but then I watched a black carriage pulled by trotters come rolling into town from up the creek, and it was surrounded by some tough customers. Sure enough, it was Carter Scruples in there, having a look for himself. He had three or four toughs on either side of him, and I recognized Lugar and them thugs who called themselves Arthur and Cleveland and Garfield, and some others I hadn't seen, but with a pair of revolvers on their hips.

I just stood there watching. I had six bullets before they'd completely cut me down, but the first two was reserved for Scruples himself. They saw me, all right, but a word from Scruples was enough so they didn't try anything, just stared at me. He was out looking at the damage, the closed-down gin mills, the shut-down mine and mill, and deserted town. He wanted to see it for himself, and shooting me wasn't on his list of things needed doing just then.

So I leaned against a post on the boardwalk and watched his slow progress.

But then Lugar came trotting over.

"He says to tell you he's not forgotten you," Lugar said. "And that isn't healthy."

"What's he doing?" I asked.

"Counting empty buildings. He's gonna take title to about fifty for free, and that makes his deal all the better. He's got two big mines full of ore, a mill, and twenty or so small mines in the district. With the buildings, he's got a deal no one can refuse."

"What happened to that buyer?"

"As if you didn't know," Lugar said.

"He got any others?"

"His brokers are looking at prospects all the time. There'll be several parties arriving here any day now."

"What's he want for the whole district?"

"Whatever the traffic will bear. He's holding out for one million even."

"What's he going to do if it don't sell?"

Lugar smiled. "We're on our way to Suicide Gulch."

"Take that one over, too. How you gonna get that Pullman Palace Car up Suicide Gulch?"

"Don't ask me. But he's going to do it."

"What happens here when Scruples pulls out?"

"It'll be sold before he pulls out. But his assistants, meaning us, will be getting ourselves into business in Suicide Gulch."

"That's mighty interestin'," I allowed.

Lugar smiled. "He ain't forgot that you ditched him and broke your contract."

"I ain't forgot it either," I said. "Tell him I'm remembering it just about once an hour, sometimes on the half hour."

Lugar glared at me and stalked off. As for me, I got what I was looking for, a handle on Scruples' plans, so I headed down the valley for Carboy's place. I'd give him a mouthful.

Pretty quick, I told him and Celia everything I found out in Swamp Creek, which was a whole lot.

"I guess I can go back to my rooms now," Celia said.

"I think you'd better stay here a while more, Mrs. Argo," Carboy said. "The danger's not past by any means. There's another buyer coming any day now, and Carter Scruples will not want that buyer to make any contact with you—or me."

"You seem to know all about him," I said.

"I do. And he's on his way. And he's coming at my invitation."

"I sure don't get what you're up to, Mr. Carboy."

"You'll see soon enough. I can tell you this much. The buyer is the biggest name in mining. A name to remember. It's Beal Z. Burt, who has made half a dozen fortunes in California, Nevada, Arizona Territory, and here. I assure you, B. Z. Burt is a man to reckon with, a man who's never bought a bad mining property. And I can also assure you that Carter Scruples will go to any length at all—anything—to keep B. Z. Burt from talking to you or to me. You'll never forget that name."

Chapter Thirty-three

Swamp Creek sure was quiet. The mercantile was still open, and the grocer, but they was plainly waiting to see whether the mines would get sold and reopened quick. There was maybe fifty people left, and not even the Miners Exchange was doing much trade. But there was a lot of good ore in them big mines, and the whole place could come back with a roar.

I never saw Carter Scruples. He was sulking up in his Pullman Palace Car on the hill. He'd sent all his thugs to Suicide Gulch to see what kind of trouble they could start, but he kept that big galoot Arnold around Swamp Creek, and once I got a glimpse of The Apocalypse sniffing around town, lookin' for someone to kill.

Cletus Carboy kept me on at his place, saying he needed me for the safety of himself and Celia Argo, which he did because two of his mine guards quit and went off to Suicide Gulch looking for better pay or maybe more excitement. So I was the main feller to fend off Scruples' assassins and thugs around there, and I done the best job I could. I got a good chance to visit with Celia, and I think she was enjoyin' it. I sure was enjoyin' seeing her all the time around there. But Carboy was right. It wasn't a good time for her to go back to her rooms in town.

He still had some groundsmen around for that big place, but they wasn't very handy with a short gun, and even less with a long one, so I was it. I toured Swamp Creek real often, picked up what I could be way of gossip, most of it from Muggsy Pitt. But the stark truth was that nothing was happening.

Until one afternoon, Carboy had a guest. A big homely feller in a dark suit that was cut awkward, like it didn't belong on him. He had some sort of briefcase with him, and a couple of leather bags. He'd rented a carriage and a pair of trotters in Butte and had driven himself down to visit Carboy. This feller looked me over like a preacher would, seeking out ever' sin I ever done, which was more than I could remember at once, and then Carboy made the introduction.

"Cotton, this is my friend B.Z. Burt," he said.

B.Z. Burt! The biggest mining man in the West! And visiting Carboy before he even went off to see about Scruples' offerings.

"Pleased to meet ya, Mr. Burt."

We shook hands.

"It's the Reverend Mr. Burt," said Carboy.

"A preacher?"

Burt shrugged. "Theology is the true road to making a fortune."

"Well, you some hellfire and damnation man?"

"Oh, no, Mr. Cotton. I belong to the Church of Self-Aggrandizement."

Big words again. Damned if I knew what he was talkin' about.

"Never heard of that one," I said.

"The Church of Make a Buck Fast," Burt said.

"Well, there's one I could belong to," I allowed. "You come to town to look at some mines?"

"Specifically, to see about buying the Swamp Creek Mining District from Mr. Scruples."

"And Carboy here, he don't mind?"

"Why should he mind?"

"Because Scruples euchred him outa his mine and mill."

"I invited him to come over from Nevada," Carboy said.

"This is getting way over my head," I said. "Maybe I'll go back to ranch work."

Burt glanced at Carboy. "Shall I divulge?"

"He's more or less reliable," Carboy said, nodding at me.

"Are you more or less honest?" Burt asked me.

"I got a saloon trick, and I've cheated a few pals into buying me drinks," I said.

"You'll do," Burt said. "I don't trust hundred-percenters."

He opened up that briefcase and extracted some documents and handed them to me. I sure couldn't make them out, even though I got half through sixth grade.

He saw me running a finger along each word and trying to mouth it, and decided to help me.

"These are letters of credit on San Francisco and Carson City banking houses," he said. "They total a million dollars and lack only my signature. If I sign them, they will pay for the Swamp Creek Mining District."

"Ah," I said.

"But of course I shall want something in return, the valid claims and mining patents and deeds to the

properties I am acquiring," he said. "In short, Carter
Scruples will supply me with the necessary papers of
ownership."

"Ah," I said.

"Even though his claims and deeds are either forgeries or actual claims obtained by nefarious means."

"Them is crooked claims all right," I said.

"And so are these letters of credit."

"Ah," I said. "Arrgh. Garumph."

Celia, she was sort of smirky sitting there. Me, I just
stared at B.Z. Burt like he come from under a rock.

He took his letters of credit and stuffed them back
into that leather briefcase.

"Time's a-wasting," he said. "There is one small favor
to ask of you, Mr. Cotton. Just in case, I'd be grateful if
you'd shadow me and if need be, protect me if something
should not be quite right. I'm heading for the Miners
Exchange in a bit."

"I'll do her," I said.

"But be invisible."

"There's only a few hoot owls protecting Scruples," I
said. "A heavyweight nutcracker named Arnold and a
rotten little killer named The Apocalypse, and his head-
man, Lugar."

"Quaint," said Burt.

He shook hands all around and then returned to his
carriage. We stood on the veranda and watched the reverend drive off, the trotters picking up a smart pace as
he headed into Swamp Creek.

"This should do it," Carboy said. "I'll burn Scruples'
forgeries, recover the valid claims and deeds, and
try to return them to their owners." He eyed Celia.
"Such as you."

"He still got them hooligans," I said. "And he can get the rest back from Suicide Gulch."

"We're thinking he'll just leave town when he gets those letters of credit."

I was feelin' itchy. "We'll see," I said.

Carter Scruples was usually a jump or two ahead of everyone else. Take that B. Z. Burt. Was that the real B. Z. Burt, or just some fake? I didn't know, but Carboy seemed to think it would all work out real good.

"Is that the real Beal Z. Burt? Seems to me he'd come in with half a dozen mining experts, not alone like that."

"Burt is known as a loner," Carboy said. "And Scruples knows it."

I waited a while more, and then went to the pen and curried Critter, who kicked me in the knee by way of thankin' me for feeding him every night. I got him saddled up, even if his ears was laid back flat, and then rode him toward Swamp Creek. My thinkin' was to look like I was just going to down a couple of beers at Muggsy's saloon, while I kept a watch on things.

I seen Burt's carriage and trotters at the Mountain House, so I knew the tycoon was getting himself settled before going on out to see Scruples. There was hardly anyone in Muggsy's place, it being before the serious drinkin' got going, and also there wasn't so many people in town any more. But he served me up a glass of foam and I was feeling a little angry at that, but he just shrugged.

"It's the last in that barrel," he said. "Hard to get any beer outa Butte. All the beer wagons are going to Suicide Gulch."

"I'll want about three of these for my dime," I said.

It sure was lonely in there, with just one lamp lit to

save kerosene, and Muggsy polishing glass and staring into space. I downed the suds and he refilled with more foam, and it looked like I was gonna have bubbles for booze that evening. But I was stationed in Swamp Creek, like Burt wanted, and ready for anything.

The first thing that happened was Carter Scruples walking right in there, staring at me a moment, and then settling at a table at the rear. He lit the lamp back there and seemed to be waiting for someone. Then Arnold, he come in, looks me over, and stations himself about three feet down the bar rail from me. He didn't look ornery, which was good, because he could pound the crap out of me. I guess he was just lookin' after his boss, parked now at that green-topped poker table back there. I glanced at Scruples, and saw he was pulling papers out of his briefcase, one after another, and soon had them in a neat pile. There was sure a mess of papers, with more words on them than I could ever read in two lifetimes.

I nodded at Muggsy, who filled my glass with foam again.

"This is it, you got your dime's worth," he said.

Arnold, he eyed my foam and ordered some red-eye. Then he lifted it, saluted me with a sort of evil smile on his battered mug, and downed her neat. It made me wonder where The Apocalypse was, but I thought I knew: outside, keepin' watch. And Lugar was back at the railroad car, guardin' the place.

Scruples didn't order nothing, but just sat there waiting for life to improve. He wasn't used to waiting, and once he got up and paced around the saloon, lookin' it over since he never been in there. He'd hardly gotten out of his railroad car up on the hill the whole time he'd spent in Swamp Creek.

I shoulda known what would come next, but it surprised me even so. In walked B.Z. Burt, also carrying a briefcase. He didn't pay no attention to me, except to glance my way and study Arnold for a moment, and then headed back there to shake a paw with Scruples, who suddenly was all smiles.

I strained to listen, but they wasn't exactly shouting. I could get the gist of it. Burt was telling Scruples that he'd looked over the district on his own, gotten out to every mine in the area, taken samples, killed a few rattlers, and looked over the tailings piles, which were always a sign of how the mine was doin'.

Scruples, on his part, was tellin' Burt how the two big mines produced three quarters of the gold in the district, and the independents had brought their ore into town for custom milling. He said he'd gradually bought out all them independents—he shoulda said shot out all them independents—and now had title to claims and federal patents, them that had come through.

They talked some, and asked for some red-eye, and Muggsy poured a couple and took the glasses back, and left the bottle on the table back there. Muggsy knew what he was doing, all right.

"Where are your most recent assay reports?" Burt asked.

"Assay?" The question had plainly caught Scruples off guard.

"You don't expect to sell me mines without multiple assays on each property, do you?" Burt asked.

Scruples coughed and hemmed and hawed around. He didn't know an assay report from a pickax. He was in to make a killing, not to do any mining.

"I couldn't think of purchasing the properties without

comprehensive assays," Burt said. "I need to know what I'm buying. We'll just have to wait for these. How soon can they be done? I imagine the samples will need to go to Butte."

"Ah, Mr. Burt, we've neglected to provide them. However, in the larger mines, the assays will be on file. I can send a man to the Fat Tuesday and the Big Mother, and you'll have reports that will be no more than a few weeks old," Scruples said.

It sure looked to me like old Burt had Scruples on the ropes.

Burt thought about it. "Sure, send a man. I'm not going to sit around here for a fortnight waiting for reports from all the mines, I assure you. I've other fish to fry. I'm surprised you haven't included assays in your papers here."

"Just an oversight, sir. If you don't mind, I'll find one of my staff and send him over to the mines. We should be ready to talk turkey in just a little while."

Burt shrugged. "Hard to make a deal on old assays for only two mines. What about the smaller ones?"

"Those were acquired for future exploration," Scruples said.

"Future?"

"Those were mostly one- or two-man operations, sir, glory holes. Some were mining gold from ledges and pockets. The two big mines and the mill are the important properties, and the ones I've decided to sell now that Swamp Creek has been half abandoned by the rush to Suicide Gulch. There's a future here, of course, good mines and a good mill, but I'm inclined to move on. I'm a restless man, Mr. Burt. You probably knew that the moment you saw my home, a Pullman car, fitted out nicely but ready to drag back to the rails and another life. Yes, I do believe I would welcome a reasonable offer, even knowing that the outlying small mines may or may not yield what you'd hope."

Sounded to me like old Scruples was backing off a little. He rose, headed out the door, and returned a moment later. "I've instructed my security man to pull the assay reports from the offices; he'll be back in a few minutes," Scruples said. "That should satisfy your wish to know whatever there is to know."

"Yes, yes," Burt said. "And how did you acquire all these properties?"

"Oh, various ways. Put an offer on the table. Acquired some from the estate of the deceased owner." Scruples was just warming up, I could tell. "But Mr. Burt, my friend, my particular gift is to discover legal and technical flaws in the claims and patents. That's something I'm sure you well know, with your own successes. Some of these properties were simply there for the plucking because of carelessly wrought claims, bad descriptions, sloppy work all around. You take Augustus Heintze up in Butte, a man who's making a fortune exploiting poorly done claims, and you can see how I've approached the whole business."

"You don't say?" Burt said, in a way that sort of gutted Scruples and hung him out to dry.

Burt hung some spectacles on his nose and studied the papers, while Scruples simply sat and waited. Burt took his time, looking at them one by one, sometimes asking a question or two.

"The district secretary named Brashear signed some of these, and you signed others," Burt said.

"The district secretary left under a cloud, and since I owned the majority of mines in the district, I elected myself the secretary of the Swamp Creek Mining District. Hence, my name's on some of the claims."

Burt seemed to absorb that for a long time. "I see," he said, and once again, I got the feeling old Scruples was twisting in the wind.

Eventually, the double doors opened and The Apocalypse came trotting in, his two popguns bobbing. He dropped some files on the green felt.

"Thank you, my good man," Scruples said. "Please wait outside."

The Apocalypse eyed me sitting there, and I knew he itched to perforate me, but he resisted, and stepped into the night.

I sipped more red-eye that Muggsy had conveniently provided, while Arnold sipped his own, looking more and more cheerful.

"Good values here, but these are dated," Burt said. "The assays for the Fat Tuesday are six months old. But eighty dollars a ton is a good ore."

"Well, yes, in the rush, we didn't get new assays, I'm afraid."

Burt sighed. "I can't buy a mining district blind, Mr. Scruples. Maybe some other time, eh?"

It sure was a fish-or-cut-bait moment, and old Scruples, he decided to fish.

Chapter Thirty-four

There was only Arnold and me, parked at that gloomy bar of the Miners Exchange, and Muggsy Pitt, wiping glass that didn't need wiping, and them two mining tycoons sitting back there in the yeller glow of a kerosene lamp. They had papers spread all over that green poker table, and was doing a deal so big I couldn't count that high on all ten fingers.

Burt, he just sort of sighed. "Can't buy a pig in a poke," he said.

Scruples, he was looking tense as a telegraph wire, and rapping his fingers on the felt like he was doing a drum roll.

"There'll be other people coming along," Scruples said.

"Who?"

Burt was saying that if the biggest mining man in the West wasn't gonna bite, there sure wasn't much of a line waiting to buy.

I sipped red-eye, and Arnold, he just stared. He was like a spring-wound doll. Pinch his nose and he'd fight.

"Maybe I can adjust for risk," Scruples said.

"I'm listening."

"I should've kept the assays current. Butte's a long way away, and it escaped me. I've had labor trouble ever since this town emptied out for Suicide Gulch, so I wasn't paying attention."

"No, you weren't. I suppose I'll head for Butte then. Thank you for the opportunity to look the district over."

Burt, he unfolded and reached for his coat.

"I can reduce the price some. That lowers the risk," Scruples said.

It was something, seeing Scruples sweaty and itchy. He was always so commanding in his Pullman Palace Car. Me, I just sipped red-eye and listened.

"Seven hundred thousand?"

"No."

"Six hundred thousand?"

"No."

Burt, he just picked up his briefcase and turned to go.

"Half?"

Burt stopped. "Five hundred thousand, the entire district free and clear, no obligations or impediments to clear title? No contested claims?"

"Five hundred thousand cash, not credit. Cash on the barrelhead," Scruples said. "At a million, I'd see things a little differently. Exchange stock, things like that. But cutting this deep, I'd want cold cash."

Burt stared into the gloom a moment, and then thrust out a hand. Scruples shook it. They returned to the green poker table.

Burt dug into his portfolio and pulled out some onion-skin papers, fancy-lookin' stuff.

"Before I came, I had several San Francisco and Nevada banks supply me with letters of credit or bearer notes. Each is worth a hundred thousand when signed, witnessed, and dated. These are drafts on the California Union Bank, the Merchants and Farmers Bank, the Miners Exchange Bank of Carson City, the Golden Gate Savings Society, and the Virginia City Savings and Loan. Most of these are two-hundred-thousand-dollar notes, but some are hundred-thousand-dollar notes. Have you a preference?"

Burt handed the notes to Scruples, who read them. I swore, old Scruples' hands, they was shaking a little.

"Ah, I'm headed for Nevada, so let's see about these Nevada banks."

Scruples read the notes, selected two of the two-hundred-thousand, and one one-hundred-thousand.

"I guess these will do," he said.

Burt, he turned to Muggsy.

"Mr. Pitt, your name is, I believe? Would you witness?"

Muggsy, he wiped his hands on his grimy apron and headed for that table. Burt had produced a nib pen and ink, and quietly signed and dated the letters of credit.

"Now, sir, witness here," he said.

Muggsy signed, wiping his hand frequently.

Burt collected the signed notes and handed them to Scruples. "There you are. Best of success to you," he said.

"And to you," Scruples said. They shook on it.

Burt, he scooped up all them claims and titles and stuff and slid them into his portfolio, along with the notes he didn't need to use.

So Scruples made a clean half million out of his bunch of killing and hammering and cheating. It sure looked good to me. He left first, along with Arnold, and I raised a hand to slow down Burt, just in case there was real mean trouble lurking out there. Burt, he nodded and let me slide out the back door to the alley, and then I eased around to the street, just in time to see Scruples and The Apocalypse and Arnold walk into the darkness, heading for the railroad car.

I studied that dead town a while more, and then slipped back in and nodded.

In the street, Burt steered me to his parked carriage and pair of trotters.

"We'll go on out to Carboy's place. Get in."

So I got in, and Burt steered them horses through an inky night and a gloomy town and out into the starlit countryside, where we could see better.

"It worked," I breathed.

"Maybe," Burt said. He was less sure than I.

It wasn't late, and there was a lamp glowing within.

We soon were sitting around the dining table, a lamp glowing in the middle. Celia and Carboy, Burt and me. I didn't fit, just old Cotton with all these rich people, but they let me sit there.

Burt, he unbuckled his portfolio and slid that stack of claims and titles and stuff onto the table. Carboy, he smiled slightly.

We'll sort it out," Carboy said. "Some are legitimate claims and titles, with forged letters of conveyance. Others are outright forgeries. Others are fraudulent, including everything Scruples executed as the secretary of the Swamp Creek District."

I sat there real quiet while them tycoons went through the stuff, item by item. There was a big heap of stuff heading for the woodstove, and a few claims and deeds and patents that was getting saved, including the papers that would prove Celia was the owner of the Fat Tuesday mine, inherited from Argo. It didn't take long actually. Twenty-odd working mines in the district, another fifty claims on discoveries, and a few stray papers.

Burt handed a claim and a mining patent to Celia. "There you are, my dear. You're now the owner of the Fat Tuesday Mine."

She clutched the papers as if they were magical.

"We're too late for some of them," Carboy said. "People like Aggie Cork, who had a good little pocket mine. Those will have to go to auction, with the money going to heirs, if we can find them.

"There's some that went to Suicide Gulch. Most of them were independents. We'll need to get word to them that they've got their mines back."

"Them that are alive," I said, thinking of all them graves.

"We can't turn back the clock," Carboy said. "Speaking of which, how long will it be before Scruples discovers he's been had?"

"Telegraph's in Butte. He could find it out tomorrow," Burt said. "But I doubt that he'll bother. He'll probably pocket the bank letters and then attempt to cash them when he gets to Nevada, where he's headed. He could either drag that railcar back to Butte, or he could go ahead in a buggy and have the car sent to him. I'm guessing he'll stick with his railcar. It's security to him, and comfort to him, and he's not in any rush to cash those letters."

"He finds out soon, you've got hell to pay," I said.

They stared at me.

"He'll come a-shootin'."

I sure had their attention.

"He's got a temper, even if you don't see it none. I seen it. He's still got enough of them shooters to make sure none of us lives long. We ain't exactly got an army here, do we?"

"You're it, Cotton."

"Then you'd better be ready. If I know old Scruples, he'll want some cash right off, and try to get money out of at least one of them letters. If I was Scruples, I'd have a man off to Butte tonight, to start the wires going. And he might have some answers before long tomorrow."

They sure was listening.

"I guess real early I'll go up to the railroad car and sniff around," I said. "Who's there and who ain't."

Carboy nodded. "Now there's something we need to do." He gathered that big heap of papers and stuffed them into the cold parlor stove. Then he poured a little kerosene over them just to start the party, and struck a lucifer and lit them papers. We all stood there, watching orange flame lick all them blood-soaked documents, them papers that caused so much ache and hurt and hatred. It sure caught our attention, the papers peeling off and turning black one by one until there wasn't hardly anything left of the whole lot, just a few valid ones they kept out. That was the first step, and it was sure a satisfying one for us.

"Well, then. Time for me to go back to Mountain House," Burt said.

"Stay here, B.Z.," Carboy said.

"No, it wouldn't be good for anyone to see me here. I'll take the rig back there and be off."

"You succeeded," Carboy said.

B. Z. Burt settled his black hat on his head and we escorted him to the door, being real careful to douse the lamp first. Then the mining man drove off in the night, and we heard his carriage creak down the road toward Swamp Creek. It wasn't late actually.

"There goes a real gentleman," Carboy said.

"I wouldn't know one if I saw one," I said.

All I knew was that Burt had skinned Scruples so bad that Scruples would learn a lesson or two from it.

"A good night's work," Carboy said.

"I'm thinkin' I'd better stand guard around here," I said. "You mind if I settle in on the porch here?"

"I'd be glad of the security."

"You may need it," I said.

I got me a blanket and a pillow and settled into a skinny wicker thing, and spent the night there, with that old six-gun of Celia's in hand, but nothing happened. Just when the eastern sky was lightening up a little, I abandon the porch, settled a saddle on Critter, and rode into Swamp Creek, which was real still and peaceful. It almost looked like one of them ghost towns, but I knew there was still a few dozen people around.

The Mountain House was dark and no one was stirring. I had a feelin' maybe I ought to escort Mr. Burt out of town a ways, just to keep him safe. I steered Critter on over to the livery barn, thinkin' to find out a few things. It didn't take long to figure out that Burt had left Swamp Creek. That rental rig out of Butte was gone, and so were the trotters. I looked around some, but they just wasn't there. Burt had flown the coop.

I spotted old gimpy Willis, the hostler, who was pitching hay out of the loft and into mangers, and he saw me about the time I saw him.

"What brings you here about the time you go to bed, Cotton?" he asked.

"None of your insults, Willis. I'm early to bed and early to rise."

"And early to tell a whopper," he said.

"You see anything of Mr. Burt?"

"Yeah, he come in here last eve, about the time I was fixing to bunk, and he asked me to put the feed bags to them Butte trotters while he collected his stuff at the hotel, and then harness them to the carriage. So I grained the trotters and fed a little hay, too, and an hour later he comes out with his satchels and gets set to go.

"I says, it's mighty dark, and not an easy trip to Butte, sir, and he says he knows the way, and likes to ride at night, and in any case dawn will catch up with him and he'll go halfway in light."

"He taken off middle of the night?"

"I warned him there's some tough grades and a few shoulders around mountain slopes, but he just shrugged it off. 'Mr. Willis,' he says, 'I used to be a prospector, used to going alone, and I used to be a hard-rock miner, working in dark, and I made my fortune by getting in ahead of everyone else, mostly when they were sleeping. I'd be first in whenever there was a rush, and that's how I got rich.'"

"He does get around," I said. "He got in here and looked at all them mines before anyone knew he was around. He works alone, all right."

"What did he come here for?" Willis asked.

"Bought up the Swamp Creek District," I said.

"The whole kit and caboodle?"

"Yep, the whole thing, from Scruples."

"Guess we'll see him again pretty quick."

"Maybe," I said. "Maybe the mines will all come roaring back."

Chapter Thirty-five

There wasn't much happenin' around there, so I had breakfast at the only café still open, run by an ex-madam with Saint Vitus' Dance, which was how she got to be so popular in her first profession. I had me some johnny-cakes and eggs, and while I was polishing that off, I heard a lot of bellerin' and rumbling.

That was the biggest ox team I ever did see, twenty yoke, forty ox, dragging a big flatbed outfit with a mess of wheels. I knew at once what was up. Scruples was movin' out. This outfit would haul his Pullman Palace Car back up to the railroad and put her on rails once again. Sure enough, them dozen big teamsters rolled up the road from Swamp Creek and turned up the steep grade to the hill where Scruples' railroad car stood.

So the tycoon of Swamp Creek was finally fetching himself to somewhere else. I followed along, like most everyone in town, to see the show. There was still fifty or more around there, and pretty near all of them got to hiking toward Scruples' place to watch the goings-on.

The Pullman rested on the crest of the hill, giving it a view of the countryside, and the lane down to the Swamp

Creek Road was steep in places. And just the other side, under a clay bluff maybe twenty feet high, was that giant black swamp that gave the valley its name.

I followed the crowd up the slope to see the show. There was Arnold and The Apocalypse sort of lording over the place and frowning at the gathering crowd. The Apocalypse was dressed in black, as usual, and wore them popguns at his belt, and was bouncing around there looking for someone to exterminate. He eyed me some, but didn't do nothing, knowing I was in the exterminating business, too.

Scruples was inside of that car, busy at something. And the only one missing was Lugar, and a quick check of the livestock pens told me that Lugar's horse was gone, so I thought maybe he'd gone on up to Butte to get a bank up there busy with those letters of credit. That made sense. Old Scruples, he wanted some cash in his britches right off, and trusted Lugar to get it.

Well, it was a show, all right. Them dozen burly teamsters knew what to do. They jacked up the Pullman and pulled out the railroad trucks and settled the train car on that big flatbed. Them trucks they put into a separate wagon that come along behind. Scruples, he never did leave the car, but he did come out on the rear platform to watch a little. He was lookin' mighty fine, all gussied up, like this was a dandy day to celebrate his departure from miserable little Swamp Creek. Old Scruples was heading for the big time, maybe Virginia City, Nevada, or some town like that where he could drink scotch with all the rest of the tycoons.

Them teamsters knew what they were doing, and had a big turn-jack and some blocks of wood, so it didn't take long to get that car settled on the flatbed and chocks put in there to hold her tight. Meanwhile, them twenty yoke of oxen had been rested and fed and watered, and were raring to go by the time the teamsters got things all set up the way they wanted.

Scruples, he finally decided he ought to say something to the bunch around there, so he hushed us with a wave of his hand.

"I've sold the district to B. Z. Burt of Nevada," he said. "He's familiar to you all. The foremost mining man in the country. I don't know his plans, but I'm sure he'll soon reopen the mines, and Swamp Creek will prosper."

That sounded good, but I was thinkin' of all them graves in the Swamp Creek cemetery, people that got in the way of this man.

The teamsters rigged up a block and tackle to ease the flatbed down the slope to the Swamp Creek road. They had some big hawsers and pulleys, and tied one end of that manila rope to a pine tree up there, and the other they wrapped around a peg on the flatbed, and pretty soon they was tugging and testing it to make sure it all was just fine.

It looked fine to me. Them fellers knew what they was doing. There wasn't much of any brakes on the flatbed, so they had to ease it down to the road with that tackle. They had some wheel chocks, too, so they could stop the descent of that flatbed and Pullman car and rig up the block and tackle to another tree lower down the slope.

Scruples, he stepped out of his palace car when all was ready, and them teamsters was getting set to lower that load the first fifty yards or so. But just then, Lugar rode in on a lathered-up nag, and handed Scruples an envelope. Scruples, he halted the show for a moment and stepped aboard.

"I'll be right out," he said. "This goes in my safe."

I sort of wondered if Lugar had got clear to Butte and somehow got some cash. He could have just about done it if he hurried that horse along and left last night. The car was sort of creaking on that flatbed, and the big hawser was sort of humming a little, drawn taut and ready to let the flatbed down the grade real slow, with six or seven of them teamsters playing out rope into the pulleys. Then the bad stuff happened. That big rope began to whine. That's the only word for it. It started whining and vibrating and shooting off strands, right where it was tied to the flatbed wagon, whining and snapping, and then she pulled apart, and that rope sailed back, and all six of them teamsters fell over, surprised by the slack.

Nothing much happened, at least not for a while, and then the flatbed creaked forward a few inches, and some more.

"Scruples, jump," someone yelled, but he was inside twisting the dial on his little old safe in there, and he didn't notice. Some of the teamsters tried to throw chocks in front of the wheels, but that flatbed, it just upped over the chocks, and started rumbling down that grade hellbent to perdition, carrying that old Pullman car atop.

The crowd, it scattered like doves, getting out of the way fast, though the flatbed wasn't going fast, just sort of grumbling along on its own path, which was straight down the road, all them wheels turning over.

Down below, where the other teamsters had all them yoke of oxen lined out, waiting to get hooked up, the teamsters hawed and yelled and got them oxen moving out of the way, so the flatbed wouldn't mow 'em down. There was no stopping it now, though one or two teamsters tried to throw chocks in there, but the flatbed just rode up and over.

Scruples, he was nowhere in sight, not paying attention, or maybe cussing the teamsters for moving his car before he was out and ready. Whatever, he wasn't around to enjoy the show.

The flatbed hit a steep spot, and that's when the slow motion quit and the fast started. Up to then, it was just all real slow, the car creaking its way, but then at that dip, the whole shebang got up some speed, and pretty soon it was going faster than a man could run, and them teamsters quit trying to throw chocks under there, and stood there panting.

It was the awfullest sight a man could ever see, that thing getting up speed, faster and faster, faster than a horse could trot. The teamsters below, they got them oxen going, and it was pure luck that the last yoke cleared out a moment before that flatbed and Pullman car rumbled straight across the Swamp Creek road.

Then, I'll never forget it, that there flatbed hit the clay bank beside the swamp and the whole deal went sailing over the edge. I never thought I'd ever see a railroad car flying, but that Pullman Palace Car had wings, and it sailed out into the swamp, and finally come down with a big thud, splashing black mud and cattails and muck every which way.

People was too shooken up to say a thing. They stood there, froze to the ground.

Somehow, that thing landed upright, after teetering one way and another, and diving nose-first into the muck. There it was, the roof of that Pullman still in the sunlight, while the rest of the car was slowly settling in the muck, with displaced cattails just about everywhere. The first thing I noticed was a mess of bubbles boiling up all over the place, bubbles gurgling around the sides of the car, bubbles boiling from the muck.

But the awfullest sight was to see that car settling down, inch by inch, as the swamp began to claim it. I never saw the like. People, they just stared. Most was far up the hill, close to the stock pens and the old bunkhouse. A few teamsters, they was down on the road trying to keep them oxen from running off.

Me, I followed that car down, and stood there on that clay bank, watching the railroad car slip deeper and deeper into black muck. The swamp was sure enough going to eat that car and bury it under twenty feet of goo.

The worst of it was, I didn't see Scruples anywhere. The muck was slowly reaching the windows and was covering the doors at either end. I thought maybe he got himself knocked out. That was a pretty serious old leap when that car taken off. I began yelling.

"You in there, Scruples? Open a window and I'll get a rope to you," I said.

I sure didn't hear any response. I went and got a rope from one of them teamsters, and tied her to a stump and worked my way out in the swamp, belly flopping my way across the top, and finally got to the car. I crawled up on the roof and began knocking on it.

I don't know why I was trying to save the man, considering all he done, but it was in me to rescue him if I could. I couldn't think of a worse way to check out than to be trapped in a Pullman Palace Car sinking into a swamp. Maybe I was just hoping to save him for a proper hanging, which is what he deserved.

Then, finally, I heard a knock about where that little office with the safe in it was. I got my ear down and listened, and sure enough there was some tapping. I knocked and he tapped. I worked over to the side and yelled, trying to get heard through the window glass.

"Open the window and I'll pull you out," I said.

But he didn't reply, and the window, which was slowly disappearing into the muck, wouldn't offer him a way out for long.

I knocked and he knocked back, but that's all. I didn't have no ax or anything, and I don't think an ax would have let me cut through all that steel, so we ended up knocking away, and there wasn't much to do.

That old car, it just got to settling farther and farther, and pretty soon there was only a few inches of metal above the swamp, and I had to haul myself up the rope or get sucked under.

"Sorry, Mr. Scruples," I said.

There was a mess of bubbles coming up, and if he was alive, he was in an air pocket in the roof that was getting smaller and smaller. It sure wasn't a good way to go.

By now there was a mess of people on the bank, and they got hold of the rope to make sure I'd have help, and they slid me over the swamp and then pulled me up the bank. I was dripping muck, but otherwise all right. That revolver of mine was plumb useless, which didn't comfort me any as I watched Arnold and The Apocalypse and Lugar run down the hill in my direction.

"Guess he's gone," I said.

The car, with Scruples in it, finally vanished into the muck, and a mess of black goo slid over the top. One end was slower to go under, and stuck there proudly for a few minutes, but finally it slid under, too, and then there was nothing at all except a mess of bubbles boiling up, and we all watched for a while as the bubbles slowed down, and then there was nothing there but swamp.

Chapter Thirty-six

We stood there on the bank of the swamp, watching bubbles come up. The teamsters looked like they wanted to crawl under a rock. The town people, they just gawked. It sure was quiet. No one could think of anything to say, so we stood there watching the bubbles, knowin' what was down there in that muck.

The sun sure was bright. There wasn't a cloud anywhere. That Swamp Creek Valley was as peaceful and comfortable as I'd ever seen it. Finally, Lugar, the head gunslick, stirred.

"Guess it's over," he said.

But The Apocalypse had other ideas, and came over lookin' for trouble.

"Guess you killed him," the black-clad little fart said.

I didn't bite on rotten bait like that. They all seen me trying to pull him out of that sinking coffin of a car.

"Cut it out," Lugar said to the punk.

"I say you killed him," The Apocalypse said to me.

I ignored him. The feller was standing there, legs spread, ready to whip out his popguns and do me. I turned my back.

"What are you, some coward?" he snarled.

I didn't see any reason to pay him any attention.

"His revolver's full of mud. Leave him be," Lugar said.

"You stay outa this. I've been waiting for this a long time," the gunman said.

I just ignored him. There wasn't nothing I could do anyway, with a barrel plugged up with black muck. I guess he knew that, and that just made him bolder.

"He tried to bail out Scruples," Lugar said, real firm. "Get up to the bunkhouse and draw your stuff; there's nothing left here for you."

"I got unfinished business," The Apocalypse said.

I didn't know what to make of it, so I ignored him. This here valley had suddenly turned peaceful and sunny, except for the itchy gunman. I didn't know what he had against me, but he sure was acting like it was real bad. He looked like he would invent something if it suited him.

"It's over. Time for you to clear out," I said.

"You calling me a coward?" he said.

This was getting annoying, except I had a gun full of mud and he had two working ones.

"You draw, coward, or face what comes next," he said.

I never could figure someone like that out, but I knew he wanted to pump a few lead pills into me. People was getting out of there fast, in fact running for cover, except for one or two.

That's when Arnold clobbered him. That old ham fist came down like a sledgehammer, and The Apocalypse was poleaxed and hit the ground hard, and was clawing at his holsters when Arnold knocked him cold with a poke at the chin.

The Apocalypse sort of quivered there. Arnold whacked a kneecap for good measure, and kicked him in the ribs to make him hurt a little. I thought I heard a rib or two cave in.

He looked at me. "Wasn't a fair fight," he said.

I should have been grateful. Instead, I was plumb puzzled. "You worry about a fair fight?"

"You don't see me killin' anyone, do you?"

I sort of liked Arnold, at least for a moment or two.

"Yeah, well, take this killer out of here or I'll finish the job," I said.

"Thought you'd say that."

Arnold was sort of grinning at me. He'd pounded the hell out of me so many times, I grinned back. You don't want to make Arnold mad.

The Apocalypse started groaning and coming back to this world, so Arnold whacked him one in the noggin. The little shooter slid back into oblivion.

"I'll get him outa here," Arnold said. "There's no pay check now."

"He killed people around here."

"Yeah, and when we get to Suicide Gulch, someone's gonna kill him. His eyes are no good anymore. He can't hit the broad side of a barn. It's just a matter of time, right?"

"He's getting blind?"

"Yeah, he makes up for it being ornery."

The Apocalypse groaned and woke up real slow.

"How come it's night?" he said.

It was broad daylight.

"Guess I hit him too hard," Arnold said.

"Where's that Cotton? I want to kill the sonofabitch," said The Apocalypse.

"He's standing right here."

The Apocalypse reached for his popgun, but Arnold stepped on his shooting hand.

"Cotton shot me in the face," The Apocalypse said.

I let it go at that.

Arnold, he lifted them guns out of the little punk's holsters and led him off. I doubted that Swamp Creek would ever see that one again. I sort of liked Arnold, even if he'd rearranged my carcass a few times. I thought Arnold would make a good house pet for Carboy. But Arnold, he'd take care of the little killer now. That's what his life would come to.

I sat down in the grass and cleaned my swamp-gummed revolver best I could, taking the thing apart and wiping it down. I'd need new rounds, since I didn't trust any in the chambers. But maybe I wouldn't need the gun now that Swamp Creek was some changed.

People was still staring into that swamp, watching bubbles come up where that railroad car went under. I guessed they'd talk about that for the next few years. The teamsters with twenty yoke of oxen stared, too. They wasn't going to get their flatbed back; it was down there under the Pullman. But they stared anyway, making sense of what happened and maybe feeling a little bad about the big rope that failed. But they wasn't talking much, and pretty soon their straw boss, he lines 'em out on the road to Butte, and they're gone.

I watched Lugar board his tired horse and ride away, sort of in a hurry. I guess he was thinkin' that he didn't have Scruples around to protect him from a noose anymore.

There was a few nags in the pens up where Scruples kept his outfit, and I thought they'd need some caring. I also thought that if there was some guns lying around up there, I'd take them to pay me for the ones Scruples lifted off me. But when I wandered through the bunkhouse, I saw it'd been stripped clean by the punks that went to Suicide Gulch. But them horses were there for the picking, so I picked one. I'd sell him off and buy my own gun and get the one I was wearing back to Celia. And while I thought about it, I'd nab another nag for her. They owed her.

Celia Argo and Cletus Carboy, they was out of town and probably hadn't got word, so I got ahold of Critter and rode out there. It sure was a pleasant day, with the whole world just grinnin' at me.

I got there about the time Carboy was taking tea, and made a mess of excuses so I wouldn't have to swallow that stuff.

"Darjeeling," Carboy said.

"I don't care what it is, it ain't as good as coffee."

But there was a plate of raspberry tarts sitting there, and I thought I'd munch on a few while I told him and Celia what happened.

"Well, sir, Scruples is no more," I began. "He sank into the swamp with the Pullman Palace Car."

That sure got their attention. I never had a better audience. So I just told the story like it happened, while Carboy's eyebrows went up and down and Celia bounced in her chair as fast as Carboy's eyebrows was bouncing. But I finally got it all told, though I didn't talk much about trying to save Scruples. I wasn't sure how they'd take that. But that was the first thing Carboy wanted to talk about.

"You tried to get him out?"

"Well, sir, I was trying to get him out for a proper hanging."

Carboy stared at me. "That was a good thing. And a brave thing to do."

"Well, it was a bad moment, when he was in their banging on the ceiling, and I was trying to tell him to open a window before them windows disappeared. But that's the last we heard from him. He's in there somewhere, and gone now."

"Tell me again about Lugar. He came riding up on a lathered horse?"

"Yes, sir, carrying a big manila envelope. I can't see as how he went to Butte. It's too far."

"Lugar didn't go as far as Butte, Cotton. He hardly got five miles out of Swamp Creek."

I sure was listening.

"I got word just an hour ago from a messenger. Beal Z. Burt was expecting trouble, and stuffed his portfolio with worthless papers in a manila envelope, including the unused letters of credit. Sure enough, north of Swamp Creek, before midnight, a masked highwayman waylaid him and demanded that portfolio, which Burt was only to happy to get rid of. The highwayman made a swift search of the carriage, using a torch, and then let Burt go. That highwayman was no doubt Lugar, and those papers are what Scruples stuffed in the safe when the rope broke."

"Scruples was tryin' to get all them titles to Swamp Creek back?"

"He was indeed, and thought he'd end up with the district back in his hands and half a million dollars, too. Ah, greed. It does inspire mad designs, doesn't it?"

I nodded. There was all too much greed around, and I thought I'd enjoy some of it myself. But my greed, it was for a herd of shorthorns, not a pile of ore.

"Where's Lugar now?" Carboy asked.

"About the time he saw there was no more paycheck, he got on his nag and got out, maybe thinking that would keep his neck from bein' stretched. I suppose he's up at Suicide Gulch by now. That's fixing to be the next hell-hole."

So that was how it spun out. I got to thinking of all them dead. Amelia Trouville, who tried to go straight, Armand Argo, who wouldn't sell out, all them owners like Aggie Cork, people who got in the way like Billy Blew, all that death for greed. I sure thought I'd stick with livestock and get away from gold and silver the rest of my life.

I seen Celia sitting there sipping that Darjeeling, so I handed her Argo's revolver and belt and she settled it at her feet. "I got a new one on my saddle," I said. "I got it from the hardware store. But thanks for the loan of this. I cleaned it up pretty good, but you might have a smith take another look."

She stared uncertainly at it. "That sounds like you're saying good-bye, Cotton."

"I am. This mining stuff's not for me."

"It's not for me either. I'm going back to New Orleans."

I stared real close at her and she stared real close at me, and a lot went through us just then. But there was no changing anything. We were sayin' good-bye, whatever the language.

"I've agreed to buy the Fat Tuesday," Carboy said. "We'll get the mines and mill going soon, and Celia will get her inheritance."

I nodded.

"There's room for you in my business, Cotton," Carboy said. "Managing the mill. I need a man who'd stay right on top, and learn the business."

I was afraid he would be coming to that, and it made me twitchy. "That's mighty kind, Mr. Carboy, but I got other plans," I said.

He didn't ask what they were, and I didn't say, because I didn't know either.

Turn the page for an exciting preview of

SIDEWINDERS: CUTTHROAT CANYON

by William W. Johnstone

with J. A. Johnstone
Coming in June 2009
Wherever Pinnacle Books are sold.

*The wise man avoids trouble,
so as to grow old with grace and dignity.*
—Sir Harry Fulton

Nobody ever accused us of bein' smart.
—Scratch Morton

Chapter One

Scratch Morton dug an elbow into Bo Creel's ribs, nodded toward the building they were passing, and said, "That's new since the last time we were here, ain't it?"

As Bo looked at the building, a nearly naked woman leaned out a second-story window and called to them, "Hey, boys, come on inside and pay me a visit."

Bo ticked a finger against the brim of his black, flat-crowned hat, said politely, "Ma'am," then used his other hand to grasp his trail partner's arm and drag him on past the whorehouse's entrance.

"You'd have to pay, all right, like the lady said," he told Scratch, "and we're a mite low on funds right now."

"Well, then, let's find a saloon and a poker game," Scratch suggested. "There should be plenty of both in El Paso."

Bo didn't doubt that. The border town was famous for its vices. That was the main reason Scratch had insisted on stopping here. They had been on the trail for a long time, and Scratch had a powerful hankering for whiskey and women, not necessarily in that order. They had come home to Texas, and Scratch was of a mind to celebrate.

For most of the past two score years, the two drifters had been somewhere else other than the state where they were born. Of course, Texas hadn't been a state when Bo Creel and Scratch Morton entered the world. It was still part of Mexico then. They had been youngsters when the revolution came along, and after that they'd been citizens of the Republic of Texas for a while.

By the time Texas entered the Union in 1845, Bo and Scratch had pulled up stakes and gone on the drift, due to Scratch's fiddle-footed nature and Bo's desire to put the tragedy of losing his wife and family to sickness behind him. They had been back to the Lone Star State a few times since then, but mostly they'd been elsewhere, seeing what was on the other side of the next hill.

The long years showed in their tanned, weathered faces, as well as in Scratch's shock of silver hair and the strands of gray shot through Bo's dark brown hair, but not in their rangy, muscular bodies that still moved with the easy grace of younger men.

As befitting his deeply held belief that he was God's gift to women, Scratch was something of a dandy, sporting a big, cream-colored Stetson, a fringed buckskin jacket over a white shirt, and tan whipcord pants tucked into high-topped brown boots. The elaborately tooled leather gunbelt strapped around his hips supported a pair of holstered Remington revolvers with long barrels and ivory grips. People had accused him in the past of looking like a Wild West Show cowboy, and he took that as a compliment.

Bo, on the other hand, had been mistaken for a preacher more than once with his sober black suit and vest and hat. His gunbelt and holster were as plain as could be, and so was the lone .45 he carried. Not many preachers, though, had strong, long-fingered hands that could handle a gun and a deck of cards with equal deftness.

Having lived through the chaos of the Runaway Scrape and the Battle of San Jacinto, Bo and Scratch both claimed to want nothing but peace and quiet. Somehow, though, those things had a habit of avoiding them. It seemed that despite their best efforts, wherever they went, trouble soon followed.

Bo was determined that things would be different here in El Paso, since they were back on Texas soil. They would replenish their funds, have a few good meals, sleep under a roof instead of the stars, stock up on supplies, then ride on to wherever the trail took them next.

It was a good plan, but it required money. Bo set his eye on the Birdcage Saloon in the next block as a likely source of those funds.

He recalled the Birdcage from previous visits to the border town. It was run by a big German named August Strittmayer who insisted that all the games of chance there be conducted in an honest fashion. Bo was sure some of the professional gamblers who played at the Birdcage skirted the edge of honesty from time to time, but by and large, Strittmayer's influence kept the games clean.

"You can have a beer at the bar in Strittmayer's place while I see if there's an empty chair at any of the tables," he suggested to Scratch.

"Now you're talkin'," Scratch agreed with a grin. "The scenery's plumb nice in there, too."

Bo knew what Scratch was referring to. On a raised platform on one side of the room sat the big cage that gave the place its name. Instead of a bird perching on the swing that hung inside the cage, one of the saloon girls was always there, in the next thing to her birthday suit. The girls took turns rocking back and forth on that swing. They might not sing like birds, but their plumage was mighty nice.

When Bo and Scratch pushed through the batwings and went inside, they saw that the saloon was doing its usual brisk business. Thirsty cowboys filled most of the places at the bar and occupied all but a few of the tables. A group of men gathered around the birdcage in the corner, calling out lewd comments to the girl on the swing.

Strittmayer had laid down the law where those girls were concerned: The saloon's bouncers would deal quickly and harshly with any man who so much as set foot inside the cage. Strittmayer couldn't stop the comments, though, and the girls who worked the cage soon learned to ignore them and continue to wear a placid smile.

The air was full of the usual saloon smells—whiskey, tobacco, sweat, and piss—and the sounds—loud talk, raucous laughter, tinny piano music, the click of a roulette wheel, the whisper of cards being shuffled and dealt. Bo nodded toward the bar and told Scratch, "Go grab a beer."

"I can handle that job," Scratch said.

Bo spotted a dealer he knew at one of the baize-covered tables where poker games were going on. The man wore the elaborate waistcoat and frilly shirt of a professional tinhorn. Close acquaintances knew him as Three-Toed Johnny because of an accident with an ax while splitting some firewood one frosty morning. He was an honest dealer, at least most of the time. Bo hadn't seen him for a couple of years. The last place they had run into each other was Wichita.

The hand was over as Bo came up to the table, and Johnny was raking in the pot. No surprise there. One of the players said in a tone of disgust, "I'm busted. Guess I'm out." He scraped back his chair and stood up.

Johnny stopped him and held out a chip. "No man leaves my table without enough money for a drink, my friend," he said.

The man hesitated, then said, "Thanks," and took the chip. He headed for the bar to cash it in and get that drink.

Bo said, "Some people say that's what got Bill Hickok killed. He busted Jack McCall at cards, then tossed him a mercy chip like that the day before McCall came back into the Number Ten and shot him."

Three-Toed Johnny looked up and grinned. "Bo Creel! I didn't see you come in."

Bo sort of doubted that. Johnny didn't miss much.

"It's good to see you again, amigo," the gambler went on.

Bo gestured toward the empty chair. "You have room for another player?"

"Most assuredly. Sit down."

"Wait just a damned minute," a man on the other side of the table said. He was dressed in an expensive suit, but the big Stetson pushed back on his head, the seamed face of a man who spent most of his life outdoors, and the calluses on his hands all told Bo that he was a cattleman. The suit and the big ring on one of his fingers said he was probably a pretty successful one. So did the arrogant tone of his voice.

"Is there a problem, Mr. Churchill?" Johnny asked. Bo could tell that the gambler was keeping his own voice deceptively mild.

By using the hombre's name, Johnny had also identified him for Bo. The upset man was Little Ed Churchill, the owner of one of the largest ranches in West Texas.

Little Ed wasn't little at all, but his pa Big Ed had been even bigger, Bo recalled, hence the name.

"This fella's a friend of yours," Churchill said as he jerked a hand toward Bo. "You said as much yourself just now."

"And that's a problem because . . . ?"

"How do the rest of us know that you and him aren't about to run some sort of tomfoolery on us?"

Johnny's eyes hardened. "You mean you're afraid we'll cheat you?" he asked, and his soft tone was really deceptive now. Bo knew how angry Johnny was.

Bo wasn't too happy about being called a cheater himself.

"I've seen you play, Fontana," Churchill said. "You win a lot."

"It's my job to win. But I do it by honest means."

So Johnny was using the last name Fontana now, Bo thought. Johnny had had half a dozen different last names at least. Bo wasn't sure Johnny even remembered what name he'd been born with.

"To tell you the truth," Johnny went on, "I don't need to cheat to beat you, Churchill. All I have to do is take advantage of your natural recklessness."

One of the other players rested both hands on the table in plain sight and said, "I don't like the way this conversation is going. I came here for a friendly game, gentlemen, not a display of bravado. And certainly not for gunplay."

"Shut the hell up, Davidson," Churchill snapped.

The man called Davidson paled and sat up straighter. He was in his thirties, well dressed, with tightly curled brown hair and a mustache that curled up on the tips. As Davidson moved forward a little in his chair, Bo caught a glimpse of a gun holstered in a shoulder rig under the man's left arm. Despite his town suit, Davidson looked tough enough to use the iron if he had to.

"I can go find another game," Bo suggested. He didn't want to sit in on this particular one badly enough to cause a shootout. "I just thought I'd say hello to an old friend."

"There's no need for that, Bo," Johnny said. He gave Churchill a flat, level stare and went on. "Bo Creel is an honest man, and so am I. If you doubt either of those things, Churchill, maybe it's you who had better find another game."

"I won't be stampeded, damn it." Churchill nodded toward the empty chair. "Sit down, Creel. But remember that I'll be watching you." He looked at Johnny. "Both of you."

"It's going to be a distinct pleasure taking your money," Johnny drawled.

"Shut up and deal the cards."

Johnny shut up and dealt.

Chapter Two

Bo wasn't sure what would have happened if he or Johnny had won the first hand after he sat down. Little Ed Churchill might have been more convinced than ever that he was being cheated.

The man called Davidson was the one who raked in that pot, however. In fact, judging by the way what had been a fairly small pile of chips in front of Davidson when Bo sat down began to grow after that, the man's luck appeared to have changed for the better.

Davidson won three out of the next five hands, with Bo taking one and Johnny the other. Bo understood now what Johnny meant about Churchill being reckless. The man was a plunger when he had a decent hand and a poor bluffer when he didn't. Bo wasn't surprised that Churchill lost a considerable amount of money in a short period of time.

The cattleman's face was red to start with, and it flushed even more as he continued to lose. Bo felt trouble building. If not for the fact that he and Scratch needed money, he would have just as soon gotten up from the table and walked away.

Scratch ambled over from the bar and stood there watching the game with a mug of beer in his hand. Churchill glanced at him and glared.

"What two-bit melodrama did you come from?"

Scratch's easy grin didn't hide the flash of anger in his eyes that Bo noted. "I'll let that remark pass, friend," the silver-haired Texan said. "I can see you've got troubles of your own."

"What the hell do you mean by that?"

"Well, from what I've seen so far of your poker playin', my hundred-and-four-year-old grandma could likely whip you at cards."

Churchill slapped his pasteboards facedown on the table and started to stand up. "Why, you grinning son of a—"

"Gentlemen, gentlemen!" The booming, Teutonic tones of August Strittmayer filled the air as the saloon's proprietor loomed over the table. "All the games in the Birdcage are friendly, *nicht wahr?*"

"Don't talk that damned Dutchy talk at me," Churchill snapped. He settled back down in his chair, though. Strittmayer was an imposing figure, two yards tall and a yard wide in brown tweed, with a bald head and big, knobby fists.

"Trouble here, Johnny?" Strittmayer asked.

"Not really," Johnny answered with a casual shrug. "Mr. Churchill is a bit of a poor loser, that's all."

"No one leaves the Birdcage unhappy," Strittmayer declared. "Why don't you come over to the bar and have a drink with me before you go, Herr Churchill? I have some splendid twenty-year-old brandy that I would be pleased to share with you."

"Who said I was going anywhere? I'm staying right here, damn it, until I win back my money!"

"I'm afraid we don't have that much time," Strittmayer said.

Johnny added, "Yeah, we'd all grow old and die before then."

For a smart man, Johnny never had learned how to control his mouth, Bo thought. Churchill paled at the insult. He glared at Strittmayer and demanded, "Are you throwing me out, you damned Dutchman?"

Strittmayer looked sorrowful. "Although I regret to say it, yes, I am, Herr Churchill."

"Do you know who I am?"

That was a stupid question, given the fact that Strittmayer had just called the cattleman by name. But Churchill was too angry to be thinking straight, Bo decided.

"Most certainly I do."

"You'll lose a hell of a lot of business if I tell my ranch hands to stay away from this place."

"Then I suppose I shall have to make up that business some other way," Strittmayer said.

Churchill got to his feet. "You'll be sorry about this," he said. "And you can keep your damned twenty-year-old brandy. In fact, you can take the bottle and shove it right up your—"

Strittmayer's hamlike hand closed around Churchill's arm and propelled the rancher toward the door. "I think you have said enough, *nicht war?* Good evening, Herr Churchill."

The whole saloon had gone silent now. Everybody in the Birdcage watched as Strittmayer marched Churchill to the door. Even the girl in the cage wasn't swinging back and forth anymore.

Churchill cursed loudly at the humiliation as Strittmayer forced him through the batwings. When the rancher had stalked off, Strittmayer stepped back inside, dusted his hands off as if they had gotten dirty, and beamed around at the crowd. "No more trouble, *ja?* The next round of drinks, it is on the house!"

Cheers rang out from the customers as most of them bellied up to the bar for that free drink. Bo had a feeling that the bartenders would be reaching for special bottles full of booze they had watered down especially for such occasional demonstrations of generosity on Stritt-mayer's part.

"Sorry about that, gents," Three-Toed Johnny Fontana told the other cardplayers at the table. "Poker should be a game of more subtle pleasures."

"I don't know," Davidson said with a smile. "I enjoyed watching that blowhard get thrown out of the place. A man like that gets a little money and power and thinks he owns everything and everybody."

Bo nodded toward the big, affable German, who had gone back to the bar and asked Johnny, "Can Churchill really make trouble for Strittmayer?"

Johnny shrugged. "That depends on how badly his pride is wounded. August does enough business so that it won't hurt him much if Churchill orders his men to stay away from the place."

"What if he tries something a little more drastic than that?"

"You mean like coming back here with a bunch of those hardcases who ride for him and trying to wreck the place?" Johnny shook his head. "That seems like a little bit much for a dispute over a few hands of poker."

For once, Johnny's ability to judge other men, which

was so important in his profession, seemed to be letting him down a mite, Bo thought. He had seen something bordering on madness in Little Ed Churchill's eyes as he was forced out of the saloon. As Davidson had said, some men got that way when most people didn't dare to stand up to them. It enraged them whenever they ran into an hombre who didn't have any back-up in his nature.

But maybe Churchill would show some sense and go back to his ranch to sleep off that rage. Bo hoped that would turn out to be the case. When Johnny said, "Shall we resume the game?" Bo nodded.

Davidson's luck was still the best of anyone's around the table, but Bo won a few hands, and was careful to cut his losses in the ones he couldn't win. He had increased their stake enough so that he and Scratch could afford a couple of hotel rooms and some supplies. He was about to call it a night when he heard a lot of hoofbeats in the street outside.

"Strittmayer!" a harsh voice bellowed as the horses came to a stop. "I told you you'd be sorry, you damned Dutchman!"

Bo dropped his cards and started to his feet, but Scratch grabbed his shoulder and forced him back down. "Everybody hit the dirt!" Scratch shouted, his deep voice filling the room.

Even as Scratch called out the warning, the glass in the two big front windows exploded inward as a volley of shots shattered them. The saloon girls screamed and men yelled curses as more shots blasted from the street. Muzzle flashes lit up the night like a lightning storm.

As Bo dived out of his chair he rammed a shoulder into Davidson, knocking the man to the floor out of the line of fire. Bo palmed out his Colt as Scratch overturned the poker table to give them some cover. Scratch crouched behind the table with Bo and drew his long-barreled Remingtons. Everybody in the saloon had either hit the floor or leaped over the bar to hide behind the thick hardwood, so the two of them had a clear field to return the fire of Little Ed Churchill and his men.

Churchill must have gathered up a dozen or more of his ranch hands in some of El Paso's other saloons and gambling dens and brothels and led them back here to Strittmayer's place. Bo didn't know if the cattleman had spun some wild yarn for his men about how he'd been cheated at cards and then run out of the Birdcage, or if Churchill had simply ordered his men to attack. A lot of cowboys rode for the brand above all, and if the boss said sic 'em, they skinned their irons and got to work, no questions asked.

Either way, lead now filled the air inside the Birdcage. The mirrors behind the bar shattered, and bottles of liquor arranged along the backbar exploded in sprays of booze and glass as bullets struck them.

Davidson crawled along the floor, and got behind the same table where Bo and Scratch had taken cover. He pulled his gun from the shoulder holster Bo had seen earlier and started firing toward the street. He glanced over at Bo and Scratch and said, "I knew Churchill was a little loco, but I didn't think he was crazy enough to come back and lay siege to the place."

From behind the bar, Strittmayer called, "Everyone stay down, *ja?*" The next moment, several shotguns poked over the bar. Each of the weapons let go with a double load of buckshot. That barrage blew out what little glass remained in the windows and ripped into the cowboys in the street. Men and horses went down, screaming in pain.

Anger flooded through Bo. Not only was Churchill trying to kill everybody in the saloon, but now he had led some of his own men to their deaths, all because Churchill was a stubborn, prideful bastard who couldn't admit that he wasn't a very good poker player. What a damned waste, Bo thought.

He could only hope that some of that buckshot had found Churchill as well, so that maybe this fight could come to an end.

That didn't prove to be the case. With an incoherent, furious shout, the rancher leaped his horse onto the boardwalk and then viciously spurred the animal on into the saloon. The horse was terrified—anybody could see that—but Churchill forced the wild-eyed beast on. Men rolled and jumped desperately to avoid the slashing, steel-shod hooves.

Three-Toed Johnny leaped up from somewhere and shouted, "Stop it! For God's sake, stop it!" He had a derringer in his hand that Bo knew had come from a concealed sheath up the gambler's sleeve. Johnny swung it up toward Churchill, but the cattleman was faster. He had a six-gun in his right hand, and as he brought it down with a chopping motion, powder smoke geysered from the muzzle. The slug punched into Johnny's body and threw him backward.

Bo and Scratch fired at the same time, but Churchill was already jerking his horse around. Their bullets whistled harmlessly past his head. Churchill sent his horse crashing into the overturned table. Bo and Scratch threw themselves to the side to get out of the way, but the table rammed into Davidson and knocked him down. His gun flew out of his hand.

"Now I'll get you, you damned four-flusher!" Churchill yelled as he brought his revolver to bear on the helpless Davidson, who lay sprawled on the floor under the rearing horse.

Bo and Scratch fired again, and this time they didn't miss. Their bullets tore through Churchill's body on an upward-angling path, causing him to lean so far back that he toppled out of the saddle. Suddenly riderless, the panic-stricken horse whirled around a couple of times and then leaped out through the one of the already broken front windows.

The shooting from outside had stopped. Churchill's men were all either dead or had lit a shuck out of El Paso. The survivors probably wouldn't stop at Churchill's ranch either. After this brutal attack on the saloon, the men who had lived through it would take off for the tall and uncut and keep going, so that the law would be less likely to catch up to them. With Churchill dead, his wealth and influence couldn't protect them anymore.

A pale and visibly shaken August Strittmayer emerged from behind the bar clutching a reloaded shotgun. "They are all gone, *ja?*" he asked.

"Looks like it," Bo replied. He heard a lot of shouting from outside. The city marshal and some of his deputies were coming toward the Birdcage on the run, he assumed. The sounds of a small-scale war breaking out had been enough to attract the law.

Bo didn't pay any attention to that at the moment, but hurried to the side of Three-Toed Johnny instead. As Bo dropped to a knee, the gambler's eyelids fluttered open.

His vest was soaked with blood over the place where Churchill's bullet had ventilated him.

"I think I'm . . . shot, Bo," Johnny gasped out as his eyes tried futilely to focus.

"I'm afraid so, Johnny," Bo agreed.

"Pretty . . . bad . . . huh?"

"Bad enough."

"Well . . . hell . . . we all draw . . . a bad hand . . . sooner or later." Johnny's head rolled from side to side. His eyes still wouldn't lock in on anything. "Ch-Churchill?"

Scratch had knelt on the gambler's other side. "Dead as he can be, pard," Scratch said.

"Good . . . At least I'm . . . not the only one . . . to fold—"

His eyes widened and grew still at last, and the air came out of him in a rattling sigh. Bo waited a moment, then shook his head and reached out to close those staring eyes as they began to grow glassy.

Strittmayer said in a hollow voice, "I never thought . . . I never dreamed that . . . that Churchill would . . . would do such a *verdammt* thing! To come back with his men and open fire on innocent people! The man was insane!"

Bo and Scratch got to their feet and started reloading their guns. "I don't reckon he was loco," Scratch said. "Just poison-mean and too used to gettin' his own way."

That was when several men with shotguns slapped the batwings aside and rushed into the saloon, leveling the Greeners at the two drifters as a gent with a soup-strainer mustache yelled, "Drop them guns, you ringtailed hellions!"